A Gap in the World

Harry could not see the face of the speaker and cupped her hands around her eyes to cut out the dazzle of the new day. Looking a little crookedly she found herself staring, not at him, but at the two young men standing silently behind him. They appeared to be identical, and she knew at once that they had crawled out of a wrong gap in the world, that they had struggled through holding on to the silken thread of her own story. She had closed one door shutting out Teddy Carnival's bleeding ghost, but had opened another. Their streaked hair fell onto their foreheads like question marks, upside down and therefore devilish. They had never been children; they had never been innocent.

Other books by
MARGARET MAHY
from Scholastic

The Catalogue of the Universe
Aliens in the Family
The Changeover: A Supernatural Romance
The Haunting
Leaf Magic

THE
TRICKSTERS

Margaret Mahy

SCHOLASTIC INC.
New York Toronto London Auckland Sydney

ISBN 0-590-41513-1

12 11 10 9 8 7 6 5 4 3 2 1   8 9/8 0 1 2 3/9

Printed in the U.S.A.   01

First Scholastic Printing, October 1988

PART ONE

Midsummer

1
A Possible Ghost

Any Christmas visitor looking for Carnival's Hide dropped down from the hilltops by a shingle road that elbowed its way across farmland already scrawled over by sheep tracks. The visitor would have to open a five-bar gate, close it carefully behind him and trust the crinkling road a little further still. Then, enclosed in a great, green, summer bouquet of poplars and silver birches, the steeply pitched, iron roof of the house, also green, rose up like a magician's sign.

At the sight of it Harry's blood skipped a little.

"Something is waiting!" she had cried to her mother many Christmases ago as the green peak came into sight. This time she said nothing, but she knew the waiting was still going on.

Jack Hamilton, her father, sitting at the wheel of a car that seemed to be finding its own way down the hill, looked at the house, and then sideways at his guest, Anthony Hesketh, an English visitor to

New Zealand, still a stranger to the three Hamilton children crowded into the back seat.

"It's haunted of course!" Jack remarked proudly, as if he were describing a particularly desirable feature. "Did Naomi mention that?"

The station wagon, heavy with holiday boxes, curved around Carnival's Hide and out into the sunlight.

In front of the house stretched a ruined lawn, nodding with the heads of meadow grasses, some of them brown and ready to shed seeds, others no more than delicate speckled patterns in the air. A path of flat paving stones, overgrown and weedy, ran down to the sea through a small, neglected orchard and a belt of native bush in dark persistent greens. For a moment after the engine stopped, the day was still, and then the nor-west wind, strong as a lion, swept through it, and everything tossed, nodded, swayed, struggled, lashed and laboured under its power.

Anthony Hesketh looked around him and then into the back seat, at Harry, half hidden by her glasses and her curtains of reddish-brown hair, at Serena, round and romantic, and Benny the youngest, only seven, already seizing the door handle.

"Is it really haunted?" Anthony asked.

"Well, it always feels as if it could be — it's sort of open to haunting," Harry answered.

"And we do have a possible ghost," Jack pointed out. "The house is ninety years old — " He broke off and looked apologetically at Anthony as he did so. "That *is* old for this part of the world, you know. And when the house was built Edward Carnival was really building it at the back of beyond."

"There weren't any roads in those days," Serena chipped in, leaning across Benny to push the door open. "Everything had to be brought across the harbour by boat — every single thing."

"Edward Carnival — he was the man who built it?" Anthony asked, but the Hamiltons were all scrambling out of their car and no one answered him.

Old, easy and single storeyed, its verandah sprawling with purple bougainvillaea, the house was welcoming yet still secret, bathed in sunshine yet spreading around itself a gentle skirt of shade, sharpened only by the gleam of stained glass in the front door. The slope of the front roof, curiously parallel to the sharp crest of the hilltops behind it, was interrupted by a single central dormer window, a little extra eye set above the steadfast gaze of other larger windows all looking out to sea under the rich fringe of purple and green.

Serena and Benny tumbled out of the car, pounded up the steps and along the verandah, Benny tossing his reddish hair like a skittish pony. He was little and thin and, being short-sighted, wore clever-looking glasses as Harry did. Serena danced and swooped beside him flinging out her arms as if she might actually sail away on them. Harry watched them a little wistfully. On her own she might have swung herself round one of the verandah posts like Benny or embraced another like Serena, but being seventeen made a difference. She was too shy to be openly happy before Jack and his English guest.

"It's summer, summer, summer!" half-sang Serena, still hugging the post, peeping round it and hoping she looked sensitive.

"It's been summer for weeks," exclaimed Benny scornfully.

"Yes but it's *extra* summer when we come to the Hide," Serena said, letting her warm glance dwell on Anthony. Harry could see she was falling in love with him, for he had a beautiful voice and looked slightly sinister behind his dark glasses, and besides, Serena enjoyed falling in love, usually choosing boyfriends of their older sister Christobel to practise on.

A few yards behind the house but further up the hill was a second grove of fruit trees and another building, half house, half shed.

"That's the wash-house and a storehouse full of old junk, and the loo," Benny told Anthony, light reflecting from his glasses as if he had put silver pennies over them. "If you can't make it, well, don't worry. Just go in the grass. That's what I do."

Jack looked mildly exasperated at this confidence, but Anthony laughed and said useful advice was always welcome.

"All the same, once you get there, everything's modern," Jack said hastily. "We flush and flow like the best people these days."

"The little stone path leads down to the sea," Serena offered, sweeping her arm generously at the entire harbour basin. "There's a boat shed down there, and an old hut."

"And where does the ghost walk?" Anthony asked. "Around the house trying to get in?"

Harry, following Jack and Anthony on to the verandah, turned involuntarily, and looked out over the sea, facing into the lunging wind, which shook the house like a prey between its paws.

"There's where he drowned," Jack said, pointing. "Edward's son, Teddy, that is — our possible ghost." Anthony turned too, and looked, almost eagerly, along Jack's raised arm.

"Open the door!" demanded Benny rattling the handle. "Please, Jack!"

"We go for a swim first thing," Serena told Anthony. "You can have a really close look at the drowning place in a moment."

"We have to tell him we've arrived," Benny said, rattling once more, while Jack slapped his pockets looking for the keys. "We let him know he's got good company again."

The key turned in the lock, the door creaked slightly, and the first strangeness of an empty house came to meet them in a hall that had several doors opening off it. Wallpaper, old and loose, had been painted a flat white, turning the walls into empty pages. Harry had always imagined that, if she ever opened the door soundlessly, she would surprise a strange story written up on these blank surfaces, but she had never been clever enough to catch it. The walls kept their story to themselves. There were no secrets — unless someone had hung an old, family skeleton carelessly among the few still coats dangling limply from the coatrack halfway down the hall. There was a bow-legged table heavily powdered with dust beside one closed door.

"Too much make-up!" said Harry, writing her initials on it with her finger. The door whined shut behind them. Serena, waving her red towel, dived into a room off the hall, while Jack ran his fingers gingerly over the blisters rising up under the painted paper.

"Edward Carnival built the house for his wife," he said, answering Anthony's earlier question. "She died having a third child, before the house was completed, and it became more of a hiding place than a home."

"Carnival's Hide," Anthony said.

Jack stopped his rueful exploration of the loose wallpaper. "Naomi's the one who knows it all," he said, "what with working at the museum among all the local history — letters, diaries. People may not have always liked young Teddy, but they gossiped about him. And Edward was quite well known, quite a pioneer of forestry. Well, that's why you've wound up here, isn't it? We've got his pamphlets."

"And the poem he wrote when Teddy died," Harry added. "It's all through here."

She swung her own hold-all gently at the door on the right. It was not closed, and swung silently open. They trooped through into a big, hot, stuffy, faded room.

"Gosh, open the windows!" Harry exclaimed. "It's full of cooked air."

The windows were pushed up, the nor-wester rushed in at them breathing its dragon breath upon them, and the room came alive with new wildness. Posters fluttered, unseen doors banged, the linen curtain, once green, now faded to lichen grey, swayed and then billowed out over the seagrass matting, while above the mantelpiece three old, curling photographs flapped up and down against the wall, apparently welcoming new company.

"There they are — Edward and Ann," Jack said, looking at the couple in the topmost photograph. Edward and Ann Carnival, young and serious in their formal clothes, held hands and stared at the camera as if having their photograph taken was something they had to suffer together. Below them, Edward, still stiffly dressed but older and wilder, stood on a beach, gesturing proudly at the sea. "See that garden there behind him?" Jack said. "He was a prodigious gardener. We still find bits of it in the tangle out there. It came right down to the sand in those days."

"There's Teddy," Benny said. "That one there."

"And Minerva!" added Harry quickly. "Everyone forgets Minerva just because she didn't get drowned."

The last photograph on the wall showed a girl of about twelve, and a slightly younger boy, both formal, both overdressed. Anthony looked intently into the small, still faces. The girl looked calmly over his head, but the boy stared down at him with an expression as inquisitive as Anthony's own. He had a head of wonderful curls, slightly tilted eyes, and a smile that pressed his curved lips together, secretive and mocking.

"He has a chilly smile for a child," Anthony said at last.

"I think he looks too clever about wrong things," Harry agreed. "Terrific curls though. We've all had a go at being in love with him, Christobel, Serena and me."

"I have not!" shouted Serena crossly from the doorway.

"Love! Grunt! Grunt!" cried Benny vigorously and put his tongue out to show his distaste for extravagant feelings.

He was using a private language he and Serena

had invented in which "moo" meant *wonderful*, and "grunt" *terrible*. They could give opinions they imagined were secret to one another in front of strangers, using this language, and it was quite catching, so that other members of the family, who had quickly got sick of "grunt" and "moo", found themselves grunting and mooing in spite of themselves.

Serena leaped into the room resplendent in a new red swimming suit with a little red frill that made her look even rounder than she really was.

"Edward saw Teddy dive," she cried, half miming the old story. "And he didn't come up. He vanished away."

"They searched, of course, and decided that high seas the day before had shifted a submerged log in some fatal way," Jack added. "So there it was. Edward's wife never entered the house and his son, whom he had carefully brought up to be a sort of noble savage, never lived to inherit it."

"If he didn't hit the log, Teddy must have been a determined drowner," cried Benny smugly, earning a surprised look from Anthony, which made Serena jealous.

"He didn't say that first — Christo did!" she exclaimed.

"You think Christo said every good thing first!" Benny cried back.

"So does Christo," Harry muttered, as much to herself as to Serena.

"The beach is actually very safe," Jack assured Anthony, who was turning away from the photographs. He still had his dark glasses on, and for a moment Jack and Jack's children and the sitting room of Carnival's Hide swam over his hidden eyes — curved, glossy shadows in a dim room. Then, as if there were no longer any need for a mask, Anthony took his glasses off, sliding them into a soft vinyl case, which he carried in the pocket of his shirt.

"What happened to the body — that *is* a mystery," Jack added. "There's no real current to carry it off."

"But what about the underwater cave?" Benny suggested and Jack smiled.

"It's scarcely a cave — more a hollow in the rocks, but I suppose it's possible a body could get caught there, and then shifted out with the tide."

"He was never found!" Serena exclaimed, staring fixedly at Anthony, anxious that he should understand every bit of the old drama. *"Never ever found! That's why we think he's still here."* She danced a step and then threw out her arms violently, catching Jack across the stomach. Anthony glanced back at the photographs, as if (Harry thought) he suspected them of watching him behind his back. Then he looked at Jack. "So here I am," he said, "in a holiday house with a ghost, a piano," (he looked around again, but at other things this time) "and a bookcase. Civilization!"

A tall bookcase stood back against the wall opposite the photographs. Harry, standing beside it, had one hand laid on a ladder which led, like a ship's companionway, up through an open trapdoor in the ceiling.

"That's Harry's ladder," Serena cried. "She sleeps up there among the Christmas decorations like a possum. Jack had a little window put up there," she went on, bouncing from one foot to the other, "didn't you, Jackie, back in the wife-swapping days."

"Who's quoting Christobel now?" Jack demanded, sounding resigned. "Let's stick to ghosts, shall we?"

He put his hand on Serena's shoulder and shook her gently. "I promise I've never ever wanted to swap your mother."

"Not you — but other people!" Serena cried earnestly. "Remember all those parties you used to have when I was little? Well, Christobel says some people used to swap over — husbands and wives, that is."

"Christobel again!" Jack groaned, shaking his head, but his irritation automatically turned into forgiveness. "Even when she isn't here she still has her say, because other people say it for her. Look, Harry — you speak out for me."

"No good! Harry wouldn't notice if anyone swapped over," Serena cried triumphantly. "She's a dreamer, and anyhow half the time she forgets to wear her glasses." Then she jiggled over to Harry as she spoke, hoping for a reaction, but Harry looked out, not in. She was staring through the window, towards the sea.

"I don't know about you lot, but I'm going to go swimming before Ma comes and we have to get organized."

"Yes, and we'll tell Teddy we're here," Benny said. "He might want to be part of a happy Christmas family for a change."

2
The Writer up under the Roof

Upstairs in her strange little room Harry dropped her pack on the floor, pleased to be up there, still hearing family voices but not having to answer them. Though the attic was called Harry's room, it was not really a room at all, simply a floor laid over the ceiling joists and insulation, a space fitted in under the pointed "A" of the roof. Its dormer window looked out to sea across curved wands of bougainvillaea, and she shared the space with boxes of Christmas decorations. A little mirror without a frame hung on a nail in one of the diagonals that supported the iron roof. She could see tents, ground sheets, rolls of wallpaper left over from previous home improvements, and many other spare things that just might be needed some day. Here at night, over many years, the house had groaned and murmured to her, peopling her dreams with old Edward, the builder of the house, meeting her eye and gesturing grandly at the sea, or with Minerva, his daughter, who had lived and been forgotten, and

Teddy, his son, who had died and been remembered. In some way the walls of Carnival's Hide were soaked with the memory of this brief life, and Teddy wandered freely through Harry's sleep, his face turned away from her, leaving a trail of salt water behind him, darker drops sometimes mixing with the clear ones. Harry was never upset by these nightly visitations. They were part of a general weather of the imagination, and perhaps someday another sleeper under the roof might dream of her, although she could not believe she would ever belong in the house as Teddy had belonged. Visitors to Carnival's Hide were always given its history almost as if it were living gossip.

Harry opened her pack and pulled out her blue towel. Under her skirt and top she already wore her swimming suit. In a moment she was ready for the sea, but she did not go down the ladder immediately, holding back to hang a few clothes along the length of clothesline that served her as a wardrobe, putting two or three books on the apple crate that doubled as a cupboard and bedside table. Then, at last, sitting on her stretcher-bed, she took from the very bottom of her pack an old peacock-blue scarf folded around a heavy, square book. She unwrapped it and opened it very carefully, as if guilty secrets might fall from between its pages like pressed flowers. This was Harry's secret. She was a writer.

Across the pages marched her own cramped, careful handwriting contrasting oddly with the passionate things it was telling about, for Harry was writing a story of mysterious and threatening love. Rereading it now, she felt she was looking between the lines and seeing a whole world beyond the black bars of writing, in which an ominous creature, come out of her head fully grown, could dip and soar and fly and fall. Writing about him, she had felt him flowing out of her head, down her arm and into her magical, writing hand, out through the pen and on to the paper, where he at once took on a life apart from hers.

Suspended over the city, Belen, the black arrow of the air, looked down on the beautiful women gathered together for an entertainment as if he were choosing which one of them he should devour. His eyes were like pools of gold in a golden face and his hair was black as jet, streaked with silver, as if it had been bleached by the moon rather than the sun. He was very strong, and had a foxy sort of smile.

Harry found that, now she was here in Carnival's Hide, the face of this imaginary creature — part-man, part-bird — could be seen even more clearly. At home she had carried the picture secretly in her mind, piecing it together out of other peoples' stories and her own dreams, but here it was in the air around her. When she moved around her space, no corner was free from her winged man, and she suddenly believed she had caught him, like a cold or measles, from the old house, which had always been infected with him. For a long time he had hibernated in a quiet corner of her head but now he was reaching out to her, navigating her blood, moving confidently through the lock of her heart. It seemed silly that she couldn't let other people see him as clearly as she saw him — beautiful, powerful and unbounded. Yet being haunted by Belen left her a little guilty, for somehow this romantic villain had become a secret lover. A wild part of herself was set free in him. She was thrilled by the things she invented for him to do, and was also ashamed of them.

Already Harry knew her story was unsharable, though she had started it with the vague idea that she might write it wonderfully well and have it published some day, but, once begun, the story had twisted and changed. Suddenly her true life was lived in the moments when the tip of her pen met the white paper. After all, in family life all the best possibilities (beauty, cleverness and the power to go out and have adventures) had been taken over before she was born and were being used up by others. Even though Charlie, her older brother, was living in an apartment in the city, and Christobel was working in another town, they still held their family places. Harry could not move up — only out. However, behind the written lines there was the space she longed for, and all of it seemed to be hers, even though she sometimes felt someone sharing it with her — swimming blindly out of it towards her. Often when she was most pleased with something she had written, she found herself believing that her industrious writing hand was being used to tell someone else's story.

"Here I am!" something was saying. "Write me down. Let me live."

Harry had a private rule, that, if she took her book out, she must add at least one line before she put it away again. After one or two false starts, her frown cleared, and her hesitating pen looped on defiantly, leaving its trail of dark story behind it.

He looked as if he had never been a child, she wrote. *He looked as if he had never been innocent.*

Brilliant, thought Harry. That's really brilliant! She was so excited with the last line, she had to stop for a moment to get over the shock of her cleverness.

Standing up, she suddenly caught sight of an owl in a copper-coloured hedge — her own face, glasses on nose, staring out of her reddish-brown hair. Harry's bangs came all the way down to her strong, straight eyebrows, her hair flowed past her shoulders. She had turned herself into her own hiding place. Yet, unexpectedly, she caught the trace of a vanishing expression that surprised her, as if, only a moment earlier, she had been not a fugitive, but an enchantress. She tried to make the expression come back; it wouldn't be ordered around. So instead she thought of Christmas, sighed and shut her eyes. Her head immediately filled with a hot golden dazzle, smelling of pine needles, tasting of salt. Holidays, Christmas and Harry herself ran into each other as they always did. In a changing world, this, at least, refused to change.

She could happily have stayed there a little longer, letting the wind come boldly in at her window and blow across her, but the sun came out, and it grew too hot under the iron roof with its regular, rigid ripple. Besides, now the upstairs space was her own again, she must leave it and go down to take over the sand and sea.

Listening to the little ones re-exploring the house, shouting about the hammock and last year's forgotten comics, reminded her unfairly of other voices in their everyday home in the city over the hills, voices that argued at midnight when other people were supposed to be asleep. Harry had another secret that was not really hers, though now she had it, she could tell it at any time she wanted to.

"But I never would. Never! Never! Never!" she said under her breath three times, like a spell.

It filled her with uneasy triumph, for simply knowing it made her powerful after years and years of being nothing but a middle one, someone over whom older and younger members of the family could cheerfully seesaw.

"Shhhh!" Harry leaned forward to whisper to her reflection. The untold secret made a little cloud on the silver glass, and the reflection obediently tightened its lips over stories that no one else must be allowed to hear.

3
Hand to Hand

Harry came out onto the verandah just as Serena
stopped being a ballet dancer in love and leaped off
over the grass with Benny. They shouted to each
other as if there were great distances between
them, then vanished among the trees, flickering in
and out of sight like jumpy figures in an old film.
But the path that had carried the little ones off to
the beach simultaneously delivered two sandy men,
loaded with waterproof bags, fresh from the sea.
Sheathed in their oilskins the newcomers swam
through the golden afternoon, shouting cheerfully
back at the children and forward to Jack, Anthony
and Harry, who were coming to meet them.

"My oldest son, Charlie." Jack introduced the
fair-headed young man to Anthony Hesketh. Charlie and his companion had come to Carnival's Hide
by sea, sailing Charlie's boat, *Sunburst*, across the
harbour, for Charlie was an enthusiastic sailor and
always took part in the New Year Regatta at Gorse
Bay, the first big bay to the east of Carnival's Beach.

"And this is Robert Huxley, a friend of Charlie's — well, a family friend by now. Charlie, you've heard me talk about Anthony Hesketh — here on a forestry fellowship." Charlie and Robert both nodded. "Robert," said Jack, "you'll be relieved to know that Serena has taken a liking to Anthony, so maybe you'll be spared the dancing and the meaningful looks for a while."

"What a false-hearted girl," Charlie said to Robert. "I wonder how you'll get by with only Christo."

"I'll manage, don't you worry," Robert said, shaking Anthony's hand warmly. "I'm sure she's chosen the best man."

"I think it's my sunglasses," Anthony said. "They give me an added edge." He looked apologetically at Robert, for Robert, his dark curls tossing in the nor-wester looked so like dashing Lord Byron it seemed wrong to take any affections from him — even Serena's.

"It'll be your accent," Charlie said. "Jack and Christobel and Serena are right into culture, and they love a good, English accent."

"Forgive him — and forgive that attempt at a beard too," Jack said to Anthony. "He's trying so hard to make himself look older." And then he asked the men from the sea if they had had a good journey across the harbour. They now began to speak with great enthusiasm in a sort of part song, praising the power of the wind (fifteen knots one moment and forty the next), the water (they'd gone over twice, but had managed to right the boat through pure skill) and the boat itself, which had survived the crossing with nothing broken in spite of the force of some of the gusts.

"Is Ma here yet?" Charlie asked.

"Is Christo here?" Robert asked in the same moment.

"Either of them could arrive at any time," Jack said vaguely. "We're on our way down for the first Christmas swim."

"Well, tell the kids to give my love to Teddy," Charlie said cheerfully. "Have you turned the fridge on? Robert and I might sit down on the steps and have one beer and then we'll come down ourselves, and tidy up *Sunburst*."

Jack and Anthony walked down the track followed by Harry. Anthony had the pale skin of someone who had passed straight from winter to summer with no spring in between. He had the trick of looking around him as if he were remembering things, and so he already seemed at ease with the track down to the sea. Then, beyond the orchard and the native bush, they came face to face at last with the harbour, held in a circle of craggy hills in the cone of an old volcano. Its grey spaces and reflecting films of water at low tide made it look more like a prehistoric estuary than a commercial port, even though docks and cranes, small as children's toys, could be seen directly opposite. Thin soil lay draped over the bones of the land, in long, curving folds, falling, always falling, down to the sea and ending in a ragged coastline of tiny bays and indentations. Native bush grew darkly in the gullies; the gaunt ridges were freckled with the gold of gorse and broom. The two landscapes ran into each other and made a new countryside altogether (not pretty, but desolate, beautiful and timeless). Towards the eastern end of the beach was the boathouse with Charlie's *Sunburst* drawn up on the ramp, and beyond that, just as if sand and seagrass had somehow worked themselves into a useful shape, was a little cabin propped up by flax bushes and wild yellow lupin. Harry saw Anthony notice it.

"That's the old whare," she told him.

"What? A-a warry? You've lost me now," said Anthony doubtfully.

"It's a Maori word for house — in this case a little, old hut," Jack explained. "We've got a fishing net in it, and one or two other things. And four bunks! It hasn't been used — oh, for about three years."

"I expect it was handy in the wife-swapping days," Anthony suggested.

"Yes, it probably was," Jack agreed absent-mindedly. He was wrapped in his own thoughts, but Harry looked keenly at Anthony, thinking he had made a sly family joke almost without anyone noticing. The breeze lifted his hair, which was a soft, light brown with fair streaks in it, not curling so much as rippling like the sea.

He caught her eye, shrugged slightly and made a gesture that took in the sea and hills.

"An extinct volcano . . . The harbour . . . Carnival's Hide!" he said. "Well, here I am."

"Here you are!" Jack agreed, but Harry thought Anthony had been using the words to talk to himself. Her imagination played a trick on her by suggesting she had seen him standing here before, even though she knew it was his first visit.

Voices came sonorously over the water. To the west, Serena and Benny were established on a large, smooth rock, higher and flatter than its neighbours. Mysteriously their reflections swam in the sea below them for, though the rest of the harbour was chopped by the wind, directly under this protecting rock, within the curve of the small promontory, the water was smooth enough to form a mirror. Their images rose and fell with the sinuous breath of the sea. Serena and Benny peered intently into the water, chanting softly to their reflections.

"What are they looking at?" Anthony asked.

"Oh, it's a private ceremony!" Jack said lightly. "Rather like a game in a graveyard. That's the very rock where Teddy Carnival dived and disappeared."

Anthony looked fascinated.

"It must be alluring," he remarked at last. "There's a definite charm about frisking around the edges of doom. I've played in a few graveyards myself."

"We've always been very happy here, ghost or not," Jack said.

"I don't doubt it," Anthony said. His face was pleasant rather than handsome, but as he spoke, staring over at the children, something enigmatic and imperative looked out of his mild, blue-grey eyes.

Harry, who at seventeen was the closest of them all to being a child herself, knew just what the children were doing and swam over to them, finally pulling herself up beside them. They lay on their stomachs on the wide, warm rock, saying a name over and over again like an incantation.

"Teddy Carnival! Teddy Carnival! We are here, O Teddy. You are not alone," they murmured.

"You'd be terrified if he did come. Don't give the sea your own names whatever you do," Harry warned them, only partly teasing them.

"He was never found," said Serena in a sonorous, melancholy voice. "There's a bottomless cave down there, and he was sucked into it."

Harry lay down beside them on the rock. The wind roared and shook its hot mane over them, while her hair dripped wet freckles on to the stone, which dried almost as soon as they formed.

"It's not bottomless, nothing like!" she said. "I've felt all over that cave and it's not much longer than an arm. It's more like a tunnel really — a tunnel left by a volcano worm."

"Don't frighten me," Benny cried, for he sometimes suffered from nightmares. "I'm not scared of Teddy. But no volcano worms!"

"She's inventing, you know how she does," Serena said. "Anyhow, Harry Hamilton, you used to call Teddy too, and give him your name. It's just a way of remembering him, like putting flowers on his grave." She looked intently at Harry, but all she could see was a curtain of hair and the tip of a nose.

"Christobel started it," Benny said, as if that made it all right, while Serena stared at Harry a moment longer, then sighed deeply.

They all three stared into the water, but the only faces they saw there were their own, differently drowned, a darker green than the green sea.

"What do you want for Christmas?" Benny asked Serena, beginning another game.

"A white pony with a cream mane and tail and a scarlet saddle and bridle," Serena said promptly, "or a lot of tame golden pheasants that will eat out of my hand and won't come to anyone else."

"You won't get anything like that," he said, shaking his head.

"I know that," Serena replied, "but you said what did I want, not what would I get!"

"I'd like a racing car or a hang-glider — blue, so I would look as if I were hanging on to the sky," Benny said. "What do you want, Harry?"

Harry was about to say she couldn't think of anything she wanted and almost thought it was true, but, as her mouth was opening, her thought turned inside out and she saw plainly that what she wanted was not nothing, but everything. She was sick of feeling closed in by people above and people below, of being good old Harry, not wonderful Ariadne, for that was her real name. She was sick of being gratefully but carelessly praised for docility when she wanted to have a turn at being the difficult, brilliant one instead, and she longed to be overwhelmed by something so whirling and powerful she could never be expected to resist it.

Being the middle one of the family suddenly seemed like an illness she had suffered from all her life, which might finally kill her if things did not change. But to wish for change was like wishing for a white pony with a cream mane and tail, or a sky-blue hang-glider. She began to play with her wish a little bit, to tell it, but in such a way that its true nature was hidden.

"I'd like a book," she said slowly, dabbling in a rock pool.

"Grunt! Grunt!" cried Benny scornfully. "Just a

book!" His glasses made him look clever, but he was a slow reader and suspicious of the printed word.

"It's a special book, this one," Harry said. She had just found a ring of white shell, the collar of some vanished mollusc, the rest of the shell broken off and carried away. "As you read my book you alter the world. You read Chapter One, look up from its pages and — hey presto — things have changed."

"Like *Alice in Wonderland?*" asked Serena, interested.

"Not that sort of change!" Harry said, peering down into the water again. "It would be just little changes to start off with, and nothing would move while you watched it. But each time you looked up, the world would have altered more and more. Things would get brighter and brighter, and the moon would come down, inch after inch, until it broke into a thousand little moons. Mirrors would begin to cry silver and leak out rainbows, and the glass people would come out searching for the one they belonged to. You'd look up from a page and see the reflections getting about, peering into people's faces, and when they found the right one they'd hug them, and from then on that person would be seen in their true beauty." Harry fell silent.

"Go on!" Serena said, profoundly intrigued. She stared at Harry as if Harry herself might be an unknown glass person in disguise.

"Oh, nothing more — only that, when you got to the end of the book, you'd feel there was a face watching you through the last page, and when you turned the last page, you'd find that you were a book yourself," cried Harry, suddenly delighted with her own invention. "You were a book, and someone else was reading you. Story and real would take it turn and turn about, you see."

She slid the white ring on to her finger. It was rather large but looked convincing on her brown hand.

"There! I've married the sea. I'm Mrs Oceanus," she said. "Everything comes out of me."

Serena pondered this all. Frowning, Benny asked, "Suppose you were hugged by a reflection — what would it feel like?"

"It would feel like a jump," Harry said positively. "A jump into a high place." She could see her water-face, blurred and misty below her, she stretched out her arm and touched it so that it broke into many different rings spreading out below her. "My book would make something happen in the outside world by the power of its stories," she said.

"There's no such book though," said Serena, "or you could get it from the library."

"The waiting list would be too long," Benny said gloomily, for he always wanted to read books based on television programmes and had to wait a long time to get them.

"I'll write it myself then," Harry promised, muttering back to the muttering sea. Now, just to bring common-sense back into the world, Benny pushed Serena, who was round and rolled easily, into the water and then jumped in after her. They swam off, bubbling and shouting and their churned-up reflections swam with them, leaving Harry to watch her own piece itself patiently together again. She thought she might not wait for it to come looking at her, but embrace it first and by taking it into herself grow brighter — as bright as Christobel perhaps. Now was the time to be bright, now school was over until next year, now she was her own person for a while. Half-smiling, she slipped gently into the water, feeling cautiously for branches that might have been carried against the rocks by a forcible tide. However, she could feel nothing except for the water, like wonderful silk, cool and warm at the same time. Even though the tide was out she could not quite touch the bottom, so she turned over in a slow somersault and dived down into the sea.

The water in the harbour was never quite clear. Particularly on a nor-west day there was always some mud suspended in it, so Harry entered a semi-opaque world rather than a translucent one. The feeling of her hair streaming behind her was wonderful. She had become a current, an eddy, a part of the ocean.

The little cave appeared like a black submarine eye watching her swim towards it and then became a plug-hole through which all the oceans of the world could run and roar, emptying out between the stars. Harry had to reassure herself that it did not go on forever by putting her hand right to the back of it, as she had done many times before. But this time something different happened. For a moment she thought a red-hot wire had sliced down and severed her hand, and then she thought it was a blade of ice, and finally she knew her hand was still joined to her, for she could feel its fingertips and bending thumb. There *was* discontinuity, but it was not in her. Her hand had found an alien space there in the tunnel under Teddy Carnival's rock, so she was in one place, and somehow, her hand was in another. This was the first terrifying thing to happen to her. The second was that another chilly hand took hers and held it very lightly. There could be no mistake. She could distinctly feel the fingertips and the ball of the thumb. Then something (she thought it was a mouth) whispered against her palm and at once her palm could see. It could see the age of the rock, the volcano in which the rock had been born out of fire, and the salt water that had slowly shaped it over thousands of years. Pictures of a rambling garden, in which a spade and garden fork stood up like witnesses, formed in her mind, and Carnival's Hide could be seen beyond them, recognizable but indefinably altered. Her mind was flooded with memories not her own; she saw, not through her eyes, which were full of salt and greenness, but through her lost hand. Shouting furiously underwater, she snatched her arm back out of the tunnel with no trouble at all, though she was uncertain if her hand had actually come with it. Her cry could not be heard, but rose in silver bubbles before her eyes, just as if she were a screaming girl in a comic book. "Eeeeeek!" would be written in the heart of each bubble, but it would stay unheard until the bubbles burst on the surface of the sea. Meanwhile, she dived upwards until her head came out. She coughed violently in the face of the wind, while salt tears, some of them from under her eyelids, poured down her cheeks. A weird, whooping sound filled her ears, but it was only her own sound, made as she struggled to get her breath again. There were screams from the beach too, but cheerful ones, for

Jack was romping with Serena and Benny, and Anthony was laughing and encouraging them. Everything was as it should be.

She had vanished for a minute — maybe less. At least she knew she could hold her breath for that long. As she bobbed in the water, lungs panting, heart pounding, a great jumble of thoughts running through her head, she found herself believing that the space beyond the rock was the same space that existed behind the lines of print in her book, and she had but managed to reach through to it and had actually touched one of its inhabitants.

Somehow she had crumpled things up by wishing to be the sea's wife, with everything coming out of her so that points in time, which had once been far apart, had actually folded together. Her hand was safe, clenched on the end of her arm — but inside her she was divided, the homely, familiar world behaving in a normal way on one side, and on the other a prospect of madness.

Harry decided to climb back on to the rock until she had got over her shock and could face the world calmly. She turned in the water and got the worst fright of all. The rock was not empty. A man was sitting there. For a moment she thought it must be Anthony because, though she knew this man, he was not a member of her family. But then she heard Anthony's voice behind her, so of course it couldn't be he. Besides, this man was undergoing a crisis of a sort she had never seen or even imagined before — not a mere, nervous twitching of the skin, but a terrible seething, as if at any moment he was about to boil furiously. For fractions of a second he ceased to exist, and though Harry's eye was tricked into carrying him over these gaps, she knew he was not continuous, only an intermittent presence trying to make a place for himself in the world. He was fully dressed and soaking wet, kneeling and staring out to the horizon, his hair dragged down by the weight of the water in it. Water streamed from every part of him.

There was no reason why people should not walk around the coast to Carnival's Beach. Though the little seashore seemed to belong to the Hamiltons, it could not really be privately owned. However, she knew this man had not picked his way round the headland as people occasionally did. He was too sudden and too wet — the source of many springs — and from the side of his face that was partly visible to her, the water ran red.

Treading water and gasping, knowing him at last, Harry imagined a face eaten away by mud crabs, and then a face untouched by water or crabs or time, which might be even more frightening. Besides, he was certainly bleeding. With every moment of recognition he became more and more real and horrifying, until Harry ducked her head under the water and tried to fill her thoughts with something else. She thought desperately of characters in her own story — of winged Belen, of mocking Prince Valery; she did everything she could to deny the existence of the man on the rock. When she came up again the rock was empty. He was quite gone.

A great shouting now began from Serena and Benny, and their pleased excitement reached over to bewildered, frightened Harry. She began a lopsided, clumsy dog-paddle, one hand still clenched, away from the rock, limp with shock and astonishingly drowsy in the water, as if suffering from an after-effect of concussion. The family were looking and listening. They began moving up the hill.

"It's happened at last," Harry said, taking a breath as she swam, but speaking with her lips under water so that words bubbled out softly. "I've gone mad from imagining things." Even if she spoke out clearly no one would take her seriously.

"Dreaming again, my poor old Harry!" Jack would say, rubbing her head affectionately. "But we'd better get a bit of speed on. That's Ma's car coming down the hill. She'll need a hand."

So Harry came out of the sea and began following her family. There was nothing else to do. The rock was empty. Her hand was still safely on the end of her arm, her ring of shell had washed back into the sea. She reared up on legs that felt as if they might yield to the strong backwards slide of the water that flung lacy wings high around her knees. Up along the track ordinary family life was going on and Harry would have to join in. But as she thought about it, it seemed no more substantial than a sea mist, which — at a given word — would dissolve into nothing, and carry her with it.

4
A Private Argument

Harry thought her father was the best-looking man she knew and also was aware from old photographs that he had always been handsome. Even now, when his face was lined and his thick, waving hair was iron grey, it seemed he had merely exchanged one kind of beauty for another. Sometimes Harry thought that being so handsome had let him off learning slow lessons like patience, but then he had Naomi — Harry's mother — to be patient for him. People who had met Jack for the first time often expected him to be married to some matching woman, someone glamorous, polished and probably younger than he was, and they couldn't always hide their surprise politely enough on meeting Naomi, who was actually a year older than Jack and a little taller, with pleasant freckles, a beaky nose, an uproarious laugh and a lopsided smile, as if one half of it were sadder than the other. However, Harry, a family listener and watcher, knew her parents loved each other, wept when they argued and sometimes embraced in the shadows like threatened lovers. Over recent years it had been Jack who feared to lose Naomi, not the other way round.

Serena and Benny bounded up to the verandah to welcome their mother, as excited as if they had not seen her for a week, instead of having left her only two hours ago. They found her already out of her car releasing Crumb, the grey cat, from his cat box, for Crumb was a portable cat and came with them every holiday.

"Moo! Moo!" they shouted enthusiastically. Then they both rushed to cuddle Crumb, though neither of them had wanted to travel in the same car with him because he cried aloud in great, hollow, melodious miaows all the time the car was moving. However, he was so furious at having been confined to a box that he began hissing in little spurts, like a kettle with a slight leak, and ran in under the house where he crouched, staring out at them with a malignant smile. The ends of his whiskers had gone into tight little curls from sitting too close to a heater one cool summer midnight a few days ago.

Harry, coming up through the orchard, could hear Serena reproaching Crumb, could hear the steps of Anthony and Jack coming out onto the verandah.

"We'll expect Christo when we see her," Naomi was saying, hugging Benny with one arm, waving to Harry with the other and simultaneously talking to someone else. (Harry could remember very few times when she had had her mother's completely undivided attention.)

"She hadn't arrived when I left, so I stuck a note on the door with Christmas sticky-tape. She's probably dropped off to visit Emma on the way here. Now, give me a hand to get this stuff into the deep freeze." Naomi began to take cartons of plastic bags and trays of food out of the back of her car, reminding Harry of the golden, tussocky, summer hills, which climbed in every direction around Carnival's Hide, open and sunny, yet, in the end, never completely knowable.

"There's enough there for several Christmases," Anthony said, looking impressed, and Naomi laughed, filling his arms with a carton of mixed vegetables.

"Oh well, you were promised a typical New Zealand Christmas, and that always involves overeating."

"A typical Christmas?" cried Serena, insulted. "We're better than typical."

"Much better!" Benny agreed, shooting out a spray of cracker crumbs. "Sorry!" he mumbled, breathing them in and then beginning to choke.

Silent and salty, Harry loped gently into a room alive and murmuring with the nor-west wind. It touched the curling spines of old books in the bookcase and ran an airy thumb across the pages of music piled untidily on top of the piano, so that these loose edges kept up a continual nervous movement all over the room. The pile of stuff being unpacked on the floor included inflatable mattresses, sun umbrellas, cartons of food, boxes of clothes, extra blankets in case it turned cold, and crates of beer and lemonade in case it turned hot, and many, many parcels in bright Christmas paper, which were being piled in the corner where the tree would stand later tomorrow.

"Jack," said Naomi, directing operations, "will you be a pet and bring those bottles of plums into the kitchen."

The plums, swimming in a tight school behind their curving glass, were a pretty pink with just a trace of gold, but they pleased neither Jack, who shrugged at them, nor Serena.

"Those are the sour ones!" Serena cried. "We're cut off here with the sour ones! It isn't fair." She clasped her hands dramatically over her heart.

"Everyone does plum-duty this Christmas!" Naomi declared. "Have them with oatmeal or cornflakes. Take the sour with the sweet."

"Who wants breakfasts with a moral?" Jack called back out of the kitchen, and Naomi gave her lopsided smile in his direction.

As things fell into their holiday places, other half-forgotten things, rediscovered, sprang to life once more. The hammock was strung between two apple trees in the ruined orchard, like a net set to catch transparent fish swimming on the tide of the nor-west wind. Almost at once it began to struggle and twist.

"We've caught the ghost of Teddy Carnival," said Serena, and then shivered and cuddled herself a little, as if her own words had chilled her, even though she had known drowned Teddy for so long.

"He won't hurt us though, will he?" Benny said confidently. "We've been down to the sea and let him know it's just us."

"I suppose Jack has introduced you to the Carnivals," Naomi said to Anthony, and he paused on his way through to the kitchen and looked up at the old curling photographs on the wall.

"We have met," he said. "Did Edward stay on, after the boy drowned?"

"Not for very long," Naomi said. "He stayed on and wrote a long rhyming poem on the event, which is almost impossible to read nowadays . . ."

"A sort of copy of a famous poem," Serena interrupted.

"It's called *A Colonial Lycidas*," Naomi explained. "And then funnily enough, he left Carnival's Hide and became a reasonable, normal man again. I mean he bought land close to a road, he entertained friends, did his experiments with tree planting, and in due course he and his daughter went back to England."

". . . but Teddy had to stay . . ." Serena added.

"Harry, are you all right?" Naomi asked, staring across the room at her.

"Why?" asked Harry touching her face anxiously. She could feel cold fingers on cheeks and chin, but they seemed like someone else's fingers on someone else's face.

"Nothing much. You just looked a bit washed out." Naomi turned back to Anthony without waiting for an answer, apparently guessing that Harry had no answer to give her. "Teddy was about eleven when that picture was taken, but it was already too late for him, poor boy."

"That's a very strange comment," Anthony said, laughing a little. "Already too late for him? He was a grown man when he died, wasn't he?"

"He was twenty," Naomi said. "Serena, remember that's Crumb's dish and don't put it with the others. No — it's just that when his wife died, Edward devoted himself to his children and invented his own educational system, which seems to have been based partly on one of those return-to-nature ideas — man being always happy close to the earth in his natural state — and partly the suppression of feeling in favour of what Edward called 'rationality'. He wanted to train them up like good forest trees, I suppose. We don't really know the details of what went on at Carnival's Hide, even though Edward wrote a book about his educational theory, because he destroyed it when Teddy died."

Harry had given herself the job of putting tea towels in one pile and sorting out the sheets and pillowcases for Anthony, her parents and Christobel. Everyone else would use sleeping bags. She was comforting her nervous hand, reminding it that there were ordinary things to touch. All the same she could feel it trembling very slightly. The tremble began in the ends of her fingers and lost itself in her wrist bones. She could feel the eyes of Teddy Carnival on her, for wherever you stood in the room Teddy watched you with his chilly smile. In the photograph or in the old gossipy stories left over from his own time, he was manageable. Down by the sea he was not.

"Edward made them garden a lot," she said. Her voice sounded ordinary enough even in her own ears. "He wanted to make this place into something like the Garden of Eden."

"But they never had other children to play with," Naomi said, "and when in due course people did meet them, Teddy seems to have been particularly — well — unpredictable. It was as if people were his toys — something entertaining he could play games with."

Robert and Charlie looked into the room from the hall.

"We've put all that stuff away, Ma," Charlie said. "We're off to the beach."

"Talking about the old ghost?" Robert asked, looking from one to the other of them, smiling. "He always sounded a bit rough to me."

From far away there came a short, sharp, tenor blast of a horn.

"Here's trouble!" said Jack, sliding in past the young men, and looking pleased.

"Come on, Robert!" Charlie cried. "You can see her in a minute. You haven't met Christobel, have you, Anthony?"

"I feel as if I have," Anthony said.

"You'll know all about it when you do," Charlie declared, taking Robert's arm tightly as if Robert might make a bolt for freedom.

"Can't I just . . . ?" Robert began.

"Oh no!" said Charlie. "Because once Christo gets her hooks into you, you won't be able to call your soul your own. If we hurry we'll be back by the time she's parked the car and shouted a few times and given everyone a hug."

"Anyhow," Naomi said to Anthony, speaking rather rapidly as if she were anxious to get a particular story over and done with, "we may even get a visit from some Carnival relatives this Christmas. We got a letter at the museum from a great granddaughter of Minerva's asking about old family relics because someone was coming over for a holiday. I think she was offering additions to the collection. I don't know what the boss replied, but he suggested I might even let them stay in the house if we weren't using it. I'd be happy to do that."

"We could learn even more gossip," Harry said.

The horn spoke again, though much closer this time.

"She's through the gate," Serena said, running out on to the verandah. Benny followed her. They danced and mooed excitedly.

Gossip in the past had talked about Teddy being amusing in a rather malicious way, but there were also stories about moods of violence. Teddy had at least once teased young men with quick, sharp words until they attacked him and had then attacked them back with particular savagery. But Christobel was coming, and Teddy had to make way. The sound of the old car could be heard turning around the house. Anthony, who had been balancing a carton on the back of a chair, carried it into the kitchen, and Harry thought of showing how independent she was by climbing up her ladder into her room and then coming down casually a moment later. "Christobel!" she would say. "Hi! I didn't know you were here." There came the sound of feet on the verandah and cries from the children. The front door banged open, the walls rang with excitement, the sitting room door burst in. Christobel had arrived.

"Here I am!" she shouted in case they were in any doubt about who it was.

"Ma!" she cried. "Holidays! Christmas! Terrific!" Over Naomi's shoulder she stared at Anthony with open curiosity. She did not wait for an introduction, but let Naomi go and moved towards him holding out her hand, speaking as she did so. "Anthony someone, I know!" she said. "Jack told me about you."

"Here on a forestry fellowship," said Jack doing his best to be in charge of the introduction.

Beauty was not enough for Christobel. She wanted to be noticed in every way, and if she had nothing surprising to talk about she simply made something up. Now, shaking Anthony's hand, she said, "Forestry! Jack — he hasn't come half way round the world to look at a million pine trees? Either he's embezzled money or had a terrible love affair, and now he's trying to find a forest at the end of the world where robins will cover him over with leaves."

"No robins here," Benny said puzzled.

Anthony did not look taken-aback. His face was too well trained for that. However, something odder happened. He blushed and, as he had no tan to hide behind, the blood rose up over his neck and cheeks and forehead until his whole face glowed with it. It was impossible not to be interested. Christobel laughed with surprise and triumph. However, when he spoke his voice was easy.

"I'll need a forest that fits," he said. "One I can go a long way into."

This answer pleased Christobel.

"Right! We'll find one for you. We'll come and visit you and put out bowls of milk like we do for hedgehogs, and after a while you'll turn into the mystical blushing man of the forest — no — hang on — you'll turn into an oracle and give us riddly answers to our questions. Terrific!" She turned her head with her own special eagerness.

"Old Harry!" she said, and it was Harry's turn to be hugged.

"You feel thinner!" Christobel exclaimed at once. "I actually felt bones. Have you been dieting?" she ended half-accusingly, looking Harry up and down as if she were thinking of buying her. "Grow your bangs out, get contact lenses, and you'll begin to pass as a human girl instead of something from outer-space."

"Don't be awful!" cried Serena. She was thrilled with Christobel's ruthlessness, and yet terrified it would be her turn next. As for Harry, she felt immediately relieved, without quite knowing why, and then disconcerted to find out that, like Serena, she badly wanted Christobel's approval.

Blow! she thought, for she had imagined she'd grown out of such old submissions. Nothing changes.

"Have you been on a diet?" Christobel demanded.

"No!" said Harry, as if scorning such vanity, but she was lying.

"Well, you look a lot better," Christobel said. "People can be as understanding as they like about puppyfat; it's not a thing you want to see a lot of. Puppyfat!" she exclaimed, and laughed. "You were more like a mature St Bernard. We could have hung a barrel of rum around your neck and hired you out for mountain rescues."

"Don't be awful!" cried Serena again. "Just because you're always so skinny . . ."

"It's for her own good," Christobel declared indignantly. "Old Harry's worked so hard at making the worst of herself she deserves a hearty round of criticism . . . that's all I can say."

"That's just about enough!" said Harry. "Any more might be too much." But this afternoon she was glad to be an uncomplaining St Bernard, mocked by Christobel just as she had always been, rather than the new kind of person who crumpled reality with passionate wishes.

"It's lovely to be home — lovely!" Christobel said fervently, one arm still over Harry's shoulders. Voices were heard outside and feet on the steps. "Oh, by the way, Ma, I forgot to tell you, I brought Emma and Tibby along with me. Is that all right?" She asked this question as if she were perfectly sure of the answer, yet time stopped between a tick and a tock. There was a little silence.

"Oh, come on!" Christobel cried. "It's only Emma! Emma and Tibby! Your adopted foster family! Remember them?"

"You could have warned us," grumbled Jack despairingly. "We've got Anthony staying."

"I dare say he's met an unmarried mother before now," Christobel said, looking over at Anthony in astonishment. "They have them in England, don't they? And there's plenty of room. Shove them in with Serena."

"Or with you," said Serena boldly.

"Not on your life," Christobel replied. "Don't expect *me* to be reasonable."

"Of course I don't mind," Naomi said. "I was just surprised because *I* asked her over for Christmas and she refused so definitely. What did you say to make her change her mind?"

"I *bully* people," Christobel said triumphantly. "I get ten times the results. Come on! A single person — well one and a half — after the crowds we are used to having. There's masses of room."

"Say 'Moo!', Tibby. Say it!" Benny was crying on the other side of the door. The door was pushed open and in came Christobel's friend, Emma Forbes, trying to hold her wriggling, heavy, two-year-old daughter Talitha, while behind her Benny leaped up and down, wriggling his fingers like spider puppets to get the baby's attention. She looked at Jack and Naomi anxiously.

"Christobel insisted," she began rather incoherently. "I tried to say 'No!' and I *did* say it. I said, 'No, *no, no!*' "

"Check!" agreed Christobel.

"But here I am," Emma said helplessly. Naomi smiled at her.

"Emma dear!" she said gently. "Of course! Look — we've missed you lately, and it'll be a treat to have a baby in the family again."

Tibby's father was known to be Sam, a lively, wandering fellow, once a regular Christmas visitor at Carnival's Hide, now vanished forever into the wilds of Canada. Her mother, Emma Forbes, was a small, kittenish girl with soft brown hair, soft brown eyes and a strong sense of survival. When her own parents had separated many years ago, Emma had adopted first Christobel and then her family, so very firmly that the Hamiltons had found themselves adopting her back, and, until Tibby was born, she shared many Christmases with them, adoring Jack and Naomi, half in love with Charlie, bossing Harry and fussing over the little ones. But now, with a baby of her own to fuss over, she had become unexpectedly independent, although Serena and Benny (particularly Benny) loved Tibby and thought she belonged to them every bit as much as she did to Emma.

"This child is pleased to see me!" Benny said. He often called Tibby "this child", adopting a grave, elderly tone.

But it was Christobel who now swept Tibby away from Emma and began to circle the floor with her in a jiggling dance.

"Dance-a-Tibby! Dance-a-Tibby-round!" she sang, adding, "Isn't it lucky she's so pretty? I'm not usually turned on by the little ones."

Tibby, one of those children whose baby hair appears quite white, roared with laughter, showing a vitality as strong as Christobel's own.

"More!" she cried. "Dance-Tibby more!" But Christobel, who did not often want more, put her down, patted her head and moved away from her.

"Perhaps we could have something to eat?" Jack suggested pathetically. "I was lured inside some years ago with the promise of food."

"Moo! Moo!" applauded Serena and Benny, giggling and pushing one another in enjoyment of their own wit.

"I'll put a cold meal out on the verandah table," Naomi said, "and hope that it doesn't blow away. Just help yourselves quickly . . . lettuce, sliced ham, tomatoes, cottage cheese, mayonnaise in the blue jug, french dressing in the little pottery one, potato salad in the big enamel bowl. Assorted drinks in the fridge! It hasn't been on long so they'll be cool rather than cold. Still, all that a reasonable heart could desire."

"Can I have beer?" asked Benny boldly. "Charlie does."

"That's not reasonable. Of course not!" Naomi said. "Put on dry clothes at once, Benny. No running around in wet togs. You'll ruin your Christmas if you get a chill. You others — I've turned the hot water on up in the bath-house so some of you can probably have showers if you want to wash the salt off you, and some of you will have to wait. And please — please don't leave wet towels all over the floor."

People separated to wash, dress, brush their tangled hair, and then began to reassemble, all glowing from the rough tongue of the lion wind.

Once upstairs, Harry sat on the floor of her loft, trying to make life ordinary again. But her mind refused to turn the seething, bleeding man into reflected light or any other natural trick. She had put out her hand and Teddy Carnival had taken it. He had always been in the air, or suspended in the water. She had breathed him in, and at last she was making him come alive. Reluctantly she put that same, fated hand under her blue pillow (trembling to see it vanish), where it met nothing worse than the square edges of her book. She took the book out and looked at it, thinking it might be the source of her madness. But at last she opened it and began to write, and as she did so, found relief, for the seeing hand and the bleeding man lost themselves, at last, in her story and became just another adventure that she had invented. She wrote on:

The Prince Valery moved through the throng glittering like a star. He was dressed entirely in white against which his ethereal golden ringlets shone. As he smiled, his expression was gentle and sweet, and only those who looked deep into his eyes saw the sparkle of amused malice in them. Everything he spoke of was made less by his words unless he spoke of himself. He praised himself outrageously, but so sarcastically that it was hard for anyone to know whether or not he meant it.

"How beautiful the Lady Jessica looks," said a friend of his. "Beautiful and happy."

"Beautiful and happy?" said Valery. "That is much too ostentatious. She certainly overdoes things."

"No, Prince — she's very shy. A modest girl."

"She has more to be modest about than most people," the Prince replied, for he hated to have his half-sister praised in front of him.

Harry hesitated, her pen poised, staring at what she had written with a certain surprise for it seemed to her rather clever. She was glad to be distracted from her earlier experiences. A moment later her pen, almost deciding for itself, began scratching like a small night creature, in a busy self-absorbed fashion, while Harry listened, comforted, to the murmuring voices rising up from below.

Suddenly Belen's black eyes fell on one particular girl, Lady Jessica, the Prince's half-

sister, slender as a silver-birch, vivid as a flame. Belen smiled, for he could see below the rose-coloured silk to the white electric skin beneath it. Jessica stopped and gazed up into the air as if she could feel him looking down at her. There were bright torches everywhere and she couldn't see up into the night where he circled above her in the air.

Harry thought she could tell that Christobel had just come from the verandah, into the room below, could tell by her step, or could sense her like an extra glitter in the light. She was opening a cookie tin. The faint, metallic twang was unmistakable.

"Oh, Ma! What's in this tin? Don't tell me you've been burning things again."

"Only baking!" said Naomi, sounding rather ashamed.

"They're the same thing with you. You burn things so often it's pagan!" exclaimed Christobel. "Buy cookies! *Buy* them! You can afford to."

"I feel guilty doing that," Naomi protested vaguely. "You know, Mother goes out to work, family life breaks down."

"Burning cookies won't stop any breakdown in family life," Jack declared. "Honestly, Naomi — here's a great one-way river roaring down at you, and you try to charm it away by holding out a cookie to it."

"Better than you, though," Naomi retorted, much less vaguely. "You just lie down and let the river run over you, then swirl off, smugly saying, 'Disaster! Just as I predicted!' Jack there *is* a definite difference between defeat and maturity, you know."

Jack flung his arms wide. He looked very like Christobel.

"Convince me," he cried warmly, "and you shall have an electric cake mixer for your next birthday."

"What a fearful revenge!" Christobel gave a shout of laughter. "He was going to get you a mink coat until you said that."

"I'll ice the burnt bits," Serena offered anxiously.

"I'll eat them!" Benny was even more generous. "I like burnt."

"That's not the point!" Christobel became indignant again. "Burnt is still burnt."

"Too true," agreed Jack. "And when things are ruined they're ruined. Put them out for the birds and forget them."

"Here — you're both sounding very sincere about something?" Christobel was asking a question. "Is it a very private argument, or can anyone join in?" Under the light voices sounded other more fervent tones left over from midnight. Christobel heard them, but Harry was the one who recognized them.

"Well, I brought some cookies," Emma said hesitantly. "Bought ones," she added.

"They'll be very welcome," Naomi told her. "Christobel, don't try and take over my fights with Jack. Go out onto the verandah and start one of your own. I'm sure you can if you try."

5

The Illustrated Beach

Harry came down her ladder to find Anthony studying the bookcase. Beyond him, Jack, who had fussily
brought his evening meal inside, sat in the best
chair, and Christobel paced up and down in front of
him with a glass saucer full of cottage cheese, pineapple and tomato, talking and waving a fork as if
conducting her own conversation. The windows
were wide open, so verandah-voices could easily be
heard.

"It's an intellectual collection of books for a holiday home," Anthony remarked to Harry as she set
her feet on the floor. "*Metamorphoses* by Ovid!" he
added with respect, pulling out one book and blowing the dust off it.

"Most of them are books no one ever quite feels
like reading, but we sort of respect them too much
to throw them out," Harry explained.

"Harry reads everything," said Serena, appearing out of nowhere at Anthony's elbow, surprising

Harry with unexpected praise. "She can read upside down, or in the bath and even in the . . ."

"You can't put *Metamorphoses* out for the Volunteer Fire Brigade garage sale, can you?" Jack asked quickly.

"Anyhow, I might read that George Eliot this Christmas," Christobel said, fired with ambition. "I loved *Middlemarch* when I finally got round to it."

Frustrated in her attempt to tell Anthony about Harry's reading powers, Serena pulled out a book, and shook it in Jack's direction.

"What about *The Book of Love*?" she cried with relish. "That's almost brand new, but Ma put it here because one of Jack's students gave it to him, didn't she, Jack?"

"Don't start that wife-swapping talk again!" Jack said wearily. This was a mistake.

"Oh, Anthony," cried Christobel, giving her father a needling smile, "you really should have been here three or four Christmases ago. It was all barbecues in those days, with wine, olives, people being sick in the bushes and a bit of fairly discreet wife-swapping going on."

"I'm sorry to have missed it," Anthony said, sounding sincere.

"Christobel just wants to forget how very respectable it mostly was," Jack protested.

"You're the one who forgets," Christobel declared indignantly. "Oh well, you were so busy making false jokes about being forty-five and trying to remember who had their steak rare. And anyhow I didn't say *you* were a wife-swapper. Emma and I watched you like hawks so you wouldn't get the chance." Jack, looking appalled, opened his mouth to say more.

"Don't apologize!" Christobel said quickly. "I wish it was still going on." She smiled rather impudently at Anthony. "Probably our greatest thrill this year will be rubbing sun-tan lotion on one another."

"It's a comedown after wife-swapping," said Anthony, "but then I'd have been at a disadvantage anyway, not having a wife in the first place."

"Never mind," said Christobel, making plans for herself, however, rather than for Anthony. "Just when you think you're going mad with the little ones kicking sand over you, Robert and I will whisk you away to Gorse Bay, where there's a tennis court and a marina, and there actually is some life at this time of year."

"Nasty life!" said Jack scornfully.

"You dear old-fashioned Jackie!" Christobel called back. "Just because people break a bit of glass at New Year! Here's to wonderful parties — that's what I say."

Memories of barbecues and wine assailed Harry, because she had been allowed to go swimming by moonlight. Lying on her back, her hair drifting out around her, she had floated limply, sustaining herself by the smallest possible movement, imagining herself to be a mermaid or a beautiful, drowned girl whom people would find washed up in the morning, and marvel over with desire and terror. On nights like that she had felt a slow heart beating in harmony, while the constellation Orion, faint but constant in the moon-painted sky, paced up out of the east towards her. At last, carrying the whole crater in her head, she allowed the laughing and singing voices to guide her home. But for Christobel and Emma, people, not stars, had been the spectacle of the summer nights, while Charlie probably remembered conversations about sailing, for many of the guests were members of the Gorse Bay Yacht Club.

Harry sat down on the edge of the verandah, legs dangling, while the wind battled to steal her lettuce leaves away, and she had to weight them down with cottage cheese and pieces of tomato.

Yet in spite of the wind and the fading light they elected to stay outside on the first evening at Carnival's Hide, watching gusts of wind sweeping in from over the sea. The ragged crests of the waves drew light into themselves and advanced in lines of broken luminosity across the dark surface of the harbour. The wind whirled in the bush, roared in the orchard, and at last attacked the house itself, rattling windows and doors, bringing the taste of salt with it.

"Midsummer!" Anthony said aloud, adding more doubtfully, "Christmas! New Year!" The festivals were rushing towards him in an unfamiliar order and would soon rattle him and sweep on by.

"Midsummer!" said Christobel echoing him. "Christmas! New Year!" She looked a little sad in the gathering dusk, watching Benny at the edge of the orchard pushing Tibby to and fro in the hammock. "Oh dear — I'm getting old so quickly. Yesterday a fifth former, today twenty-one, tomorrow thirty. Where's it all going? I want to be happy — I mean *wonderfully* happy, not just getting by. I do want marvellous chances, don't you?"

She was sitting on a cushion between Robert's

and Charlie's chairs, but neither of them answered her.

"I've got Tibby," said Emma, looking around Robert, and added apologetically, "OK — so it doesn't sound very trendy, but Tibby's my chance. And I never ever feel that nothing's happening. I often wish nothing was." She supplemented her social benefit payments by cleaning out a small factory, a block of offices, and a doctor's rooms.

"We think Christobel will marry Robert," Serena confided in Anthony, leaning intimately over his shoulder. She had enjoyed a large secret meal of peppermints ten minutes earlier. "She's been going out with him for ages, but she keeps on falling in love with other people."

"Never for long at a time, and never in front of him," Christobel shouted, overhearing this. "Mind you, fancy being married to an accountant! Fate worse than death, really." She rubbed her head affectionately against Robert's knee as she spoke.

Harry felt the house quiver, as if it were alive in its core, but whether it was straining towards something or away from it she couldn't tell.

The beast from a thousand fathoms! she thought, trying herself out. Maybe the volcano worm.

She was not frightened now, for her afternoon memory had become confused with her own invented stories. The hand that had lightly taken hers belonged to no one more substantial than Prince Valery or the winged Belen and threatened no one. The wind licked her hands and face with a hot tongue of air. Benny, who had been looking after Tibby, suddenly hoisted her on to the verandah looking disgusted because he had caught her drinking milk out of Crumb's saucer.

"Poor thirsty Crumb!" he said with a sigh, while Crumb himself, apparently electrified at this news leaped on to the back of Charlie's chair, wailing despondently. His tail was so thin it looked like a wire covered in dense grey fur. "Puss! Puss!" said Tibby, crinkling her fat, dirty fingers at him.

Robert looked at Tibby in the curve of her mother's arm.

"Hey — she said, 'Puss! Puss!'" he exclaimed. "She's talking."

"Of course she's talking," Emma replied, laughing at him. "She's a big girl."

"Big enough for a front-row forward!" Robert took his hand from Christobel's shoulder and extended it towards Tibby. "Hey, Tibby, say some more."

Delighted at finding herself the subject of attention, Tibby beamed at him and offered an unpainted wooden giraffe with gnawed ears. Robert took it politely, but Tibby snatched it back quickly.

"Mine!" she said. "Mine Dum Dum!"

"That's what she calls it — her Dum Dum!" explained Emma, enchanted by this cleverness.

"Oh, well — we've all got to begin somewhere!" Christobel said tolerantly.

"You hang on to that Dum Dum, Tibby!" said Robert heartily. "I wouldn't mind one myself."

So they sat and talked about nothing except themselves and the friends who might be calling in on Christmas Eve until Christobel grew restless and exclaimed suddenly, "What did I tell you, Anthony? Boring already."

"I *like* it quiet," Naomi protested. "I love it quiet."

"Oh, you great, old earth-mother you!" cried Christobel. "Did you remember to put the milk bottles out? Right. Then Robert and I will go off into the twilight and bring them in. It's about a mile to the milk box, Anthony, can you imagine!"

"And I must put Tibby to bed," Emma said, to the instant fury of her child who flung herself passionately on the ground shouting, "No bed, Mummy, no bed!"

"Gosh, I don't envy you," Christobel said laughing, vanishing into the dusk with Robert, and slowly other people began to think of the things they might just fit in before the day was gone forever.

Whatever it was that Harry had felt stirring in the tumultuous evening, now crept like a tide, unseen but all pervading, a faint stain working its way into everyone's vision, a whisper so low it was felt, not heard. Something came closer and closer, invaded the house and moved among them.

Out by the rocks at the end of Carnival's Beach, Christobel and Robert, having brought the milk in, but drawn by the whirling dusk, kissed, talked softly, then embraced and kissed again.

"Oh Christo," groaned Robert. "Oh Christobel!" and seemed to have some unexpected dilemma beyond immediate physical passion. But Christobel spoke quickly and restlessly as if she thought he might be about to introduce a difficult subject.

"Don't you feel we're being watched? Oh well, who cares! But still . . ."

"Serena?" Robert, diverted, looked out into the wild, deep twilight.

"Someone more chilly! Teddy Carnival, say! Are you there, Teddy?"

Curiously, there was a response. A voice cried wordlessly back, harsh and musical and desolate, a seabird hidden by the dark. Christobel shivered in the warm evening. "A goose is dancing on my grave. Let's walk a little, Robert darling. I love this warm wind, and I must say it suits you. How can an accountant wind up looking so much like a romantic bandit?"

In the kitchen Naomi wrapped cheese in a plastic bag, put empty bottles down beside the fridge and put new bottles in to chill. An ordinary, pleasant, unexciting Christmas is what we need, she thought, and then — who knows? "Wet towels on the verandah rail!" she said aloud, reminding someone she felt come into the room behind her, someone smelling of the sea. However, when she turned around, the kitchen was quite empty.

Emma, sitting with Tibby, drowsy at last and almost asleep, thought Naomi was looking in at the door.

"What's so strange about it all is that it really feels like coming home," she said uncertainly. "I thought it might have changed." There was no reply. "Are you absolutely sure it's OK for me to be here, baby and all?" She turned, but the room and the doorway were both empty.

Suppose, thought Harry, sitting at her peaked window, suppose I was accidentally *welcoming* someone through when I took that hand.

The night sighed around her bare shoulders, but then there was a perpetual sigh in the air, even between the gusts of wind, as if silence itself was breathing into the enchanted dark. She could hear, faint but unmistakable, the sea sidling around the rocks, sucking and fretting at the land below the trees. In the orchard, a shadow moved as if someone were standing there looking up at her, but when she put on her glasses and looked again it was nothing but an accident of night. She climbed into her sleeping bag at last, turned out her light on its extension cord and went to sleep, beginning to dream, as she dreamed every night, tumultuous dreams she would not recall in the morning.

Some people wake up to alarm clocks. Harry sometimes woke up to poetry. Scraps of verse, titles once seen on covers she had not bothered to open, childhood poems and mottoes rose and fell in a slow, continuous fountain in her mind. "So small a part of time . . . dull would he be of soul that could pass by . . . no longer at peace under the old dispensation . . . the sea, the sea . . . 'twas brillig and the slithy toves . . . whistled and warbled a moony song to the echoing sound of a coppery gong in the shade of the mountains brown!" Harry was aware of the silence behind the poetry, even before she was properly awake. The wind had dropped; the high cloud had gone; it was going to be a lovely day. As Charlie and Robert tiptoed up and down the verandah before setting off for *Sunburst* and the early morning harbour, Harry took out her exercise book, her pen marking the place where she had finished writing the night before.

Wicked Belen now had Jessica in his power. She was helpless, shrinking before him, but secretly thrilled by his strength and sneering beauty. Her helplessness provoked violent passion.

> *They fell together onto the quilt of fallen blossoms as if on to a bed of silver and ivory. "Now you will be mine," said Belen. "You can't escape. In the end you will beg me to possess you."*

What am I describing? Harry thought uneasily, but once again it seemed that Christobel, Emma, Anthony, Jack and Naomi became the ghosts of her imagination. The little ones barely existed. Once again her true life was being lived through the beautiful lovers of her story, eternally ravishing one another among flowers and jewels. She wrote until she felt empty of words, light and free enough to go properly into the day.

Wearing her track suit she came down into an empty morning. The sun was not up; it was very early. The day was unmarked, yet Harry, turning her head, remembering yesterday, was pricked by a sense of warning. "Watch out," she muttered softly through her teeth, pulling the laces of her sneakers tight. Whatever happened in the world beyond the door, her feet would be under control.

Crumb, cushioning a chair, smiled enigmatically at her, like a cat that has seen all but will tell nothing. Harry stuck out her tongue at the cat and, anxious not to risk waking Christobel by accidentally opening a door too loudly, climbed through one of the open windows on to the verandah. She had begun early morning jogging in November, determined to grow thinner, and had come to enjoy the rhythm of thought it set running through her mind. However, at Carnival's Hide, east, west and south all ran up hill, and north out into the sea. In the end she began by going down to the beach where the sand was silver above the high tide mark and damp and brown below it.

Someone had been drawing faces in this firm, damp sand, and not only faces but animals and birds. A procession of creatures capered and clowned along on stick-like legs, turning whiskered faces to look at her. Humans, horses, cats and owls all wore the same crescent smiles. But the sea was devouring this smiling procession from the feet up. Falling on her knees beside it to stare more closely, Harry watched as the sea foamed and swallowed a winged cat and then ran back again leaving an expanse of glistening sand as pure and shining as if nothing had ever been drawn there, and on this newly virgin surface Harry, still kneeling, saw greyness form. A lopsided, man-shaped darkness slowly grew, apparently oozing up between the shining grains, but it was really appearing because the fiery rind of the sun had pushed up over the edge of the eastern hills, and all things now flung shadows towards the west. Harry had seen, soft and dim as yet, the early morning shadow of a man taking shape — a man standing very close behind her — and as the light strengthened from moment to moment, she now saw two more, as if the first shadow had brought attendants from the land of shade. Harry sighed a deep and private sigh, then turned her head very slowly.

Three strange men stood behind her. They could have touched her if they had wanted to.

"You're alone on Teddy Carnival's beach," said one, not asking a question but sounding as if he were giving her a warning. The voice was breathy and excited, but faint like the voice of a man recovering from a long illness. As the sun rose and the shadows darkened, it would perhaps grow stronger still. Harry could not see the face of the speaker and cupped her hands around her eyes to cut out the dazzle of the new day. Looking a little crookedly she found herself staring, not at him, but at the two young men standing silently behind him. They appeared to be identical, and she knew at once that they had crawled out of a wrong gap in the world, that they had struggled through holding on to the silken thread of her own story. She had closed one door shutting out Teddy Carnival's bleeding ghost, but had opened another. Their streaked hair fell onto their foreheads like question marks, upside down and therefore devilish. They had never been children; they had never been innocent.

6
Visitors

"I'm sorry we frightened you," said the man who had spoken to her. His breathy voice was apologetic, but Harry could see he was not really sorry at all, and that he did not even want her to think he was.

All three men looked at her attentively as if she were the stranger on the beach and they were at home there. Since he was her own height, their spokesman looked very directly into her eyes. He had a wide, almost Mongolian face, the skin slightly pitted. Chickenpox or acne had given him a texture that oddly improved him, making him less soft and girlish than he otherwise would have been. A black, peaked cap was perched rather insecurely on ringlets of tarnished gold, the curls no thicker than her finger, and under the double shadow of the cap and the heraldic mane his eyes were a beautiful green like clear sea water.

"What I intended to ask you was whether that house up there was Edward Carnival's house." He paused, but not long enough for her to reply. "We're Carnivals ourselves, you see, working our way back home, you might say."

Once again his words conveyed a different meaning from the one they appeared to have, for they were light-hearted. But everything about this fair-headed man suggested menace to Harry.

"I did get a fright," she admitted, glancing back at the drawings vanishing under the wet palm of the tide.

The crescent smiles on the cats and mermaids were caricatures of the smile she now saw before her.

Behind the fair man, the two other young men nodded politely at her, identical in height and feature, though one wore a red shirt and the other a blue. Harry let her eyes touch them without lingering. They looked handsome and strong, their eyes of a brown so light and clear it reminded her of honey straight from the comb. The waves of black hair, flopping heavily on to their foreheads, were streaked with a lighter colour, too light for the sun to have bleached it. The streaks matched one another exactly, and as if they guessed that this odd effect disconcerted her, both men suddenly smiled identical foxy smiles. In their own way these two appearances shared between three men were fascinating and were also entirely familiar to Harry. "It was Edward Carnival's house once," she said. "But he's dead. It's ours now."

"Dead?" exclaimed the fair man. "Oh, a man who builds a house never really dies."

"It's always his house at heart," said the dark man in the red shirt.

From somewhere beyond them a faint, regular sound made itself heard.

"Edward's heart-beat," he added, with a peculiar smile.

"It's just someone coming down the track," Harry said firmly, though once the idea of a beating heart had been put into her head she almost believed it. She was pleased at the prospect of other company and turned eagerly as Anthony Hesketh appeared from under the trees, wearing a blue towelling beach-coat over his swimming suit, a scarlet towel slung over one shoulder, and his dark glasses (although the sun was not yet dazzling enough to hide from). It was impossible to tell just what he thought of them all, confronting each other in the early morning, but after a slight hesitation he came down on to the beach by the uneven steps as if he'd been doing it for years.

"Good morning!" he said. "It looks as if it's going to be another amazing day."

"A day of amazement," said the fair man cheerfully. His air of menace vanished, whisked away so quickly it might never have existed. "For us, anyway. We've been haunting this part of the coast for a long time, looking for a way back to Carnival's Hide and at last we've found it. We're Carnivals who have stopped hiding — relatively speaking . . ."

"Relatively speaking, we're relations!" said one of the dark men.

"Uncertain relations," finished the third. Their voices crowded in on top of each other, as if they only had one voice to share between them. The fair man got possession of it and talked on triumphantly.

"And we do hope we'll be allowed to cross the ancestral threshold," he said to Anthony, possibly thinking he was a member of the family.

"I'm sorry," Anthony said in a puzzled voice. "Did you say you're related to old Edward Carnival's family in some way?"

"Directly descended!" said the man in the blue shirt.

"Direct as a blow!" said his red-shirted companion, smiling again.

"English then," Anthony said briskly. "Like me . . . It's a small world." Harry was grateful to him for coming between her and the men on the beach.

"I'm off," she said. "You're probably going to start working out whether or not you both come from London and know the Queen, and I can't join in."

She thought they should probably be watched carefully, but if she stayed she might find herself inviting them up to Carnival's Hide, even though she was still not sure how real they were. Light certainly stopped when it came to them, and their shadows were as black as her own. Harry went on up the hill, under the native trees and into the orchard, leaving Anthony, an innocent guest, to cope with them, glad to be free of rules of politeness. If someone wanted to talk to you, you had to pretend you wanted to talk back. It was amazing how hard it was to break rules of that kind.

Down towards the orchard came the little ones, already dressed for swimming, trying to flick each others' legs with old beach towels. Beyond them

Emma, carrying an orange bucket, walked along the verandah on her way up to the wash-house.

Carnival's Hide was waking up for the day. For once Harry was glad she would not be alone. There were times when a good family made her feel lovingly guarded and safe.

In the kitchen Naomi was making a pot of tea and there was a cup to spare for Harry, who wrapped her long fingers gratefully around it because such warmth was always reassuring, even on a warm day when it wasn't strictly necessary.

The most unwilling morning people were always Jack and Christobel. They both liked sleeping in, and Jack also liked breakfast in bed if he could get anyone to bring him any. However, the first morning at Carnival's Hide was always a difficult morning to sleep through. A few minutes later — minutes that Harry had spent holding her tea, hand and hand about, staring at the bookcase — Jack wandered through from the hall. The mere presence of his elegant dark-blue dressing-gown made the whole room seem sophisticated. He rumpled her hair in passing, and she knew, without raising her eyes beyond the silk dressing-gown, that he was wearing the brave smile he used first thing every morning, and especially on early ones.

"It's not like you to be up early," she remarked, not really getting at him but wanting to hear his voice.

"The baby woke me," he replied. "She's certainly determined to get her way." As he said this the door from the kitchen opened, and Emma came through on her way back from the wash-house, a naked Tibby clinging to her like a monkey child, giggling into her hair.

"Good morning, Emma and child!" Jack said, looking at them gravely. "It's a lovely day."

But at that moment there was a serious disturbance across the hall, for Christobel was getting up too — Christobel, who valued her sleep. Normally anyone who woke her up, even by whispering or tiptoeing too loudly, was likely to get shouted at and ordered sternly out of the hall. You could hear her waking up and then getting up, coming closer and closer like a southerly storm. First she would yawn once or twice, yawns so deep and loud they sounded like cries. Then she would begin a series of exclamations, mostly of disgust, as her feet met the floor, and groan as she stood upright. Benny, Serena and Harry always found it easier to get out by a window rather than risk waking Christobel and being yelled at. Even Charlie was careful. But when she did appear, having yawned, stretched and exclaimed, the day began to sparkle in sympathy with her high spirits. Jack, hearing these first yawns, groans and cries, went into the kitchen to get himself breakfast, but his timing was bad, and he came out with a bowl of Naomi's sour plums at the same moment that Christobel came bursting into the room.

"Where *is* everybody? Emma — Harry — but I don't really count you two. Where's everyone else?"

"I'm here," said Jack, sounding resigned. Christobel waltzed over to him.

"Hello, darling Jack," she cried, joyously, kissing his ear. "Oh my! What elegant ears you have. They smell of after-shave too — very sexy. Where's that Anthony? No use him thinking he'll be allowed to sleep his broken heart away. If *I'm* up — *everyone* has to be up."

"Oh, stop it, Christo," Jack said, clutching his bowl of plums and vaguely kissing the air where she had been a moment earlier. "Don't be irritating."

"Sorry!" Christobel said, but not at all repentantly. "That Anthony looked so secret behind his glasses I couldn't resist having him on a bit. Didn't he blush!"

The room was filled with a soft light as day was reflected in obliquely by the silver wood of the verandah. Outside, the sun was becoming hotter and brighter, but inside, the second-hand sunbeams were gentle and pale on walls and ceiling. The first cicadas were tuning up. Their songs would cut into summer like ecstatic little saws. There were no breakers to boom on the shore, but the movement of the sea was constant, a secretive rustle in the air.

Christobel was wearing an old dressing-gown of Naomi's, worn through at the elbows. Her long feet were bare, and her fair hair, sticking up in unbrushed spikes, looked almost luminous in the gentle light of the room.

"You've started eating those plums," she cried at Jack. "Traitor! You used to have standards, but lately you've chickened out."

"I'm older than you," Jack said defensively. "Life's too short for chasing rainbows."

"Me for rainbows every time!" exclaimed Christobel. "I don't ever want to learn better."

"What if you caught one — a rainbow I mean?" asked Harry. Christobel thought she detected a satirical note in her sister's voice.

"Aha!" she cried. "I can see you're trying to make out I'm one of those frivolous girls who'd cut a rainbow up for hair ribbons. But what I'd do is learn all its tricks and turn into it, so everyone would see me up in the air, all colours. And now I'm going to make myself a slice of rainbow toast — and let the rest of you suffer over the plums."

She moved towards the kitchen door but stopped as a snatch of sound came in at the window, faded and came again. It was the sound of several voices all talking at once.

"The little ones," Jack said. "I rather hoped we wouldn't see them until lunch time."

"It's not just them." Emma moved to the window. "Oh, they're bringing strange men with them. Where on earth could they have picked them up at this hour in the morning?"

Jack groaned slightly, but Christobel grew immediately alert.

"*Possible* men?" she asked. "I mean, here I am, awake and fancy-free, deserted, really, until Robert chooses to come home again. Well, he'd better watch out if there's going to be any other talent around."

"What do you mean 'possible'?" Jack said, sounding rather irritable.

"Emma knows my style," Christobel retorted significantly.

"*Highly* possible," Emma reported back to Christobel just as if they were both sixteen, still at school and assessing a new boy. "More than possible — actually *probable*. One short and two tall."

"I know who they are," Harry said. "I met them on the beach and left them talking to Anthony . . ."

"Oh God, another early riser . . ." Christobel muttered in the background.

"They said they were descendants of Edward Carnival and that they came from England and were looking for Carnival's Hide."

"At *this* hour in the morning?" Jack exclaimed incredulously. He had made little headway with his plums which he now put on the edge of the table, automatically smoothing his hair with one hand. Though unprepared for visitors, he managed to look distinguished.

Serena burst in.

"Dad, I mean Jack, guess what?" she cried all in one breath. "There are these men come to see us and they're Carnivals and want to see Carnival's Hide. Our house is getting famous."

"Quick, get the postcards," Christobel said. But steps were already sounding in the hall. They stopped and there was a long pause.

"The waterlily wallpaper's gone," said a low, unrecognizable voice sounding blank and disbelieving. Then the door opened, and in came the men from the beach, real beyond all doubt, drawing their reality from the acknowledgement of others and the room, and perhaps even the photographs on the wall, the fair man in front of his dark companions, all ushered in by Benny. The first person the fair one saw was Christobel, and he did not immediately look beyond her. Harry thought his face brightened like a hunter's when natural prey comes into view.

It was to her he spoke rather than Jack, who had struck a graceful and easy-going early-morning attitude a little beyond her.

"Do excuse this early-morning break-in!" he said. "We didn't imagine for a moment we'd find you, let alone get such a warm invitation. Serena's told you who we are?"

"Brothers?" asked Jack. "Carnivals?" The fair man looked over at him. The pleasure on his face deepened if anything. He inclined his head, smiling.

"We're travelling, and checking up on family history as we go."

"Fancy!" Christobel said. "I thought you must be the King of the Rainbows." But she could not disconcert the fair man, or make him blush.

"And so I am!" he answered at once, his tentative smile becoming a beaming one. "How clever of you to recognize me when I'm travelling incognito."

Christobel laughed.

"Sit down, anyhow," she said. "Ma's the actual house historian, but we can tell you most things — show you some books. Let's see! We've got a photocopy of *A Colonial Lycidas* (that's about the boy who drowned off the rocks down on the beach), copies of original Carnival photos there behind you on the wall, and copies of two pamphlets on forestry . . ."

"*English Forests in the Antipodes*," quoted Serena. "That's why Anthony came to see us."

"And besides, I'm thinking about breakfast, so there'll be tea and coffee in a moment," Christobel said in an inviting voice. "Don't worry — we like odd visitors at odd hours. We're used to them."

"You probably don't mean a word of it, but we're willing to be easily convinced, because we've come such a long way to . . ." The King of the Rainbows hesitated.

". . . to find out!" said the red-shirted one, taking over, his voice sounding so like his brother's that it was almost as if the same man were still speaking. "To find our beginnings."

"And endings," said the blue-shirted brother. "Either will do."

"Well — this is the master of the house, dashing Jack Hamilton," Christobel said. "And that's Emma over there with her pet marmoset, Tibby, and I'm Christobel — oh, and that statue over there is my sister, Harry. She's well done, isn't she — looks almost alive."

"You're obviously not local," Jack said, shaking hands. "Are you from the English family, or the Australian one?"

"English," said the King of the Rainbows, staring with great interest around the room. "And this actually is Carnival's Hide? What's happened to the hall? Where's the waterlily paper?" he asked sternly.

"Well and truly gone," Jack said, looking amused. "There have been a lot of changes over the years, though I can see the waterlily-patterned paper has become a family legend. You're not entirely unexpected you know. My wife, Naomi, works at the museum and they had a letter a while ago saying that some members of the family might be coming our way. And anyhow," he added, looking at them, and then up at the photographs on the wall, "you look the part."

"But who *are* you?" asked Christobel. "I mean we could call you Carnival One, Carnival Two, Carnival Three and so on, or you could give us your names."

"Well, we're travelling brothers," said the King of the Rainbows lightly. He spoke without hesitation, leaving Harry uncertain if she had imagined a flicker of irresolution in the green eyes that touched her and moved restlessly on to the bookcase. "I'm Ovid. The red one is Hadfield. Blue — Felix. And we're wandering along on one of those fantastic quests, hoping to save the world from the powers of darkness, boredom and so on."

"Your parents certainly liked wild names, didn't they?" Christobel remarked. "So did Jack. I'm Christobel." Ovid took her hand, looking into her eyes as if they had a deep and vaguely disreputable understanding. Harry sat down in the chair close to her ladder and watched them keenly. They still alarmed her, but here among her family she was a match for any ghost or storybook spirit the sea might cast up on the beach.

"My book would make something happen in the outside world by the power of its stories," she had boasted yesterday, sitting on Teddy Carnival's rock. Striking as he was, it was not the King of the Rainbows who had frightened her. He was strange, but he could easily have been just another Christmas visitor, a true travelling Carnival, climbing out along lost branches of the family tree. It was the dark brothers at his elbow who had made her skin creep with fear. But it was no use. Even if she brought out her story, underlining all the descriptions of Belen and pointing out how closely they corresponded to Hadfield and Felix, no one but she could tell how exactly and unnaturally they matched. Everyone would think she was merely copying the outside world. The possibility that the outside world was copying her was unbelievable.

"So! You're actually descendants of the old Carnival family?" Jack was asking, staring at Ovid, just as intrigued as Christobel, for, like her, he enjoyed bright, astonishing people. Under their double regard, filled with the beginnings of admiration, Ovid seemed to pull brightness out of the air.

"I carry a reference with me," he declared, and dramatically opened his hand towards Christobel. Colour flowed between his fingers. Incredibly a rose bloomed in his hand, petal after petal unfolding. "It speaks for us all," he said. Christobel and Jack were first taken aback, and then entranced.

"You're a conjurer!" cried Christobel.

"We have to earn as we go," said Ovid lightly. In rapid succession he worked five more roses out of the air, drew a gold ribbon from nowhere, tied their stems together and passed them to her.

"Silk!" she said, feeling their petals. There was a trace of relief in her voice. "For a moment I couldn't help wondering . . ."

"You'd better have that cup of coffee. I think there's some that's actually hot," Jack suggested. "Sit down for a moment. Harry will get some for you."

The three Carnivals looked at Harry as she stood up. Now she detected a difference between Hadfield and Felix, thinking at first that one had darker eyes than the other. However, it was simply that the pupils of his eyes were larger, and these dilated pupils made him seem like a beast merely disguised as a man.

"Don't your brothers speak?" Christobel asked inquisitively.

"Yes, but only to the point!" said the one in the red shirt. Crumb writhed sensuously about his legs, purring loudly.

"We're champions of silence," said the blue-shirted Felix, smiling at Harry hesitating in the kitchen doorway, as if he too were about to offer a rose drawn from the living-room air.

"They try to make it sound good, but really they've got nothing interesting to say," Ovid declared, as Harry went into the kitchen and closed the door behind her.

The coffee in its big, glazed pot was barely warm. Harry very carefully made some more, giving herself a breathing space . . . imagining the brothers as spirits of the past, as mermen come up into the land of grass and air to lure Christobel and Jack, too, out beyond their depths. All the time, surprise, interest and even pleasure flowed under the door into the kitchen.

When at last she carried mugs and the big coffee pot out into the living room she found the entire family sitting around listening to the breathy accent of Ovid Carnival, and occasional interpolations by his brothers. All three had the same soft, smoky tones, and all three spoke in a leisurely fashion as if they measured time in seasons rather than hours. Yet there was nothing rustic about them. Like actors, who, having started off a little doubtfully before settling down and becoming sure of the parts they had to play, they were beginning to enjoy themselves. There was a sound like a little motor in the room. Crumb was almost flinging himself against the red-shirted brother who casually scratched his head between the ears, causing him to dribble with ecstacy. No one else seemed to notice this remarkable display from a cat who was normally aloof with strangers. Harry looked sternly at Crumb, thinking he was making a fool of himself.

Ovid spoke as easily as if he had known them all his life. Her family stared at him, fascinated and puzzled, but not entirely surprised, being completely used to unexpected visitors. Harry could see Naomi was suspicious but amused and, looking from Christobel to Jack, rather resigned. Anthony Hesketh, himself a guest and perhaps not entitled to pass judgement on other guests, was nevertheless listening as if he were an established member of the family.

"The resemblance is quite strong," Jack said. The photographs of Edward Carnival and Teddy and Minerva were being passed around. "Isn't it astonishing the way family faces persist?"

"Isn't it just!" Ovid said, idly patting Tibby on the head as she went past him, though he looked like the sort of man who'd gladly ignore a baby. "We've always thought that we looked like real Carnivals. And we've tried to exemplify the name too. It's an odd one, isn't it?"

"I've always thought it sounded very jolly, like being called Birthday Party or Monster Circus," Christobel told him.

"It means something like 'goodbye to flesh'," Hadfield volunteered. "People used to eat a lot and celebrate just before Lent. They used all their appetites excessively before attempting to exercise self-control — 'Carne levare' (that's 'a leaving off of meat'). 'Carne vale' — Carnival."

"Don't try to be clever, dear, that's my job. In our family I'm the head, and Felix is the heart, and Hadfield's a simple predator." (Hadfield smiled lazily.) "If our name *does* mean 'goodbye to the flesh', don't we contradict it just by being here?" And now he looked briefly over at Harry. They were true Carnival performers, but tossing words, not balls and batons, through the air, juggling for a living. Jack, Christobel and the little ones watched, eager and mystified, Naomi withdrawn, yet recognizing signs of a familiar response in her family. Anthony seemed just as perplexed as anyone could have expected him to be. Harry recognized an expression of irresolution.

"Well, you look like it — like Carnivals, I mean," Serena cried enthusiastically.

"Oh yes," Ovid agreed, pushing his hand luxuriously through his ringlets. "Our faces are our fortunes. We're bound to do well."

Under his hair, at the very hairline, the trace of a shocking scar was momentarily revealed. Long healed as it was, it had left a blue-white puckered seam, slightly glossy, and suggesting that, at some time in the past, someone had tried to scalp him. Harry thought it looked like a hieroglyph of death. She was not the only person to notice it, for there was an immediate silence. Then Benny leaned against Naomi and put his arm around her neck. She squeezed his brown hand, crusted with a few tiny crystals of sand.

"We come from a lonely place . . ." Ovid said. "Like this, but lonelier."

"We had to be our own company," Felix put in, "or else invent it."

"When we were children we made a whole kingdom out of the garden tools." Ovid looked around the room dreamily.

"King Trowely, Lord Rake-Rake . . ." Felix continued.

"The beautiful Fork sisters, Raven and Sylvestina, a hoe called Bagnold. Well, you can imagine!" Hadfield had picked up the account easily. "It was a private land, and we invented a private language to use there."

"We talk in grunt and moo!" exclaimed Benny proudly, detecting allies and growing easier.

". . . and Suriel the Spade, the benevolent angel of death — an executioner. Isn't that a strange one?" Felix said, reaching over to brush the hair back over his brother's forehead. "But it was all long ago."

"It sounds a strange upbringing?" Naomi was really asking a question.

"Oh well," said Ovid, shrugging. "It happened that our father lived remotely, so of course we had to, too. It seems to have given us a singular quality. On the one hand we're ordinary enough . . ."

". . . but on the other, we fall on our knees whenever we see a garden trowel and take off our hats to rakes," said Felix.

". . . and our heads to spades," said Hadfield.

"People do give us funny looks from time to time," Ovid conceded, and all three looked critically at one another, while the family tried to appear as if the last thing they were likely to do with visitors was to give them funny looks.

"Don't you feel lost, now you're out in the world?" Naomi replied sympathetically. "After all, you're none of you very old — and . . ."

"Yes and no," said Ovid anticipating. "As you see we travel in threes like fairy-tale princes. We juggle, eat fire, do magic as we go along, and we . . ."

". . . struggle for power . . ." Hadfield said, unexpectedly smiling.

"Oh yes, we do that!" Ovid agreed. "I'm the best at it, and Felix is the worst. And of course we devoutly believe that we're the only real men in a world of spirits, but that's human nature. I just know Christobel thinks the same thing, even in the heart of a family."

"It takes one to know one." Christobel was unabashed.

"Anyway — now you're here you must stay for breakfast, real or otherwise," Jack suggested heartily. He was bewitched by the strange brothers boasting of their oddity, laughing at themselves while they did so.

"Stewed plums," Serena cried anxiously. "Mum says we've got to eat them up."

"Do you like stewed plums? Bottled ones?" asked Christobel. Her voice was quite innocent, but Ovid gave her his beaming smile as if they shared an understanding.

"It's a national dish," he said lightly. "Our appetite for stewed plums, even rather sourish ones is — oh, it's infinite, isn't it, Hadfield?"

"Absolutely infinite," Hadfield agreed.

"Or even more!" concluded Felix.

Naomi laughed suddenly. "Where are you heading for?" she asked.

Ovid shrugged. "Wherever we get to," he said. "Anywhere we stop is where we're hoping to get to."

"But you happen to have stopped here," she said dryly. "Well, you're very welcome."

"And you're very tolerant," Ovid observed. "It's a virtue I've been spared myself."

"You'll need massive tolerance to eat the plums," Christobel assured him.

"Only self-interest," he answered. "I've got plenty of that."

Naomi, half-thinking of seating people at the table, looked around the room in sudden confusion.

"Who was the idiot who pulled the furniture round?" she demanded. "Where's the cane table? Ovid, you sit over there and the twins on the settee."

Harry actually saw Ovid recognize that a chance had been offered to him.

"It's understandable and all that," he began apologetically, "but there's a tiny mistake. We're more than twins — we're triplets — all born under the same star in the same hour."

Everyone stared silently at Hadfield and Felix who met their stares with identically enigmatic expressions, quite free from shyness.

"I'm fraternal of course, a separate conception

I'm glad to say — quite unique really," Ovid explained, as if they were in a classroom. "Whereas Felix and Hadfield are mirror-image identicals. Hadfield, for example, is left-handed . . ."

". . . sinister . . ." Hadfield pointed out with relish.

". . . and his heart is not in the right place. It's merely on the right *side*, and that's the wrong side for a heart to be. He's a reversed man — a dextrocardiac to give the technical term."

"Dazzle everyone with science! Hadfield and I are entantiomorphs," Felix said and added, "It goes very deep. We're Siamese twins really, but the join doesn't show."

"It's another conjuring trick," Christobel told Ovid. "Here I was thinking you were unique, but you're just part of a set."

"Not a matching one," he replied. "Besides, I'm its head, and they do what I say, or they mostly do. Hadfield occasionally gets the better of me, and Felix is always giving himself airs, not that it does him any good."

"I'd never get any airs at all if I didn't give them to myself," Felix argued. Ovid ignored him.

"It suddenly occurs to me we've left our packs down on the beach and the tide's coming in."

"You're walking round by the beach carrying packs?" exclaimed Naomi. "For someone who isn't one of nature's hitchhikers you certainly find ways of punishing yourself."

"I was hating every minute of it," Ovid said warmly. "But could we put the packs in your boat shed for an hour or two while we set the good example?"

"Shove them in the whare," cried Christobel. "You might even like to stay on when you find out how nice we are. Come on! I'll show you."

As Christobel led the brothers out of the room, Felix glanced at Harry again, but there was still nothing to be learned from his expression. Then they were gone.

"Ask them to stay, Ma!" begged Serena. "Christmas magicians — moo!"

"Christmas tricksters! Grunt!" said Naomi, pushing her hair away from her face. "Three funny young men, I'd say."

"We're used to all sorts," Jack pointed out.

"Oh well, I can see they've engaged your interest," Naomi said, a little grimly. "I think Ovid knew just who to smile at."

"But they *are* Carnivals — well, Ovid is anyway," Jack said, glancing up at the photograph on the wall.

"Oh, they can bunk down in the whare if they want to," Naomi said carelessly. "I don't expect they'll bother me much. I've had too much practice with mixed Christmas visitors, not to mention mixed Christmases . . . You're very quiet in your corner, Harry, dear."

"She always is!" cried Serena proudly. "She's Harry the Silent." She stared at Harry and sighed deeply.

"Well, Harry the Silent, a penny for *your* thoughts," Naomi asked lightly.

"You don't get all that value for a mere penny," Harry replied. "How about a higher offer?"

"Later on!" Naomi lost interest in Harry's

thoughts. "The day's well and truly begun and our Christmas duty is to get back out into it again."

Harry did not go out with the others straight away. She was glad to climb her ladder and be on her own for a while. Once in her room, she lay on her bed and read her book through all over again from the very beginning, frowning and muttering to herself.

When at last she came down her ladder she was surprised to find Anthony waiting silently in a room that she thought was empty.

"Hi!" she said vaguely. "I thought you were down on the beach with the others."

"I will be," he replied, "but I wanted to ask you something, and I was shy of asking it in front of everyone else. Were those young men — those Carnival brothers — threatening you when you were down on the beach?"

This question astonished Harry, and while she wondered for a second what to say, Anthony answered his own question for her.

"I could see they were," he said. "What did they say?"

"It was partly anyone being there at all," Harry explained. "At that hour, anyway!"

"They're not what they say they are," Anthony said in a positive voice, and then added in rather more puzzlement, "though they may be Carnivals — in fact I'm sure they are. But don't let them trouble you, or threaten you again, will you? If you can't tell anyone else, tell me because I saw you there and I'll believe you."

"It wasn't anything they actually said. It's mostly

their style," she explained. "And there *is* one other thing — but no one *could* believe it — not even you."

"I can believe six impossible things before breakfast," Anthony said lightly. "Six afterwards too, plums and all. Try me!"

But Harry could not bring herself to say that Ovid looked rather like Prince Valery, and the entantiomorphs, Felix and Hadfield, exactly like the marvellous winged man, Belen.

"They're not what they said they were," he repeated obstinately. "Though God help me, almost nobody is, I suppose," he added rather gloomily. "Not even me. But don't forget."

"I won't," said Harry fervently. "You're right, no one's just what they seem to be, except people like Christo, who couldn't be any different if they tried. She seems beautiful and she *is* beautiful," she said wistfully.

"But that's probably not all she is," Anthony added. "Well, let's take each other down to the beach where your father has promised me a wonderful day on the edge of the sea."

"He books them in advance," Harry said. "But there's plenty around at this time of the year. It's rain you have to queue up for."

"All the same, sunshine mustn't be wasted," Anthony replied, and they went down to the sea side by side.

7
In the Sun

The Hamiltons and their friends spread out like a
Christmas tribe along the beach below Carnival's
Hide, the only people in the world, for there were
few signs of man to be seen from the beach. Earth,
air, fire and water had once played, turn and turn
about, over the hills around them, like huge careless
children, and the Hamiltons now sunbathed and
swam in the ruins left by those games, baring their
backs and legs on the shifting margins of sand and
sea.

Robert and Charlie sailed in, excited and rav-
enous, and having obediently eaten plums well beyond the call of duty, helped blow up the inflatable
mattresses and put up the sun umbrellas. The little
beach baked in the summer day. Harry, swimming
with the others, found that, as her arms stroked
down below the surface of the water, the memory
of yesterday's experience visited her unpleasantly.
The opaque green water had become frightening
because of what it might conceal. In the end she

went to the boat shed, got out the blue canoe and set off to the two little islets just beyond the western headland — Kingfisher and Heron — neither of them any larger than the living room at Carnival's Hide.

From here, on a doll's-house beach, she could see Jack talking to Anthony and then retreating up the track with Serena and Benny running and mooing beside him, Charlie stalking behind. Robert and Christobel set off in the opposite direction, making a temporary beach family of themselves by taking Tibby for a walk. Anthony talked to Emma.

This morning the beach had been lonely and mysteriously illustrated with smiles. But now it was a cross between a garden in the Land of Oz, bedded out with huge, flowering sun umbrellas, and the summer camp of shining, well-oiled nomads, sunglasses on their noses like headlights of darkness, ready to pack up and go when the sun deserted them. From the beach Emma and Anthony saw Harry, the Robinson Crusoe of a doll's-house island.

"You've been here many times before, I gather," Anthony asked Emma, who nodded and smiled a little ruefully.

"You see when my parents separated — years ago it was — I don't know — it was very strange. They pulled apart and somehow I just dropped away between them. One moment there was a home that seemed more or less like anyone else's and then — nothing. (Well, my father was around — but not really *there* — and my mother was gone.) I was friends with Christo anyway, and I began going home with her after school, and the Hamiltons just seemed to me like one of those great, big, wonderful storybook families — dashing father, loving mother, brothers, sisters, garden, pets, holidays, stories by the fire, birthday parties — the whole bit. I longed to be part of it all."

"And aren't you?" Anthony asked.

"Oh, I was," said Emma, nodding. "Naomi just scooped me up — of course I wanted to be scooped — but then, later, when I was expecting Tibby, she wanted to scoop her, too. I mean, to adopt her — properly adopt her. And it might have been giving her the best chance if I'd said yes, but I just couldn't. I couldn't! Naomi and I didn't quarrel, but we've always been just a little bit uneasy and apologetic to each other ever since. As for Christo, she thought I ought to have had an abortion or get Tibby adopted, and when I didn't she got browned off with me, and it was all messy. Much more messy than you could possibly imagine."

"You don't think much of my imagination then," Anthony said, his eyes narrowing as he smiled.

"I didn't mean that!" Emma protested. Then she laughed too, relaxed a little and let him see a brighter, easier face for a moment. "Well — one's own messes always seem like the greatest messes of the world," she said. "I'll edit a book of them one day. Anyhow — touch wood for this Christmas." She put her fingers against her own forehead.

"And your Tibby looks completely happy with everything," said Anthony watching Robert and Christobel lift the little girl over a tiny stick, whisking her up a bit so that she screamed with pleasure, took her feet from the ground and swung on their arms to make them whisk her once more.

"More swings!" she shouted. "Please — more swings."

"Before they get back I'm going to swim out to the Heron," Emma said suddenly. "Because, though Tibby's terrific, it's so nice to be without her for ten minutes — able to go in any direction I like. If Christo's getting sick of her, could you keep your eye on her just for a moment or two?"

"Of course!" said Anthony. "Off you go. Harry's on her way back."

"Harry . . ." said Emma, looking reflective. "Christobel used to be really hard on her when she was a fat, bookish little thing and wanted to join in with us and we couldn't be bothered. Oh, well — it's too late now . . . but you think of things like that afterwards. When you've got one of your own, I mean."

Anthony watched her walk out up to her knees in the green water and then fall forward into a long dive. Her arms flashed as she swam and the water boiled to the rapid beat of her feet.

". . . and here we are, back where we set out from," Christobel said a moment later on his left. "Do you know what that means, Tibby! It means the world is round. That's what it *does* mean, doesn't it, Anthony?"

"Proof positive!" Anthony agreed, watching her fold herself down on her inflatable mattress, like some leggy, elegant bird settling itself to rest. She picked up Tibby's wooden giraffe and gave it to her.

"Mine!" said Tibby, seizing it. "Thank you. Mine Dum Dum."

"Just listen!" Robert said. "She really knows

what she wants, doesn't she? Hey, do all little kids talk as well as Tibby, or is she clever?"

"Has Jack run off and left you? And Serena?" said Christobel to Anthony, ignoring Robert's questions. "How hideous! I don't know how you bear it, sitting there with no one to admire you. For instance, I've been speaking very sternly to Robert about going off this morning and leaving me to languish."

" 'Nagging' is what you've been doing," Robert said. "Besides you didn't do too much languishing. As far as I can make out you've filled the whare with magicians."

"But only out of desperation," said Christobel, looking vaguely in the direction of the whare. Between their sunbathing place and the whare, *Sunburst* was drawn up on its ramp, and the halyard, striking against the aluminum mast, rang a sad, silvery bell, muffled rather than clear, as if ringing from under water or through a mist that blurred sound as well as sight.

"Poor little Teddy Carnival, still being rung for," Christobel said. "And here's old Harry, home from the sea."

Harry, beaching her canoe, saw Christobel's gaze discover something worth looking at and turned to see the Carnival brothers, suddenly emerged, walking towards them — Ovid, in a white towelling beach-coat, a peacock's feather pinned to it like a flower, Hadfield and Felix, at his heels, two well-behaved dogs being taken for a walk. Ovid's coat looked new, very similar to Anthony's blue one. His brothers simply wore their familiar red and blue shirts hanging open over the most remarkable antique swimming suits.

"Now there's a very patriotic note!" Anthony observed lazily, looking at the red, white and blue.

"I'll be very surprised if there's one single patriotic thing about Ovid," Christobel said. "He's an empire of one."

"And doesn't it take one to know one?" Ovid called across to her, echoing her words from earlier in the day, though he did not seem as if he could have been close enough to hear. "I earned my empirehood the hard way. That's why I insist on it now." As he came up, his sunny smile embraced everyone, after which his eyes particularly turned to Christobel. He took off his coat and shook it sharply. Spangles, flowers, paper butterflies and little hummingbirds, made of silken tissue so fine they actually fluttered in the air before settling gracefully on the sand, fell from its folds. One of them landed on Christobel's wrist and immediately its image, blue and grey, appeared on her skin. Christobel looked delighted at this casual magic, but Ovid was already talking as if his trick did not deserve the tribute of a moment's silence.

"I see you're overwhelmed by my swimming suit," he observed. "Don't you love sarcastic clothes?"

"It's amazing!" cried Christobel. "They're all amazing. Where did you get them?"

"Memory's wardrobe!" Ovid replied. "We've had them a long time."

"We're attached to them," said the red-shirted brother. He smiled sideways, hunching his shirt forward over his shoulders, but the blue-shirted man looked down at himself almost scornfully. Harry had read in many books of men whose hot glances stripped girls naked. This glance, turned on himself, made the blue-shirted brother seem as if he himself were really naked, there among them. Ovid turned his old swimming suit into a fancy dress. His brother wore his as if he were playing a scornful game so that they would not be too frightened at seeing him entire.

"It's terrific!" Christobel applauded again. "But I think it might be going a bit too far on a hot day."

"Too Far! Now that's a fabulous kingdom," Ovid cried. "Help me to get there. I've never been allowed to, and it's made me so cross."

"Once perhaps," said the red-shirted brother, smiling over at him and holding up one finger. "We got there once . . . and now we're back again."

"I *long* for Too Far," Ovid said, speaking more loudly than his brother and drowning his incomprehensible words. "But mine is a lonely struggle. Is there room for me to recline at your feet and look admiringly into your eyes?"

"Moo!" Christobel said, catching Serena's very tone. "With Robert beside me, and you at my feet, and Anthony on the left, I'll feel really well set up. This is Robert, by the way."

Ovid beamed at Robert as Christobel went on to introduce his brothers.

"And this one is Felix."

"Hadfield," Hadfield corrected her.

"Hang on a moment!" Christobel said, disconcerted. "You were colour-coded. Blue Felix, red Hadfield!"

"He's right, though. He does know who he is even

if they do seem interchangeable," Ovid said. "Have you louts changed shirts?" He looked at them severely.

"We put on the wrong ones this morning," the blue-shirted Hadfield said, stretching like a lion, smiling lazily. "You know what it's like in the morning. We're correctly dressed now."

"Hadfield's Hadfield, and I'm me. Simple!" Felix said, smiling a smile Harry believed should belong only in her book. He had a force of his own, but it was different from Hadfield's, quieter, more watchful and harder to name.

"Oh, well — I suppose you know best." Christobel subsided slightly. "I hate saying that!" she added plaintively and sighed. "I can't seem to say it sincerely even when it's true."

"I would never ever say such a terrible thing, so it never *is* true," Ovid asserted, "but then, I'm the creator of the universe, of course."

Harry, on the edge of the group but not part of it, thought Ovid was casting a dangerous spell. This morning he had somehow made Christobel offer him coffee, had bought her attention with silken words and with silken roses. Now his brothers performed another trick on his behalf. Felix turned to speak to Anthony. Hadfield asked Robert about the morning's sailing and received an answer quite as enthusiastic as if Charlie had given it. It had been a wonderful morning. They had been carried along effortlessly like men in a dream. In the beginning, the flow of water past them, the very air dividing around them, had been a soft and pearly grey, then the hills had been burnished by the rising sun. Robert was filled with an exhilaration he yearned to share, and Christobel not only refused to share it, but resented it, and reproached his enthusiasm for something other than herself.

Harry thought she had just witnessed a deliberate movement that had cut Christobel off from her true friends and left her alone with Ovid, who radiated both admiration and mockery in such a way that Christobel could not be sure if she were being truly admired or simply teased. Strangely enough, Harry thought Ovid was not sure either. Wearing only her plain sunglasses, she could not be certain of smiles or frowns, even voices were not always helpful, though sometimes her short sight made her other senses more alert. There were other paradoxical times when, with the edge of sight gone, hearing seemed to lose its edge, too. All the same she thought she detected an unwilling fluctuation in Ovid's tone, as if something about Christobel forced him to be warm when he intended to be merely tricky.

"Emma's on the way back!" Christobel said, as a faint splash made her look out to sea. "She'll be thirsty. People say I don't think of others, but I do. Robert, could you be a dear, run up to the house and get a few cans of beer or fruit juice or something cool for her, and get something for the rest of us, while you're about it."

"Will you give up nagging me about sailing if I do?" Robert asked, with a small challenge lurking under his easy words.

"Are you trying to bargain? Well, all I can say is the quality of slavish devotion isn't what it used to be!" Christobel exclaimed indignantly.

"I'll go!" Harry said, just as Anthony suddenly

said to Felix, "How did you know I was interested in conservation?"

"You've got the look of it," Felix suggested. "Why not? Or someone mentioned it." He got to his feet and looked very directly at Harry as if his entire conversation had simply been a way of filling in time until that moment. "I'll come and help you carry things, if you like," he said to her. "Just tell me slowly and clearly what you want me to do, and I'll probably be able to do it."

"I can manage by myself," Harry said — or thought for a moment she had said. But she hadn't actually spoken and Felix was already standing beside her. It was too late to say it now. "Thanks," she said instead, and they walked off up the track together.

8
The Honest Man

Harry made up her mind not to talk to him more than was strictly necessary, for she thought she might be worked on like Christobel, but as they walked along the hazy ribbon of path leading back to Carnival's Hide she stumbled, and Felix turned and held out his hand to her. Harry's fingers curled protectingly down over her palms, but Felix merely smiled faintly and took her arm above the elbow. His touch, unexpectedly cool considering what a hot day it was, was very gentle but impersonal.

It was odd, considering this, that Harry felt a strange little twist, high up under her ribs, cutting her breath short and startling her as if she had had a thrilling splash of cold, salt water on hot, bare skin.

"Warm day," he said, in a solicitous voice.

"I'm short-sighted," Harry explained. "I tripped because I'm wearing ordinary sunglasses not my proper ones."

Glancing down at her feet she saw her toes had

curled themselves up tightly in her sandals. That little twist had made itself felt even in the soles of her feet.

"Short-sighted?" Felix said. "You're seeing something different from me, then?" He looked up into the canopy of bush under which they were walking, as if he were now seeing it differently himself.

"I've got used to seeing things a little bit blurred," Harry said.

"You might even get to prefer it," he agreed, surprisingly. "I don't trust sharp edges myself."

"It's nothing like that," Harry said. "I mean it's not philosophy, just vanity that makes me try to go without glasses. Sometimes they make me look as if half my face was further off than the other half. I can do without that."

Felix laughed (out of surprise, Harry thought). He did not let her arm go.

"And sometimes I don't mind being cut off," she added, detaching his fingers from her arm, trying to be polite but firm. She saw him watch her hand very carefully while she did this.

"Is your name really Harry?" he asked, moving on beside her.

"Ariadne, really," she explained, "but I don't match up with it; it's too grand. I've always been called Harry."

They entered the little orchard that lay below the grassy slope leading up to the house. Harry reminded herself not to start talking, but found she was already asking a question.

"What about you — are you always called Felix?" She was driven to challenge him a little, even though silence was safest.

"I've been called a lot of things in my time," he said. "But you know what they say — a child of many names is dearly loved."

Harry had never heard this particular saying. She thought he sounded as if he were ridiculing himself.

"Is that your mother in the hammock? Have we crowded her off the beach?" Felix asked. He seemed genuinely concerned.

"No!" said Harry, peering in the direction of the hammock. "She likes a chance to get away from us and catch up on her reading. You know what mothers are."

"I don't, you know," said Felix. "I had one, but she died. I knew my father twice as much as I needed to. I suppose that was a sort of compensation."

A smudged cocoon hung between vague leafy branches.

"Pass on by!" Naomi shouted as they hesitated. "Don't give me any news or ask me any questions or tell me anything."

"See what I mean?" Harry said. All the same, she had to ask two questions. "Where are Charlie and the little ones? Where's Jack gone? It's unnatural down on the beach, almost civilized, really."

"They've gone to get the tree," Naomi said, and Harry felt an electric touch of mystery and pleasure at the thought of the tree, realizing with regret that this was the first tree-choosing expedition she had missed out on for years and wondering if she had suddenly grown too old for tree-choosing.

"I hope they get a good, big one," she said as they left the old orchard behind.

"Tree?" Felix asked cautiously.

"Haven't you ever heard of Christmas?" Harry was bewildered at her own voice, which seemed to have found a challenging life of its own, but Felix did not seem worried, and simply laughed.

"Oh, yes, Christmas! Well, we never really had Christmas. My father thought it might give us unreasonable expectations, and he believed that unreasonable expectations were what was wrong with society. Well, he certainly made sure we didn't have any, bless his dear old heart. But we had our own festivities — we invented them to spite him . . . Compost Week and the Great Dig and King Trowely's Elevation. Do you have any of those?"

Harry found, rather to her irritation, that she was curious about King Trowely's Elevation. However, she chose not to reply.

"Ovid and I did the inventing: Hadfield doesn't invent, but he helps with the celebrating. And we celebrate midsummer, too!" Felix went on.

"Midsummer and Christmas come too close together here," Harry said. "I think it's midsummer tomorrow, but there's no special party for it."

They climbed the verandah and walked into the white, blank hall of Carnival's Hide. Light reflecting in from the verandah penetrated the coloured glass and put a narrow stripe around the room, and as Felix turned, his face was striped, too, with a narrow, rainbow-coloured mask. He gave her a confiding, cunning smile. Harry ducked her head and walked primly past him through the living room, collected her true glasses from their case on top of the piano and moved on into the cool farmhouse kitchen that lay beyond the living room. Together, she and Felix made up a big jug of apple and orange juice, adding ice cubes, and sprigs of mint and pineapple sage from the ruins of the kitchen garden beyond the back door. They paused there for a moment to admire the flat heads of seeding parsley. Each wide green umbel was composed of smaller stars, alive and growing.

"Carrot flowers are beautiful in the same way," said Felix idly, sliding his fingers under the flat, lacy head. "When I was a gardening child, I used to let a few carrots go to flower every year if I could get away with it. I liked the smell of them, too. Now then — why do you look as if you don't believe me?"

"I believe about the carrots, but I'm not too sure about you being a child," Harry said seriously. "You remind me too much of someone who wasn't. Did you really have a mother and father?"

"What sort of question is that?" asked Felix, looking astounded. "Of course I did. One of each, in the beginning. Mind you, we quarrelled most dreadfully with our father. Ovid — well, you heard him say he wanted to create the universe, and so did my father. I suppose in a way we *were* his universe. Well, there's only room for one universe-creator in a single family."

"It's been done already," Harry said, unimpressed.

"If a job's worth doing, it's worth doing twice." Felix followed her back into the kitchen, like a wolf playing at being a pet. She loaded him up with a tray of green plastic tumblers, hesitating to look at him directly because he was very attractive, and just by standing in front of her, confronting her with his hair and skin and debatable smile, he confused her into something very like shyness.

"He's doing quite a heavy line with Christobel — Ovid, I mean!" She meant her voice to sound light-hearted, but it betrayed her again and came out disapproving.

"I'm not his keeper," Felix answered smiling.

"No! I think he's yours," Harry retorted. It was as if somehow she had already watched Felix submitting to his brother in another life, but Felix ignored this, concentrating instead on turning her accusation back to front.

"Well, I must say *I* thought Christobel was very struck with Ovid. He's a glittery little fellow, isn't he? Or perhaps his fine old swimming suit admires her white bikini." He sounded anxious to divert her. "Do you think that clothes have a life of their own, and maybe have unsuitable affairs with opposite styles? I mean — you look at some people — their clothes go on flirting long after the people inside them have lost interest."

Harry grinned reluctantly.

"I knew I could make you smile," he said, immediately triumphant. "You've been looking at me much more darkly than I deserve, you know."

"You might deserve it," Harry suggested.

"How?" asked Felix inquisitively.

"By being a wolf in sheep's clothing," Harry replied. She had said something that amused Felix, for he laughed and assured her it was the other way around. "I'm a baa lamb, really!" he answered her.

"I'm alongside the wolves, maybe — but bleating not howling."

Now was the time to set off for the beach with their trays, but, though she almost resented it, there was a dangerous pleasure about the company of someone who looked so like Belen, the black prince of the air.

"What do you mean?" she asked, but Felix smiled and said, "We're all conjurors. Don't take me too seriously. Smile again."

"I'm not a great smiler at the best of times," she said absent-mindedly, for she was still puzzling over his words, poising her tray on a tall stool that stood at the end of the sofa. And then she sighed. "I want a simple Christmas," she went on, though he had not suggested it would be otherwise. "If I were in charge, that is."

Just at that moment, it was true. Yesterday's extreme wishes had multiplied her villain, and now she was obliged to bargain with him. All she wanted today was the tree in the house, the old songs with their promises that the world would be remade with the birth of a baby, and to be Benny's age, sitting with her family on Christmas morning, opening her presents and finding them all surprising and marvellous, no matter how inconsequential. She wanted everyone kind and affectionate, not passionate and tormenting — everything open, no maggoty secrets and silences, and no arguments with other, darker arguments hidden in them. Somewhere, waiting to be found again in the approaching season, was an old, innocent self, sexless as a tennis racquet, living in a time before Jack and Naomi wept at each other late at night, and before she had made Belen a body and wings of words or allowed Prince Valery to joke at the expense of innocence. In those days she had floated on her back in the moonlit sea, watching Orion swing himself up from the water to lie over her, while the finished people, the adults, on the shore had laughed, eaten, drunk, flirted and even embraced secretly in the shadows. But that old innocent self would not come again. It was gone forever, and something else was trying to replace it.

"I don't want it all mixed up with love," she complained clumsily, and then felt herself colouring. However, Felix seemed neither embarrassed nor confused.

"Love?" he exclaimed. "This is nothing but politeness. I'm only carrying a tray of glasses for you."

"Not you!" Harry replied. "I was thinking of Christobel and your brother. There's a threat of love between them, I think, and *she's* almost engaged to Robert, and *he's* very tricky, isn't he? Well, you all are," she added defiantly, feeling his close physical presence as part of the threat, too, though she could not say so. "Be honest!"

"You can't say you want things simple and then in the next breath ask me to be honest," Felix replied. "They're different things — for instance, Hadfield's simple and I'm honest. Our hearts are on opposite sides — remember? Anyhow, you aren't being altogether simple and honest with me."

Neither was she.

Staring up at him uncertainly, Harry now saw an odd thing. Along his hairline ran an identical scar to the one she had seen on Ovid, the same white seam as if his hair had been sewn on with silver-blue glossy silk. Harry could only believe it was the same scar, but displayed by two different men. At some time in the past they had suffered exactly the same accident. The momentary easiness she had felt for Felix, gently mocking but companionable, vanished, and she said, hearing the hostility creeping back into her voice, "How did you get that scar on your forehead?" Felix opened his mouth, shut it again, and then smiled with the air of one about to give an eloquent and exact answer.

But there was a sound outside. The station wagon, a pine tree tied to its roof rack (the same roof rack that in winter carried the family's skis up into the mountains), had drawn up alongside the verandah.

"Oh it's *such* a story!" said Felix. "I'll tell you some other time."

Harry found she did not want to know too much about the scar.

"Here's the tree!" she cried, becoming entranced and losing her guarded expression, her mouth growing soft with happy memories. "We won't need to carry the trays down now," she said. "Everyone will want to come up and help decorate. Will you want to decorate, too?"

"Why not!" Felix stared out at the tree. "If we're invited, that is. In my land I'd invite you to the Great Dig."

"How about King Trowely's Elevation?" Harry asked, feeling light-hearted all of a sudden. "I like the sound of that."

"Of course. I'd even knit you a flag to wave. I was brought up to be good with my hands."

"Prove it by decorating!" Harry said, as Serena and Benny burst in shouting the praises of the tree they had chosen. A moment later Charlie and Jack carried it into the living room and the air became charged with the scent of pine needles and the green spirit of a northern season.

9
In the Dark

The presence of the tree struck Harry like a green wand. They set it up in its proper corner, all needles and cones, tears of gold on the rough bark. A piney scent filled the room. One Christmas became all Christmases. Scrambling into her loft, Harry passed down to Felix and Serena boxes of Christmas decorations overflowing with long crepe streamers, smelling of past celebrations. Christobel came in with friends and followers. Naomi left her hammock.

"Spread everything out! We'll make it absolutely beautiful this year," Christobel cried joyously.

Anthony, already surprised at the sight of a midwinter tree in a midsummer house, even though he had been warned, was surprised again by Christobel who had suddenly sounded no older than Serena. The little ones skirmished around — Tibby, first astonished and then pleased at the entertainment offered, Benny and Serena full of triumph at having chosen such a beautiful tree. However, none of the

Hamiltons reacted with anything like the enchant-
ment that the Carnival brothers showed. All three
looked at the tree with a fascination as direct as
Tibby's but much more complex. And all three were
astounded at the Christmas decorations unpacked
from layers of tissue paper. There they were
again — the golden balls and silver bells, the
painted canaries and peacocks Jack had brought
back from Australia, the Christmas lights, the little
drums and trumpets, the gilded angels with violins
and flutes, the icicles of glass that would shiver and
shine through a nor-west day and never melt, and
at last the crib with wooden people and animals.

There were almost too many ornaments for the
one tree, but it was a rule that all had to be used.
Christobel exclaimed over a tuft of pine needles
caught in the wired feet of one of the birds, a re-
minder of last year's tree, which had also lifted
green arms in the same corner of the same room,
while Jack put on a tape of Christmas carols. The
room suddenly rang with clear, pure singing. To
Anthony, it was a winter's sound, processions of
carollers coming through snow, but to Harry it was
midsummer's voice, and *her* choir marched along
the beach of Carnival's Hide, following an uneven
ribbon that high tide laid right around the world.

"More on the bottom branches! More!" Benny
said, while Ovid greeted each new decoration as if
a display of eastern jewels were being unpacked
before his eyes.

"And I wonder just what we think we're celebrating," said Jack, ironically, changing the tape.

"Being a family . . ." said Serena in a holy voice.
"The mother, the father and the baby . . ." She

looked sideways to see if Anthony was appreciating her sensitivity, inclined her head, held out her arms and pointed her toe. Ovid stared at her incredulously.

"Family!" he exclaimed. "You might just as well celebrate battle, murder and sudden death."

"Oh, it's not as bad as that," Jack said. "I'm quite happy to celebrate being a family man." For a moment he spoke as dryly as Felix.

"It's easy to be contented with a situation that gives you unlimited power," Hadfield remarked with his faint, ominous smile.

"How cynical!" Christobel said. "I'm on Jackie's side. He was never ever bossy."

"You wouldn't know if Jack was bossy because you're bossier," said Serena, made bold by surprise.

"Well, you *all* need someone to tell you what to do," Christobel said, quite unabashed. "You should be grateful, getting good advice free."

"In our case we became what we were made to become, as close as we could," said Hadfield. "Not that my father was pleased, even then. He got more or less what he planned for and then found he didn't want it. But I don't think there's anything very remarkable in that."

"Well, I think family life's wonderful!" Emma exclaimed defiantly. "And Christmas too!"

"You certainly must," Ovid commented. "You've gone further than most to get it for your very own. But I call it all battle, murder and sudden death, and I'll prove it on any ground."

"Perhaps it's man and nature we celebrate," suggested Naomi. "At Christmas, I mean. There's the tree invited in, and the year about to seesaw again."

"But the tree doesn't come in willingly," Hadfield pointed out, smelling the piney gum on his fingers. "It's *made* to come."

"Giving presents!" said Benny virtuously.

"Getting them, you mean!" Christobel declared, looking rather like a Christmas decoration herself. "When I was Benny's age I loved everything I got, but now I worry every year in case someone spends good money on something I can't be properly grateful for. Oh well, that's maturity, I suppose."

"It's the thought that counts," said Serena sententiously.

"Gosh, you're pompous, Serena!" Christobel declared. "I know just as well as you do that that's the proper thing to say, but if people are going to spend money on me, it might as well be for something I like."

"A present's got to be a surprise," Benny argued.

"Yes, but a *nice* surprise, not a nasty one," Christobel amended. "So I give people little clues about what I would like."

"You gave me an actual list," Robert said from under the tree, where he was helping Tibby wire a bird to a low branch. She was delighted and ran to seize Emma's arm, pulling her over to show her just where the bird was perched and to receive a hug and a lot of praise from Emma, Naomi and from Robert himself.

"Where did you get the tree?" asked Anthony.

"It's a thinning from a plantation over the hills," Jack said unrepentantly. "It would have gone anyway — its trunk was twisted."

"The money goes to the Volunteer Fire Brigade," Serena pointed out virtuously.

"Forget the Volunteer Fire Brigade," exclaimed Ovid. "What a lucky tree! Who wouldn't choose to blaze out for an hour rather than live a thousand years and never be seen? I was never given the chance, but I still will, if I can."

"I'm not too sure about the tree, however," said Anthony.

"We must put a star on the top." Christobel held a silver star with a heart of red glass. "Where's a good, tall chair?"

"I'll lift you!" Robert offered, and bent down, putting his arms around her knees so that she sat back on his shoulder. Christobel, amid applause, was lifted high and sat laughing, feeling Robert's cheek pressed against her thigh. She carefully hung the star on the top of the tree, Jack sat down at the piano, and the first of their Christmas parties began — just a little party to celebrate the coming of the tree into the house.

"There go the three wise men," said Charlie when the Carnival brothers left much, much later, waving and vanishing into the twilight. "And I'm going to follow their example. I want an early start. We went really well this morning."

Jack read *The Night Before Christmas* to Benny and Serena and anyone who cared to listen, and then followed it up with *The Tailor of Gloucester*. He read wonderfully well. Christobel sat down beside him on the sofa and listened with them. After a while she put her arm around his neck and her head on his shoulder so that he was draped in his children.

"Wonderful Jackie!" she said.

Listening to the old stories, smiling when she caught his enchanted eye, Harry felt the ghost of

Christmases past in the air around her. But the stories ended. She climbed her ladder, put on her cotton nightgown and slid into her sleeping bag to write boldly of Jessica, safe in the arms of her hero Conrad, but unable to forget the thrilling violations of Belen, her enemy-lover. Yet Harry herself was unable to burn with Belen or Jessica as she had done. The winged man had somehow lost his fluidity, his easy graceful flight, in the last twenty-four hours. It was almost as if he had put on weight.

"Harry," called a low voice from the foot of the ladder, and she opened her trapdoor and looked down to see Emma standing below her, gazing up appealingly.

"Do you remember if Tibby had her Dum Dum on the beach this afternoon? She won't go to sleep. I think if she had the Dum Dum where she could see it . . ."

"I know just where it is — at least I think I do," Harry replied. "She was burying it in the sand. I'll nip down to the beach and get it."

"I'll go!" Emma said. "I don't want to bother you."

"No bother! You know I like walking at night," Harry replied, and as this was indeed well known in the family, Emma made no protest.

A little later Harry found the Dum Dum, just where she had remembered seeing it late in the afternoon, but did not return to the house straight away, being suddenly interested in the signs their sunbathing had left on the beach behind them. There among the sticks and stones was a plastic tumbler, piled around with sand so it would not be easily knocked over. Christobel's yellow towel lay like an oblong splash of afternoon sunshine carelessly forgotten by day. There were two cigarette stubs, and several deep holes in the sand, just where it was dark and firm. They looked the sort of holes that might have slim, supple rodents living in them, but they were places where the pointed feet of the sun umbrellas had been driven deep into the sand. The canoe, like a long, blue-painted fish, paddle sticking out in an unwieldy fin, lay stranded out of reach of its native element. Further down the beach she heard, once more, the faint persistent chime of the halyard striking the mast. Harry, carrying Dum Dum by the neck, stood entranced with the mystery of night-time and the sea. She wandered on a little, letting the flashlight put out its sudden finger of light and touch whatever it found, giving things, suddenly rediscovered, significance they had lacked in the daytime when they were part of a jumble. A black stick looked like a frightening lizard crouched to spring at something; some orange peel resembled a cluster of strange flowers glowing on the outside, creamy white on the inside with a few grains of sand cupped in the bottom of them like stamens. A severed head, streaming bloody hair, turned its face away from her light, but after the first surprise she recognized a clump of common red seaweed. Harry shone the flashlight up into the air, watched it make a column of light that grew diffuse and vanished away, doing little to support the weight of night around it. There was starry Orion sprawled upside down on the curve of the universe, the hanged man of the fortune-teller's cards. The remains of yesterday's nor-wester ran a warm, dry hand over her forehead. She made one last sweep with the flashlight then stepped back directly into the arms of someone standing behind her.

"Switch off the flashlight!" commanded a soft, familiar voice, but for the third time in two days Harry thought she might be about to die of fright. It was not a thing you could ever become used to.

"Who is it?" she asked, amazed to hear her voice light, high and trembling, ragged in a night of warm winds and of melting darkness.

"I'm Felix!" he said. "Can't you tell?" Harry found she had automatically surrendered the flashlight.

He moved silkily, touched her hair softly, but without real tenderness.

"Did my flashlight bother you?" she asked apologetically. "I was just looking for Tibby's Dum Dum!" She took a deep breath only to realize he was actually holding her breast and thought at first it must be an accident of mutual confusion, though Felix did not seem confused.

"I don't sleep," he answered. "Night's my true habitat." He paused. "So now's your chance to give in to darkness," he whispered, as if he were tempting her. "Go on. I know you want to," he murmured.

"The beach is becoming too haunted," Harry declared. "I'm going back to the house. Give me my flashlight."

But he did not let her go.

"Stay on and *really* know me?" he said, in rather a terrible voice.

Harry stood completely still for a moment, wondering if she could make herself thin enough to slide out of his embrace. At last she said, "How about knowing you in the morning?"

"Yes, but we won't be the same people then," he objected. "Don't we all become different people once the sun goes down? For instance, I drink blood after dark."

"Emma's waiting for me," Harry said, "and anyway I don't want to stay." She did not like the feeling she was accessible, whereas, holding her from behind, he remained secret and powerful. And then the thought came to her, that somehow, through inventing wicked Belen, she had laid a command on Felix so that he must come out of the dark to waylay her and refuse to set her free.

"Let me go!" she demanded stiffly, but he only laughed and said, "Don't hurry, Harry," in a voice that only pretended to be pleading. His touch was not an accident, but an assault, and Harry realized, with immediate outrage, that she was not going to be allowed to return to Carnival's Hide unhindered.

10
A Gross Compliment

The following day the wind turned to the south and a different cloud mottled the sky. Rain threatened but did not fall.

"I don't know," Harry, half-awake, heard Robert say doubtfully below. "It's not such a nice day today, and besides, Christo wasn't very pleased that I went off with you yesterday."

"Oh, hell!" Charlie said. "If you give in now you'll give in for the rest of your days. I'm warning you."

"Well, I'm not too sure about this Ovid Carnival. He's a clever talker," Robert grumbled.

"Bit of a poof, I thought," Charlie said. "Come on! He's more keen on himself than he is on her. They're too much two of a kind to get on for long."

"Since when did you get clever over things like that?" Robert asked sourly.

"I've got Jack for a father and Christobel for a sister," Charlie replied. "And I know a lot more about people than I can be bothered talking about. That's why I like boats. They may be tricky, but they never make you feel guilty. Come on. Hurry up!"

Neither said anything for a while though the room was filled with activity.

"Don't things look a little bit funny to you?" Robert said suddenly. "Someone's shifted the chairs about or something."

"Nothing ever stays put in this house for long at a time," said Charlie.

Harry could hear the long buzz as he zipped up his oilskin. Their voices drifted away down the track, for though Robert expressed doubts about sailing, he could not resist it. The house grew quiet again as they made off into the morning, grey, not only because clouds covered the sky, but because the sun had not yet risen behind them. When she was sure they had gone, Harry got up, put on the pants of her track suit with a dark green sweater, and climbed down her ladder. The room had indeed altered again. The flow of the furniture was unfamiliar, as if all the chairs had taken one pace back and a half-turn to the right, and Harry, staring at them, was suddenly convinced the bookcase had vanished. She found herself remembering wallpaper with a dense, flowery pattern, and not the familiar wooden shelves. She turned in consternation and saw with relief that the bookcase was safely there. She could see the very books Anthony and Jack had looked at only the day before, pushed in flat on top of other books on the shelf.

Harry looked at them severely through her glasses before she went out on to the verandah. She ran off with the angular defiance of someone refusing to be constrained against her will. There was something furtive in the way she skirted the house and turned along the easterly slopes.

Over the next twenty minutes the eastern cloud lifted a little, rolling up like a slow curtain. A strange, red glow crept out from under it, filling the sky with a clear, furious light against which the hills with their spiky crowns were plastered flat and black, having no more dimension than a shadow. The rolled edges of the clouds were touched with gold and rose colour, deepening second by second to an intense brightness.

Ovid Carnival walked naked across the beach and into the water, which was as smooth as glass and coloured like burning blood. His fantastic curls blazed, apparently quite undisturbed by a night's sleep, each one edged with a fine line of brilliance as if outlined with a fiery pen. Across the water, the departing *Sunburst* looked like nothing less than its name, the curve of its gently swelling spinnaker catching and reflecting the fierce light. Ovid shouted, but not as if he were summoning anyone, only as if his feelings were too strong to be held in. One of his brothers appeared at the door of the whare and then, also naked, crossed the beach and joined him in the water, looking like a man of some splendid, barbaric tribe, whereas Ovid looked like the spirit of the bloody sea.

Up on a ridge behind them, Harry found herself accidentally looking down on them. On the hillside she became an upstairs self and, filled with the proper power of the writer to bear witness, did not feel she was spying, but was like the sun, naturally entitled to see everything the day had to show her. She watched as Ovid ran up over the beach and his brother followed him, stopping halfway to fling out his arms rather as if he were trying to embrace the world. His head tilted back, he stopped midstride, and Harry suddenly realized that she might have been seen. Drops of water shone on the young man's shoulders as if he were set with jewels, but at least he was wingless. She turned and ran towards home, through the living room, and climbed up into her bedroom once more.

In turn Naomi woke, stared at the ceiling and then turned to her husband who lay beside her, eyes closed, blushing in the reflected light of the wild sky, still in the power of a fabulous but deeply disturbing dream. However, she suspected he was not asleep.

"Jack," she said. "Jack, dear!"

He smiled by way of an answer.

"How's it going so far?" and then answered herself by adding, "I told you it would be all right."

"Burnt cookies!" he replied, still with his eyes closed.

"It isn't!" she protested. "That's too simple. Cookies are only cookies, but people are people."

"Great!" he said, almost as if he had been Christobel, but with a wearier sarcasm.

"It was nice watching them all decorate the tree."

"Very nice," he said. "Sad, too."

"But someday we may look back on this Christmas and think — well, not that it's been our happiest perhaps, but meaningful," she said, trying to convince herself as much as him. Now Jack opened his eyes.

"Naomi, what a terrible word!" he exclaimed. "Forget 'meaningful'. I don't expect anything to mean anything anymore. I'm going along one day at a time, enjoying everything as much as I can. And I'd sooner spend that time with you than with anyone else — there now!"

"You haven't got much choice," she said doubtfully.

"I've got as much choice as anyone ever has," he protested, laughing and melancholy all at once. "I'm not that old! What *is* that dreadful noise?"

"It's the little ones meeting for the first time today," she said as voices rose in a great quarrel and objects banged in the kitchen. "I hope they don't disturb Christobel," he said in a resigned voice. "You'd think I'd be used to it by now. I seem to have spent the last twenty years with that sound going on in the background."

"Why can't they whisper?" he said.

"Jack, they think they *are* whispering," Naomi told him. There was a loud shrill scream from Tibby, followed by a lot of shushings, rapid footsteps and the rattling of a window as the little ones made a quick exit on to the verandah. Jack listened and then said, "Well, the day's begun. Let's try and stop Serena dancing *Swan Lake* all around Anthony today."

"She's got a susceptible heart," Naomi said with a sigh.

Jack groaned. "Oh God!" and closed his eyes again. "Terrible! Shoot us all! It's kindest on the whole."

The fiery day grew dull once more as the sun climbed across its band of clear sky, then hid behind the clouds again. Naomi heard the lids of cookie tins being opened, as the little ones stole cookies, and shortly afterwards the squeak and thump of Harry's trapdoor as she returned from her run, and then again as she came downstairs for the second time that day.

Thank God for one reliable member of the family, Naomi thought, for Charlie always sailed away, and Christobel needed everything before she felt secure, and Serena suffered from love and art, and Benny got asthma and bronchitis. Harry's silences were sometimes worrying, but at least silence demanded nothing.

Downstairs, Harry made off to the bathroom building with her towel in her hand. Ten minutes later, returning with wet, washed hair falling around her face, dressed in blue jeans and a yellow shirt, she met Felix coming up from the whare with a bowl of strawberries, oranges and black cherries.

"Hello!" he said cheerfully. "I've seen you already today! And tell me — just how shortsighted are you?"

Harry stared at him fixedly. His voice was so easy. She thought she must have made a mistake.

"Are you Felix or Hadfield?" she asked.

"Which do you like the best?" he asked. "I'll be that one. I've brought a few nutritious scraps because we had dinner here last night and we can't eat you out of house and home. Where would you like me to put them?"

"In the kitchen," Harry said in a chilly voice, and he looked at her startled.

"Here — what's this?" he asked briskly. "Are you shy? I thought I should be the one to be shy, but perhaps it's different these days."

"I despise you too much to let you offend me,"

Harry said very grandly. Felix watched her storm through into the living room ahead of him. Then he followed, and, looking at him out of the corner of her eyes, she could see his expression grow sharp and calculating for a moment. But he smiled and lowered his eyelashes as modestly as if she had paid him a compliment.

"Don't be like that!" he begged in collected tones, putting his groceries on the table. "We all make mistakes. And it is the better part to forgive. Shouldn't I have been swimming naked? It was such a wonderful feeling — one of the reasons for having skin at all — and so early in the morning that I . . ."

"Forget that!" Harry cried. "You're trying to put the blame on me to get out of being blamed for last night."

Felix's mouth fell open slightly, and his eyes shifted as if involved once more in a private calculation.

"Oh that!" he said at last. "Was it so very dreadful?"

"I suppose it doesn't seem much to you," Harry said. "But if you're on your own in the dark — it's like . . ." But she couldn't say what it was like. Felix sat down on the piano chair. He struck a note on the piano and listened to it dying away. When he looked up again, there was comprehension on his face. His guardedness had quite vanished.

"The greater the temptation the more forgivable the crime," he said at last, with a slight lift of his voice at the end of the sentence that suggested he was not certain about this idea. "It's love with its heart on the wrong side."

"It isn't!" Harry said passionately. "It's nothing to do with love."

"Isn't it?" Felix said, striking another note. "Well, we live and learn. *We've* never been certain where one thing left off and another began. It must be nice to be so sure."

"I am sure," said Harry. "I'm sure now."

"I expect I was carried away." Felix smiled to himself. "And sometimes, if you persist, other people do come round to your way of thinking." He lifted his honey-coloured eyes to hers with sudden concern. "Did you tell Jack and Naomi?"

"No!" she said shortly, moving to the foot of her ladder.

"Why not?" he asked her, looking first relieved, then inquisitive.

"Why should I? There wasn't any point in making a great fuss, because I reckon I managed pretty well on my own."

Saying this she climbed her ladder and vanished through the ceiling, though she continued to listen, heard Felix go through into the kitchen, presumably to put his gifts on the table, and heard Naomi come out and exclaim with pleasure and surprise. They came back into the living room together, Naomi saying, "Well, of course, it did cross my mind you might be common or garden parasites . . ."

"Hardly common! Not Ovid!" Felix answered in a slightly distracted voice.

"We've had all sorts in our time, I can tell you," Naomi said. "Were you really carrying all that stuff around with you in your packs?"

He did not answer, for the door burst open and Christobel came in.

"That bloody Charlie!" she exclaimed. "This is the second morning running he's pinched my boyfriend. Oh, well, that's all right! On his own head be it. I shall just love somebody else, that's all. How about you, Hadfield?"

"Felix!" said Felix.

"You'll do! I'm in no mood to be choosy," said Christobel.

"He came bearing gifts," Naomi said. "Lovely oranges, some strawberries . . ."

"Gold, frankincense and myrrh," finished Christobel.

"Black cherries, fairy gold." Felix sounded mystified. "It might all vanish at midnight."

"Joke! Joke!" cried Christobel. "Ma, shake Balthazar there awake, and let's start the day with coffee. I want something with a lot more *aggression* than tea."

The kitchen door shut and the voices were lost once more. Harry lay on her bed staring at the corrugations of the roofing iron only a few inches from her nose and began to wonder why she had not told Naomi or Jack about the hot, brief struggle in the dark, during which she felt that, if she did stumble and fall, she would be entirely lost. Her assailant had been very strong, but she had been slippery with sun-tan oil, hard to hold and completely furious. Once free, she had run up the track sobbing with anger and had then stood by the front door of Carnival's Hide breathing herself back into being herself, strong and above all else, silent. When she was sure of herself, she entered the house, restored Dum Dum to its grateful owner, with no more breathlessness than could be explained by her run up the hill. Though she did not look forward to meeting Felix the following day, she did not feel it would be an impossible encounter, for she had total right on her side. But then, after putting her light out and trying uselessly to sleep, she put it on again and reread her description of Belen and Jessica falling on to the apple blossom. Only when she had crossed these words out, burdened as they now were with a horrid fatality, did she feel set free, not only from a faulty story, but from a troubling idea that need no longer trouble her again — the idea that it might be exciting to have choice taken away from her.

Yet then she wept a few tears quite unexpectedly as she went to sleep and wondered why she was feeling so sad. There was a poem she had once read about Leda assailed by the god Zeus in the form of a swan. Leda had been "caught up and mastered by the brute blood of the air." Crossing out her story, Harry might be saying goodbye to her chance to be Leda all over again.

As she turned this thought over and over, struggling to patch a meaning out of it, she heard the door open.

"No one!" said Ovid's voice, filled with soft tension. "Where is he?"

"The room's changed," Hadfield said, sounding entertained. "Is it you doing that?" He laughed his weird laugh, so amused and so hollow, empty of real feeling.

"All of us, I expect." Ovid was intrigued, too. "We must make an almighty displacement."

Hadfield then said something in a low voice, which Harry could not hear.

"Remember . . . ?" Ovid's lighter voice was easier to hear than Hadfield's.

"Of course I remember," Hadfield replied. "We've got the same memories. It could have been wonderful to live here if we'd been allowed to be happy. Say the word and I'll pull it down board by board. I've not got much else to do. I need diversion."

"My God — you certainly do," Ovid said. "Well, you must be fed and I'll feed you."

"I carry all the heavy stuff," Hadfield remarked. "But then, on the other hand, it's easy to keep me happy. Not so easy to please Felix. He might take over, without Papa here to beat him out of us."

These mysterious speculations were interrupted by the kitchen door opening and Christobel coming out accompanied by the smell of coffee.

A moment later she exclaimed, "For goodness sake, Hadfield — what's happened to you?"

"You notice it, do you?" Hadfield said in a leisurely voice. "I thought you might."

"It's classic!" Christobel exclaimed. "I've never seen a black eye like it. You can't have got that just walking into the door."

"I had help. I can't take total credit," Hadfield admitted.

"Isn't it gratifying?" Ovid put in. "It seems I don't know my own strength. Last night we went for a midnight swim and Hadfield, being so much more brutal than I am, tried to duck me. I lashed out with great sincerity and — well — you can see the result. I'm terribly proud of it."

"You poor fellow — it must be dreadfully painful," Naomi, coming from the kitchen, said sympathetically. "You should put a cold compress on it."

"Oh, it was nothing I didn't deserve," Hadfield replied with remarkably good humour. "I was sorry for myself at the time, of course. Are you going to comment, Felix? This is the first time I think you've seen it!"

"Better you than me!" Felix said. "You should stick to what you're good at, Haddy."

"Well, at least it's blown your chances of posing as one another for a while," Christobel said. "I'd think the worst, of course, except that there's no real talent around, outside of me and Emma, and I know that it wasn't me, and Emma's being very single-minded about motherhood these days. Never mind! How do you have your coffee?"

"Black to match!" Hadfield said.

Up in the attic Harry combed her damp hair, plaited it and boldly went down the ladder to breakfast.

Hadfield was indeed the possessor of a notable black eye, but he met her stony stare with a smile so guileless that she was taken aback, even wondering if she had imagined the violent midnight embrace and the jarring shock that had run up her arm as her blow struck home. There was a small cut just below the eyebrow, but it was not deep. It was sealed with a thin, black line of dried blood and the bruising was already extending around it. He smiled at her, as if her arrival had brightened a dull morning, but Felix did not seem to notice her descent. He was carrying coffee and toast through from the kitchen, silhouetted against its large cupboards and the red bar stools, reminders of Jack's days as a flamboyant host.

"It's not going to be much of a sunbathing day today." Christobel had opened the window on to the verandah wide and was peering out critically. She looked tousled but somehow exquisite in her faded silk dressing-gown. Her pretty lips curved in a hopeful smile. "Let's pack up lunch and take off into the hills. We could borrow the Volkswagen, couldn't we, dear little, sweet little mother, since my car's so unreliable, and wind up in Gorse Bay, eat lots of fish and chips and see what's going on there. There's usually something happening. Terrible, but something! They might have a band at the pub, for example."

"I suppose that would be all right," said Naomi doubtfully. "There's enough petrol to get you to Gorse Bay, I think."

A moment later, Harry was deserted by both mother and sister who went to check the petrol gauge of the car, and she was left alone with the three brothers as she had hoped, and feared, she might be.

She turned to Felix and said, "He *said* he was you!" feeling no further explanation was needed.

"But you believed him!" Felix said reproachfully.

"I thought your name might be more effective than mine," Hadfield said, without showing the least sign of shame. "But I overestimated your influence."

"Besides, regardless of any confusion over names," Ovid said, "the evil-doer was the one who sustained the injury. You have to admit that's justice."

"In its way, it was a compliment," Hadfield suggested. Harry could not believe he was so completely unrepentant.

"It sounds absolutely gross!" declared Felix.

"Oh, well — yes — a gross compliment," amended Hadfield amiably.

"Gross compliments are the only ones *I* care to receive," Ovid said merrily, studying his reflection on the back of a shiny spoon. Harry was completely disarmed by their lack of shame. The night-time act, threatening and dangerous, lost its reality under such flippant treatment.

"What did you hit him with?" asked Felix, peering without sympathy or condemnation at Hadfield's eye.

"Tibby's wooden Dum Dum!" she said coldly. "I hit him as hard as I could. Don't do anything like that again."

"That has to depend on the opportunities you offer me," Hadfield said, smiling with his teeth lightly clenched, looking genial but pitiless.

Harry could scarcely believe what she had heard. She stared at Felix and understood he was more upset than he seemed to be. He met her eyes, looked briefly into them, and then closed his own.

"He could have killed you," he said. "He's like that."

"I'm all crocodile brain," Hadfield replied, yawning lightly. "I'm the simplest of the three."

Ovid placed his hand on Hadfield's arm, but spoke to Harry. "Harry," he said in a very gentle voice, casting a quelling look at Felix. "Let me give you a warning. In spite of everything, it really is Felix you should watch out for."

Felix made no comment, frowning more to himself than anyone else.

"And now," cried Ovid, as if the subject had somehow been happily resolved, "we are going to go to Gorse Bay, it seems. Are you coming, too?"

"No!" Harry replied. "I like it here," for she thought that her fear and anger of the night before represented something too real to be joked away. Felix looked at her thoughtfully, but said nothing.

"She wants to get on with her novel, I expect!" Ovid speculated wisely to his brothers. "I do wish that I was creative. You must let us read it some time before we go."

Harry felt as if the floor had dissolved under her feet. The three brothers looked at her with satisfaction, and more than at any previous time she felt helpless before their combined regard. All she could say was, "It's not finished. It's not the sort of book you show to anyone, anyway."

She turned away, but then looked back and saw them almost as if they were posing for her, Hadfield looking a little to the left and Felix to the right, while Ovid, balanced between his identical brothers, smiled directly at her. But then Felix broke the symmetry by shifting his eyes to her face and giving her his own faint smile and a look that seemed as if it must be conveying a message, passing it in the language of light, from eye to eye.

The door opened and Anthony came in, looked at her tense face curiously and then at the three brothers. However, he said nothing.

Breakfast continued. When it was over Harry went up to her room and hid her book among the empty boxes that had held Christmas decorations. She did not come down again until she had heard the Volkswagen drive away, carrying the Carnival brothers and Christobel to Gorse Bay. Growing over-anxious, she stayed upstairs long enough to take her book out from among the boxes, to crawl over into the further reaches of the roof and to slide it into a gap between iron and wood, taking care to cover it with dust and cobwebs. Only then did she feel it might be safe.

11
Fairy Godmothers

Carnival's Hide, emptied of Christobel and the Carnivals, became very quiet for a while. Then the little ones came in from their canoeing and, shortly after, Charlie and Robert from their sailing.

"There! What did I tell you?" said Robert, on hearing Christobel had gone. "I don't suppose you can blame her."

"They've only gone to Gorse Bay," said Charlie. "We'll catch up with them later." But Robert sat on the verandah, staring rather moodily out over the orchard, looking more like Lord Byron than ever. The sun came out for a little while, flooding over him, hot and bright. Someone touched his knee and he looked down to see Tibby standing there, holding up a little blue car for him to admire.

"Rrrrrrrm!" she said, making sweeping gestures in the air. Inside, Serena and Benny began a long wrangling argument about whose turn it was to wash the dishes and whose to dry. Robert picked Tibby up and sat her on his knee. She waved the car in the air again. Her fine curls smelled of some pleasant shampoo.

"You're doing an aeroplane, not a car," he said, and gently took the car from her, running it along the flat arm of the wooden chair, making car noises, changing gear and tooting.

"Mine!" said Tibby, made a little anxious by this expertise. "Mine little car!"

"I know!" agreed Robert surrendering it. "You don't want to let just any joker drive your car." Tibby held the car for a moment and then passed it back.

"Don't let her be a nuisance to you," said Emma, coming up the steps behind them. She had been pegging out washing.

"We're quite happy with each other," Robert said. "Sit down for a moment. Let's talk about something."

"Like what?" asked Emma, sitting down and holding out her hands to Tibby, who showed no wish to leave her present situation. Robert did not reply.

"Are you feeling lonely?" she asked. "Do you mind that Christobel didn't wait for you?"

"Of course I mind," he said. "But, after all, I went sailing. Do *you* mind that she goes off without you these days?"

"She asked me to go" — Emma sighed — "and I was tempted. But I can't just leave Naomi with Tibby all day, and maybe most of the night." She hesitated and then said, "Nothing will come of this Ovid Carnival. I just know there's nothing permanent about that."

"The thing is, Christo likes things unexpected and unpredictable, and I need things orderly," he replied gloomily. "We were suited for a while, but not any more. Still, I can't imagine being without her."

"I can't see you having an easy life together, I must say." Emma grinned faintly.

"No!" he agreed. "I get hacked off sitting just talking all the time, and outside of a bit of tennis, she doesn't like sport. But we're like old habits to each other."

"Well, it must be years!" Emma said. "Years and years."

"About five," Robert agreed, looking nostalgic. "But you'd remember. Back when you girls were fifteen. Late-night shopping."

"It seems so dreadful now," Emma said, but looking as if she might be about to giggle. "Christo and I used to set out looking so — so *wholesome* — then we'd get to the Square and shoot round all the chemist shops and department stores, trying out their tester ranges of make-up — lipstick, eyeshadow, gallons of perfume."

"We could smell you coming from way down the street, Sam and I could," asserted Robert. "The old Morry used to smell like a garden." (Robert was referring to the old Morris Minor, which had been their travelling house, as well as their transport, in those long-past days.) "I remember my dad saying to me, 'Either you've had girls out in this car or you're going out with the wrong sort of boy.' I don't think Naomi ever caught on, did she?"

"She always trusted us," Emma said with a sigh. "I'm never, ever going to trust Tibby."

"Long time before you have to bother about

that," said Robert, looking rather tenderly at Tibby, as if he didn't believe she would ever really get to the stage where she would put on illicit lipstick and perfume from chemist's testers and deceive her mother.

"I just can't imagine Sam walking out on you!" Robert said suddenly, in an angry and bewildered voice. "He was a bit of a chauvinist over girls, I suppose, but not a chauvinist *pig*. I thought he was all right, Sam."

A burst of Christmas music came roaring out on to the verandah and then decreased in volume as the tape recorder was turned down. The phone was ringing. A moment later Naomi appeared on the verandah followed by Jack. Harry hung in the doorway like a dark ghost.

"The Taveners, no less!" Naomi said. "They're having a barbecue this evening and we're all invited. I've got some steak in the freezer so I'll take that and we'll pick up some wine in Gorse Bay. Who's coming? They've given themselves a swimming pool as a Christmas present this year, so think about that!"

"They've got the sea a few minutes from their door and they build a swimming pool," Jack said in a slightly jealous voice.

"They like to be one up on nature," Harry observed. "Suppose God had given them wings, they'd still want an executive jet."

"Sneer if you like, they're still good friends. It's not their fault they're rich," Naomi said. "So who's in?"

"We've only just got here," Harry said. "I'm going to stay at home and read."

"I'll go," said Charlie. "I'll try and catch up with Christobel and come home with her."

"I can't take Tibby," said Emma. She had expanded a little earlier, laughed and relaxed with Robert. Now she began to look stern with herself once more.

"She doesn't sleep very easily, does she?" Jack said. "It's certainly not a suitable place for a baby. Lots of rare treasures on low tables." Tibby looked up at him knowing herself to be under discussion. Jack guiltily avoided her gaze.

"I'll babysit. No hassle!" Harry said to Emma. "Everyone knows you're the world's best solo parent. You'd get the sparkling crown and the sash and the silver cup, so you can take it easy for one night."

"Why not?" asked Robert. "Christobel's run away. Don't make me go out on my own. Be a woman of the world again."

"I suppose you think I can't be," Emma said, with a little provocation in her voice as the memory of past glory took hold of her again.

"I'm sure you can!" he said. "Try!"

"My clothes are all so old — pathetic-old, not picturesque-old."

"You've got a reasonable pair of jeans," Naomi said with sudden enthusiasm. "We'll rifle Christo's room for that pretty top — you know, the full one gathered on to a yoke. I think you could wear that. We'll set your hair, if you wash it. There's even an old hair dryer out in the wash-house, too."

If you can't be Cinderella yourself there is a lot to be said for being fairy godmother. The idea of making Emma wonderfully pretty for the Taveners' party thrilled Naomi and Serena, and even Harry grew interested. Jack, exclaiming that the atmosphere was becoming rather too specialized, suggested that the men drive around the hills and show Anthony some of the wonderful views from the crater's rim, but Robert elected to stay behind, saying that if he was going to escort Emma he wanted to have a say in how she turned out.

"It's only the Taveners!" Serena said. "You don't have to go in pairs." But Robert said that he and Emma were going to go as a pair anyway.

"You're being revenged on Christobel," Serena said, thrilled and reproachful, and Robert, blushing slightly, told her that he and Emma were such old acquaintances that Christobel would think he was silly if he didn't go out with her in the circumstances.

Charlie, Jack and Anthony had driven for miles, rising up over long tawny spurs, dropping into gullies of bush. They had a pub lunch and returned to find the midsummer transformation well advanced.

"Well, hello, Cinderella!" Anthony said. "Tibby won't know you."

"Wouldn't it be terrible if Christobel came back now," Serena said. "Everything would go grunt."

"No, it wouldn't," Emma said. "I'd just go out and dance by myself."

"Does she have to be home by midnight?" asked Benny.

"We all will be!" Naomi said firmly. "You, too — we can't have the station wagon turning into a pumpkin."

"And Daddy into a rat!" Benny said.

"I really am a rat, Benny. See my whiskers,"

said Jack, pulling a rodent face and stroking imaginary whiskers so that it was possible for a moment to believe they were really there.

"Forget Cinderella. It's midsummer's night!" Harry said. "Everyone will get flower juice squeezed into their eyes and fall in love with the first person they see."

"Don't be silly!" cried Benny, looking alarmed.

"It's in a play," Serena told him in a lecturing voice. "It's Shakespeare, isn't it, Harry?"

"Shakespeare! Grunt!" grumbled Benny, though he had enjoyed seeing Emma changed, her hair trimmed and curled, her jeans pressed. She wore a Victorian cotton blouse of Christobel's with a slightly frilled collar and many delicate pin tucks. Its designer had certainly never envisaged it ever being worn with blue jeans, but it suited Emma's heart-shaped face and steadfast brown eyes.

"She looks like the cover of some magazine, but I forget which one," Serena said.

"I've got a lot to live up to!" exclaimed Robert.

"Isn't it silly?" Emma said, laughing a little self-consciously. "I know clothes don't matter, but I always used to enjoy dressing up. And it just wouldn't be the same if I had to take Tibby with me. It's really good of you, Harry!"

"It's not that good," Harry said. "She's no trouble except at bedtime and I was staying anyway. I won't put her down until late and maybe she'll go straight to sleep."

A little later the barbecue party set off for Gorse Bay, and Carnival's Hide belonged only to Harry and Tibby, heirs to an empty house and a great, wide silence, which the sea and the wind, sighing and muttering, emphasized rather than broke into.

Harry and Tibby went inside and put the tape of an Australian band on the tape recorder. It was not a Christmas sound. The band sang about their own continent, " — living in the summer for a million years."

It seemed the voice of her own country to Harry. Relieved of the pressure of other people in the house, she danced first with Tibby and then on her own, whirling around, spinning like a wild bird with a plaited crest, caught in a gale of sound. At last, tired out, she stood still, listening intently, then laughed and took Tibby down to the beach and paddled her up and down the edge of the sea in her blue canoe, moving in water so shallow that the canoe caught continually on the sand and had to be pushed free with the paddle. There was no life jacket that fitted Tibby, and besides, Harry had no wish to go any deeper. It was like being in water and on land at the same time. She sang the songs of her own childhood aloud, and as she did so, the cloud that had dogged much of the day finally broke up and peeled away. The hills were covered with a curious late light — pinkish lavender on the long slopes — and it occurred to her she was actually singing summer back over the harbour. The silence, when she stopped singing, seemed to be not one silence, but many, rushing together to form a huge, brooding, complex quietness that lowered itself over everything, smothering all sound. Harry found herself suddenly breathless with the expectation of a voice that would speak and set her free of the spell of the last hour — an hour that seemed as if it had lasted for ever.

In due course, she made Tibby a supper of tomato soup and scrambled egg, something they had always had for Sunday tea when she was a little child. She read Tibby a story, played a game with her, sat her on her pink pot and then pinned her nappy on her. When she put her to bed, Dum Dum and the blue car stood beside her to watch over her during the night. Harry examined Dum Dum closely, but there were no incriminating bloodstains. In retrospect, she was awed with her success with this unlikely weapon and wondered if she could have blinded Hadfield by striking him.

"Serve him right!" she said, but without conviction.

"Serve him right!" said Tibby, copying her stern voice, and then laughing as if she had made a successful joke.

Was Hadfield mortal? Could he be harmed or even hurt? He had seemed entirely without resentment, unnaturally so, as if he had no pride to hurt, let alone skin and bones and nerves. Unlike Felix or even Ovid, Hadfield seemed to have a hollowness at heart. She knew he could bleed and suffer shock, but beyond that was a void, or he must have felt shame or anger.

Tibby went to sleep, and Harry came into the living room and turned on the Christmas-tree lights. They shone red, blue, pink, yellow and purple — so many little points of colour winking on and off, that the tree was alternately light and dark. The pile of parcels under the lower branches of the tree had been secretly added to since yesterday. She put on the tape of the carols, which obediently filled the house with lovely sounds, and since there were no neighbours she turned the tape recorder up very loudly, going outside and lying in the hammock for a while as the music sounded out over the seeds of summer grass, over the neglected orchard and native bush, even out over the sand and sea.

When she went inside, she saw Christobel's red silk dressing-gown hanging like a soft ghost of its owner over the end of the piano. Harry put on her cotton nightgown, then borrowed the dressing-gown and felt herself transformed, walking differently under a new silk surface. In this way, at least, she could become Christobel for a little while. She could try out what it might be like to be beautiful. Among many thoughts, thoughts of the Carnival brothers came and went — flamboyant Ovid, Hadfield, hollow and frightening, and Felix, who had let carrots come to flower in the gardens of his childhood — and suddenly it seemed to her, sitting grandiose, silken and solitary as she was, that they were all three really a single creature, come out of her own imagination, with which she must now wrestle like Jacob with the angel. So she sat, dreamily watching the tree, sniffing to remind herself of the scent of pine and looking into the deep shadow of the branches, dark between the angel's wings, the iridescent sides of the bells and birds, the solid shapes of presents waiting to be claimed and opened and possessed.

All the time, dancing before the tree, singing on the beach or lying in the hammock watching the stars, Harry was waiting for a particular voice. Her pleasure in her solitude was all the more intense because she somehow believed it would be interrupted. With Hadfield beaten off, there would be a true ambush. Yet when Felix did appear, he did not try to surprise her at all. She felt a vibration on the path, a soft but firm tread on the verandah.

"It's only me!" he shouted cheerfully, before he came into the room smiling. "But which me? Guess!"

"Is it Felix?" she asked.

"Who were you expecting?" he said, sitting down beside her.

Harry turned to face him, and immediately, with a movement both gentle and mischievous, he lifted her glasses from her nose. The shapes of the Christmas-tree lights blurred, as if tight buds of colour had burst into flower. The bells and angels lost definition and the Christmas tree became a glittering ghost holding its arms high, less in praise than in apprehension on her behalf.

"There now!" he said. "Look with your own eyes. Tell me who I am." As he said this, the lights went out, and they were plunged into momentary darkness together.

12
Felix Halted

The lights on the Christmas tree flashed on once more, and she saw his indistinct face dyed with colour, as if he wore the paint of a barbaric initiation. She saw too, even in that brief, blurred image, that Ovid had been speaking the truth when he said that Felix was the dangerous one, sitting beside her, holding her glasses — her clear sight — gently in his long fingers, smiling and sure enough of himself and of her to play a dangerous game with attraction. Harry said nothing.

"How clearly can you see me?" he asked.

"Clearly in my mind!" Harry replied, rather incoherently. "I'm getting to know your kind of thoughts."

Felix appeared to consider this with arrested interest.

"I don't know!" he said. "I could still be Haddy. You've made a mistake once already. We're reflections."

"No," said Harry. "It's nothing to do with the

way you look, or whether you've got a black eye or not, so you might as well give me back my glasses."

Not only was she immediately sure that this was true, but she wondered how she could have confused him with his brother in the first place, for simply by sitting down beside her he changed her in a way that Hadfield had no power to do.

"Anyway reflections are opposites," she said. "You more or less said so yourself."

"You accused me falsely this morning. I hate that," Felix murmured reproachfully, his voice close to her ear. "And then you didn't even apologize."

"I thought it might be a plot," Harry said, remembering that she had been ready then to think he was almost the same person as Hadfield and that they were both Belen. She felt him touch her hair as Hadfield has done the night before, a light touch that came and went, giving her no time to be frightened or indignant, and with this touch came a thin needling thrill that made her shiver, though not with cold.

"I like your hair — that and the way you slow light down," Felix said. "Did you know you could do that?"

"No," said Harry.

"It slows down crossing your skin," Felix explained. The lights went off once more, and in the dark he touched her lips with the first two fingers of his right hand, a soft touch as if he were anxious to know, for purposes of his own, just where they were. She sat as still as a girl of stone. "I've watched it often in the last couple of days," he went on. "It says in one of your books there that light leaves the sun travelling at one hundred and eighty-six miles a second. That means it tears along for ninety-three million miles through space — then reaches you and hesitates."

"How fast is it in kilometres?" Harry asked. She was not sure why, but she thought he had paid her a magical compliment and did not want to be softened by it.

"Either way, it's fast," Felix said. "Shall I make you a cup of tea? I mean I'd like one. I've walked miles and miles to get here, all the way from Gorse Bay, walking and working out good things to say."

It was an unexpectedly innocent suggestion. Harry had been preparing for something different, and he had now cunningly shifted his ground. Still, as he spoke, he was putting her glasses on his own nose, looking through them as if he were trying her on, by searching for the exact world she saw through them.

"Goodness, you are short-sighted, aren't you?" he said, pulling them down his nose so that he could look at her over them.

"Give them back!" commanded Harry.

"You *do* look a little naked and helpless without them," he commented. "But that's reassuring for me. You look at me so sternly when you're wearing them."

"I suppose you think you're seeing me in my true beauty," Harry said sarcastically, putting out her hand, and felt rather than saw this simple act affect Felix almost as if she had actually touched him. Then he laughed, stood up and walked into the kitchen. A broader light flooded through the open door as he began to make tea.

"I don't mind your glasses actually," he called back to her. "But then I'm easy-going."

She could hear him plugging in the electric jug, looking for tea, taking the lid off the teapot and knew without seeing him that he was performing these small, domestic acts with the pleasure of someone mastering strange skills.

"Are the others at Gorse Bay?" she asked.

"Everyone in the world is at Gorse Bay," he answered. "I can't remember when I last saw so many people. It really annoyed me — wherever I turned there was someone about to bang into me. I left! Besides, Ovid is going to start a fight. I know the signs, and I thought he just might use it to match me up with Hadfield again. He's very treacherous."

"A fight!" Harry cried, delighted to have something else to be outraged over.

"Hadfield *needs* a fight from time to time," Felix ran on placidly. "Are you worried about your sister? What's she like with a broken bottle? Competent, I'd say. She'll probably enjoy it. It's exciting, if you fancy that sort of thing. Oh, and we ran into a young woman called Debbie Tavener who told us that your entire family, with the exception of you and the baby, was going to spend midsummer eve by their swimming pool. I could hardly believe my good luck," he said, leaning in the doorway with the light behind him. "So here we are, the baby asleep, you changing colour by the lights from the tree . . . It's like playing house, isn't it?" He yawned slightly. "Would you like an early night?"

"It's late already," Harry said.

"If you can make light slow down, then I might manage to stop time." His voice was speculative, as if he thought he might really stop it. "It must have a natural tendency to hesitate at midnight on the shortest night, don't you think? Just long enough to give the year time to turn around and begin swinging back on itself. We could have a time on our own, outside of time."

"You're not being straightforward," Harry mumbled.

"Well, Hadfield was straightforward, and look what you did to him," Felix said reasonably. "Be fair! I've had all the humiliation of being wrongly accused, and none of the pleasures of the crime."

"I'll apologize," Harry said quickly. "I'm not too proud."

Felix sighed. "Oh dear," he said, "it might be a bit late for that. You should have apologized straight away, because I've brooded on it all day, and I've come to like the idea of being guilty more than the idea of being forgiven."

"Gosh, why do you think I'd feel better about you than I did about your brother?" Harry cried.

"I'm a whole lot nicer," Felix said with a smile. "Besides, you could help me to be the powerful one." He turned his head. "Listen — there's the kettle." He had reverted to a busy, domestic voice. Harry had certainly never expected that he might try and talk her into bed in such a homely way. In fighting off Hadfield, she thought she had successfully repelled Belen, but she had not imagined he would return, cunning and indirect, touching her with nothing but words, and those interspersed with tea-making.

The light went off in the kitchen. Heraldic in the Christmas glow, Felix carried in a tray of cups, milk, sugar and the teapot, wearing its respectable, knitted tea-cosy. He looked as if he were sweating colour. Seeing her glasses still poised on his nose, Harry longed for their definition and control once more. With sight blurred, everything seemed blurred, even her own feelings. "Do give me my glasses!" she begged. Felix ran one finger lightly around the rims.

"Come and get them," he invited her.

"That's enough!" Harry said. "I'm not scared of you. Maybe you don't realize it yet, but you're only a sort of invention of mine. I wrote you and I can probably rewrite you, or even cross you out if I have to."

The thought she was giving voice to frightened her, and she stopped with a gasp. The lights went off again. Felix spoke out of the blackness in a detached voice.

"What do you mean — you *wrote* me?"

"I invented you!" she cried passionately. "I truly invented you. You're identical with a — a person in my book, you and Hadfield, but there's really no such person, so maybe there isn't any you, either. Not these days anyway."

"Is he the hero?" asked Felix after a pause.

"He's the villain," Harry replied, very sternly. "The hero is completely different from you."

"The villain?" he said laughing, in charge of himself again. "Come off it! What's villainous about me? Name one thing — just one."

Harry was too intent on her revelation to be diverted.

"Who are you and your brothers?" She broke off,

and corrected herself. "*What* are you, more likely. You're not real people."

He was silent again, then looked back over his shoulder to where the photographs of old photographs watched from the wall. "Well, perhaps I do look like a character in your book . . ."

"Exactly like him!" she exclaimed quickly.

". . . but where did the look of that particular character come from in the first place? Nothing comes from nothing. Who is who's invention?"

Harry looked at him stubbornly.

"I mean Ovid's fair," Felix continued, "and Hadfield and I turned out dark. We're tall and he's not. His face is round and our faces are long — and yet we do look like sons of the same father, I think. You can always tell Jack's daughters and Edward's sons. We're Carnivals. So who was the father of your villain? Mad, old Edward — or dead Teddy?"

Harry suddenly felt free to act. She leaped up, shot across the room to the light switch and turned it on. They blinked at each other in the open illumination. Then Felix slowly took off her glasses and passed them back to her.

"All right! Put them on again!" he told her. "Seeing's believing, they say, and I'll stand up to any test. I mightn't be completely real, but I'm real enough."

Harry did look at him and saw his face empty of expression, just as it had been when she saw it first. She spoke furiously, her words falling over one another in their effort to find a way.

"They asked your name yesterday morning." She moved over to the bookcase. "Look!" she commanded imperiously. *"Metamorphoses* by Ovid, *The Book of Love* — that's edited by John Hadfield. And on the next shelf down, *Felix Holt* by George Eliot. We'd even talked about those books the day before — that's why they're pulled out and not pushed in again properly. I knew at once Ovid was reading those names off this bookshelf: Ovid, Hadfield, Felix Holt."

"Felix halted!" he said, staring at the bookshelf. "It's a big jump though, isn't it, from saying our names aren't our own to saying we're actually not real." He looked back at her with a peculiar expression as if he were caught by something he now saw or heard in her. "We've had to fight to be real every step of the way, and by now, I promise you, we're real enough!" He gave the last words a faintly threatening emphasis. "And the tea's real enough to be getting cold."

"But you — " she persisted. "First you're disguised with a book's name and then as my villain. You could be any shape at all, sitting here on our sofa and drinking our tea. You and Hadfield have made yourselves up out of my ideas," she ended resentfully.

"You should be ashamed, then, having such thoughts!" Felix said meanly. Just for a moment he was indistinguishable from Hadfield. He pushed his streaked hair back from his forehead.

"Did you invent my scar, too?" he asked. "Does your villain carry the brand of Suriel, the garden spade?"

"That's not fair, it's a family riddle," Harry said, though she now began to guess a terrible answer to it. Then she grew silent and wary, for as his fingers touched the blue-white seam an expression of intense and private horror came over Felix's face.

"My father — now there *was* an author! Wrote us in. Wrote us out," he said alarmingly, talking more to himself than he was to her, words coming more and more rapidly. "I fought back — we fought back, but we had to go. And he's gone himself now." His horrified expression changed, grew easier and even mischievous. "Well, here we are again," (Harry thought a memory had made him a little mad for a moment) "sneaking in at the back door," he said. "I didn't have a chance the first time round, and I wanted a chance." He looked at Harry huddled beside him. "What on earth can we seem like to you?" he asked in a changed voice.

"I don't know *what* you seem like," Harry cried, differently alarmed now because he sounded concerned, sorry for the frightening and mysterious words he had uttered only a moment previously, and she felt herself being disarmed. "At least, I do in a way. You're a snark, and I might softly and silently vanish away and never be heard of again."

"A snark?" Felix was at a loss. "What are snarks?"

"They're in a book by Lewis Carroll," Harry explained, but she could see the name meant nothing to him.

"They don't sound rational," said Felix. "I was brought up so rational I had to deny my own existence, but we'd all do that if we had to account for ourselves by pure reason and didn't have any gift of faith. Ovid did the best out of it. He was encouraged to get by, without Hadfield and me. And Hadfield and I — who should have been one — became two. No stranger than any other mirror-image twins, of course."

"I can't quite get what you're on about," Harry said. "The meaning comes towards me, but just when I think I'm really going to catch on, it goes away again."

"Little presents!" Felix said. "Ovid gives Christobel roses and I give you riddles. You might come to love me for my mystery. It's as honest as I can be." And then they grew silent once again, staring at each other watchfully.

"What's your true name?" Harry asked.

"*Carne vale!*" said Felix laughing and shaking his head. "Farewell to flesh! Even if I told you, you couldn't tell anyone. Who'd believe you?" he ended cheerfully.

"Oh, don't worry, I know!" Harry pushed her hair back from her face. "That's why I haven't tried to say anything. But how could you think I'd — I mean you might change into anything."

"I'll promise you this," said Felix at last, "we're not vampires or snarks. I think we're here because — we were *owed* something, I suppose. We were owed, and we were stubborn about being paid, whereas most people would have written it off as a bad debt. You see, we were sent to our account with all our imperfections on our head."

"Shakespeare?" Harry asked doubtfully. It sounded familiar.

"Forbidden reading for us. Too fantastical," Felix said, still cheerful. "We stole it and read it secretly, like a wicked book. It's wonderful, read like that."

"Felix," Harry said bravely, asking the question

she had been trying to ask all evening, "are you a ghost?"

"Can you see the wall through me?" he asked.

"No — but I'd be silly to get fond of a ghost, or of anyone likely to go away, wouldn't I?" Harry said.

Felix now fixed his clear gaze on her so intently that she grew shy, thinking of her flowing hair half across her face and the red silk surface she had purposely put on earlier in the evening.

"I might tell you," he said at last, "if you tell me what sort of villain you've invented. For instance, why don't Hadfield and I look like your hero? What have you been writing up in your room? If we're even partly your inventions, what have you been inventing?"

His expression was mischievous, but, unexpectedly, a little frightened too.

"It's none of your business," muttered Harry, trapped.

Felix shook his head.

"I think it is," he said, "if your inventions are really settling down over us. I mean, what actually happens in your story? Forget Hadfield! What am I likely to find myself doing?"

"I didn't tell you to walk home from Gorse Bay," Harry said hastily, though not telling him she had still half expected it.

"I *did* think it was my own idea," he said, "but it might have been more your idea than mine."

This thought frightened Harry. It was like a wild stab of fear, and as it stabbed, the Christmas-tree lights stabbed, too, flaring out so brilliantly that the whiteness of the overhead light was cancelled out by a moment of dazzling, multicoloured brilliance.

"I'm not scared of your conjuring!" Harry shouted. Felix seemed to tower over her.

"It isn't just me," he shouted back, sounding frightened himself. "You're the one who makes a wish and then puts her hand through rock and time. You're the one who's so much in love with your villain that I'm forced to stand in for him just to get here. Hadfield, too!"

Harry felt, furiously, that in some way he had insulted her, but there was nothing insulting in his wary glance — rather the reverse. So she held her breath and let anger slide away from her, and even felt glad that there was someone else who could ask these questions too.

"I don't know," she said desolately. "I don't know any answers."

The truest thing left for them to do was to cross the space separating them and kiss like experimenting lovers. Felix smiled again, and for the first time she saw the beginning of a different smile from the one he shared with Hadfield.

"You never know," he said. "You could be my dangerous lucky chance, perhaps."

"Well, at least you're warned," cried Harry, pleased at being both dangerous and lucky.

Felix took a lock of her hair in his hand and rubbed it like a stationer assessing the quality and weight of paper.

"A touchstone, say," Felix said. "To tell me if I'm true gold and to make me powerful; so I can have a turn of making Hadfield and Ovid do what *I* say."

Harry thought she understood what he was talking about.

"It must be nice to be the powerful one," she said wistfully.

"I tell you what — let's kiss just once and then be nothing but good friends," Felix suggested, as if he thought it might be possible.

There was the sound of the van outside, and they both heard it with annoyance and relief, even as they put their arms around each other and kissed, softly and clumsily at first, like blind people exploring surfaces that might suddenly give way and surrender them to an abyss. They heard the first family footstep on the verandah.

"But how could I be dangerous to you?" she hissed quickly. "Hadfield didn't think I'd be dangerous to him."

"You were, though, weren't you?" Felix managed to make his whisper sound ironic. "Besides, Hadfield's only Hadfield. I'm all heart." He sounded as if he were making fun of himself. Harry knew he did not want to let her go. But the handle of the door was turning, so he held out his arms as if releasing a flock of wild birds, stepped back one step and picked up his cup of cold tea.

13
Midsummer

The family returned, tired and cross in many ways.
Naomi and Jack were on edge with each other because Naomi believed Jack had drunk too much.
Benny had developed a slight wheeze and had to be
reassured in case he worried himself into an asthma
attack. Serena had gone to sleep in the car and was
cross at having to wake up, put herself to bed and
go to sleep all over again, and Robert was disappointed to find Christobel was not home yet. Even
Anthony seemed more withdrawn than usual.

"She'd never be home before midnight," Harry
said, astonished that Robert could think she would.

Only Emma's happiness was unclouded. She had
swum in the new, blue pool, and danced with Hugh
Tavener and with Robert.

"After midnight!" she said with a sigh. "Back to
the ashes again. Was Tibby good?"

"Was Tibby good?" Robert asked, at almost exactly the same moment, and they looked at each
other, startled, and then laughed.

"You're a born father, Robert," said Jack, with a peculiarly savage note in his voice.

"I think I probably am," Robert said, apparently unaware of Jack's sad sarcasm.

"God help you!" said Jack. "It's a terrible talent."

"Hey!" said Harry. "That's not a nice thing for a father to say in front of his child."

"And not even true!" said Naomi.

"Grunt! Grunt!" cried Emma cheerfully.

"I'm out-numbered, am I?" said Jack. "What about you, Hadfield or Felix — whichever you are? Do you have an opinion?"

"Good or bad," Felix said, "it's a talent that's often over-exercised." This answer made Jack look at him more closely.

"Didn't you go to Gorse Bay with the others?" he asked, looking from Felix to Harry.

"Yes, but I came back early," Felix said, since there was no point in trying to deny it.

"Far be it from me to play the stern father," Jack began rather fuzzily, "far be it from me . . . but . . ."

"Jack!" cried Naomi warningly. However, Jack became angry at being warned.

"Don't go trying to protect me from my own excesses," he shouted at her. "I *am* older than Benny, you know."

"Yes, but Benny's sober," said Emma with a giggle. She was light-hearted and teasing because she was still happy.

"Thank you very much, Emma!" Jack said. "Don't forget you would have been better off yourself with a sterner father than — than I've ever been."

Robert turned indignantly, as if Emma had been insulted in some way, but Jack's attention had returned to Harry and Felix.

"I hope you've been behaving yourselves, that's all," he said.

Harry saw the features of her sensuous villain take on an entirely unfamiliar expression. Felix looked disapproving.

"I've been absolutely exemplary, that is, as dark strangers go," he said. "And as they go, I must go, too, because it's late and you'll all be tired. Goodnight, Ariadne. Goodnight all."

"Who does he think he is, calling you Ariadne?" Jack said, as the front door closed. "It sounds a bit pompous."

"You chose it for me. Didn't you mean me ever to be called by it?" Harry asked.

Emma and Naomi stood looking at each other and then at Jack as if they might speak on.

"I'm going to bed," Harry said. "Goodnight, everyone."

"Goodnight," said Robert and Anthony.

But the attic was no longer the refuge it had been. Belen and Jessica, her previous upstairs companions, were banished to dark corners of the roof. Having brought them to half-life, she now saw they were crippled creatures and wished to abandon them like a heartless mother — yet they were there and she felt responsibility for them. Her father had said the ability to reproduce was terrible, and in a small way it was a writer's gift as well as a father's. Down below, she could hear Jack shout something, hear Naomi shout back and a door bang. A little later she heard Emma and Robert talking companionably below, heard them falter and fall silent, then begin talking again very quietly in a different, more intimate manner. Once Robert exclaimed, as if he had been given astonishing information. Harry was filled with an intense desire to open her trapdoor a little bit more to hear what they were saying, or to peep down at them and perhaps surprise them kissing. She would see not only Emma and Robert, making do with each other in the absence of Christobel and runaway Sam, but herself and Felix too. For, now she was an upstairs observer again, she was suddenly curious to know what they had looked like — romantic and skilful, or clumsy and unpractised. She touched her lips tentatively, for she had begun to suspect that the gentle kiss, easily given and received, had been a trickster's kiss, more disturbing than it had seemed to be at first — not just a kiss but a promise. Before the temptation to spy became uncomfortably strong, Emma and Robert began talking again in louder, public voices, and a little later she heard them going in different directions to different rooms. Still she could not sleep. The year had turned. Midsummer was over. They were falling into summer's second half, back towards autumn and winter.

When at last her mother's car drove quietly in, and goodnights and soft laughs fluttered in at her window like moths, she was still awake. The door opened below, a floorboard creaked. Charlie's voice was faintly heard as his footsteps sounded along the verandah, then Christobel's, and then another silence.

Christobel, however, did not go straight to bed. She climbed Harry's ladder, lifted the trapdoor and looked in through the triangle of darkness.

"May I come in? I don't bite." She did not wait for Harry to say either yes or no. "This must be the most impossible place in the world to get into, unless you've got three hands."

Nevertheless, she wriggled in quite cheerfully, bending down to prevent herself banging her head on the sloping roof. Then she sat on the end of Harry's stretcher-bed, clasped her hands around her knees and said, "I don't feel quite sleepy. Shall I tell you the story of my life, or just the history of the world?"

"Did you have a nice evening?" Harry said, sure that that was the proper question.

"Wonderful!" exclaimed Christobel. She hugged herself. Her eyes shone in the light of the naked bulb on the end of Harry's extension cord. "Harry — I'm in love with Ovid Carnival."

To do her justice, Christobel did not expect this announcement to be received with any particular surprise. She had fallen in love too many times, and talked about it too freely, for the announcement to have any novelty. Besides, her recollections were of the adventures of the evening, as much as they were of Ovid.

"It was amazing," Christobel said. "I've never been with anyone who behaved like that before." She seemed exhilarated and bewildered. "They actually fought — Ovid and Hadfield did. And they actually won. It made me wonder if people who talk against violence just can't be bothered putting themselves through the trouble of having to cope with it."

"Someone's always going to lose though," Harry said, "and be hurt."

"But we were in a pub — The Caledonian," exclaimed Christobel, as if she could scarcely believe it. "It was a pub brawl."

"Who started it?" asked Harry.

"I can't remember quite how it started." Christobel looked vexed. "The thing is Ovid — I mean, the mere way he looks starts fights, and he doesn't back off. A really big chap with a shaved head grabbed at him, but Hadfield got between them, and the next moment — well, it's hard to describe what happened next." Christobel stopped. There was a hesitation in her general excitement. Something disturbed her, something she had to consider all over again before she could talk about it. "Remember Ovid talking about the Kingdom of Too Far? I know just what he means, you know, but . . ." she stopped again. "I think it was close to being too far tonight," she confessed at last. "I could see Charlie thought . . ."

"When did you ever care what Charlie thought?" Harry asked in astonishment.

"No — I know!" Christobel looked surprised at herself and smiled a little foolishly. "You probably wouldn't realize it, but Charlie has a lot of judgement, in a funny way. I know it looks as if he hasn't got a thought in his head beyond sailing, but it's not that he hasn't got opinions. He's not thick. Hadfield *was* a bit too much. At one stage there, there seemed to be about six men going for him and he

just — he demolished them. He smashed them up."
She winced slightly. "Then someone shouted that
the cops were outside (they always have at least
two at Gorse Bay over the holidays), and the lights
went out — it was pitch black, people staggering
everywhere. Ovid grabbed my arm and we took off
through the dark . . . (Ovid says they've had to
escape from so many places it's like an instinct by
now) . . . and we scrambled out the back among a
thousand beer crates, up over a wall, strolled across
the road, got into the car and waited for Charlie
and Debbie who were still inside. Then we took
Debbie home and came on home ourselves. It was
just the most exciting evening I've spent in a long
time, but now, talking about it, I feel . . ." Christobel left yet another sentence unfinished. "At the
time it was terrific adventure. I felt really alive."
She played a little with a lock of pale hair falling on
to her temple. "It was as if Hadfield had no nerves,
as if he couldn't feel pain." Unconsciously she traced
on her own face the shape of Hadfield's black eye
and then asked, "Was Robert very upset when he
got back and found I wasn't here?"

"I think he felt a bit miserable," Harry said, and
Christobel murmured uneasily.

"What am I going to do about him?" she asked.
"I looked forward to seeing him so much this Christmas, and the first evening was lovely, but now I
have to make myself remember that he's still
around. Just like that! I don't want to hurt his feelings either. Isn't it awful?"

Harry had nothing to say. "He's bound to go
away," she pointed out at last. "Ovid, I mean —
not Robert. And he's not nearly as good-looking as

Robert. You wrote in that letter just before Christmas that you were only going to fall in love with wonderfully handsome men from now on."

"I said that would be my New Year resolution," Christobel corrected her. "It's over a week to New Year yet. Besides, Ovid mightn't be quite as handsome as Robert, but he can pull roses out of the air. And I like to be with someone who makes me laugh, not just at funny things, but laugh with surprise."

Harry realized that, whereas she had a voice in her head talking about the world, turning everything she saw into stories and descriptions, Christobel needed to watch expressions on a face and to hear words on live, moving lips in order to understand meanings most vividly.

"I know I fall in love easily," she now admitted reluctantly. "Lord knows I don't mean to, but it happens before I can think my way out of it, and then I work really hard to make the other person love me back. But as soon as they do, I begin to lose interest. Everything gets comfortable, but the fury goes out of it, and I like a bit of fury. Robert's just not furious."

"Robert's had Emma for company," Harry said, because it was late, and Christobel seemed as if she might need reassurance, even though she was the one who was disturbing other people. At Harry's words her face cleared, and she gave a beautiful smile, turning her eyes up to heaven a little so that for a moment she resembled an ecstatic angel on an old-fashioned Christmas card.

"Right on!" she exclaimed with profound relief. "I'd forgotten Emma. Well, at least he wasn't stranded with Anthony, Jack and Naomi. What do you think of Anthony, incidentally?"

"All right — but not easy to know anything about," Harry said.

"Well, I think he disapproves of me and thinks I'm a shallow prattler. Ovid said I should teach him the limitations of disapproval."

"What does that mean?" Harry asked cautiously. "Does he mean you should try to fascinate Anthony too?"

"That's a stately way of putting it," Christobel said, laughing. "Shall I try? Just for practice?"

"I don't think you need practice," Harry replied. She thought Christobel had told her story and would go, leaving her to her own dilemmas, but Christobel hesitated.

"Harry — are Ma and Jack all right?" she suddenly asked.

"What do you mean, all right?" asked Harry, fencing. "They seem OK, don't they? Jack was lashing around a bit tonight, but he'd had a few drinks — you know."

Christobel sighed very deeply.

"I shouldn't have enjoyed tonight so much," she said. "It wasn't very classy. And my feelings are so sudden and I'm not trustworthy. Whenever I feel doubtful about myself, it really comforts me to think about Jack and Naomi — boxing along, being good on my behalf. It sort of lets me off the hook."

Harry did not know what to say.

"How could they be good on your behalf?" she asked uncertainly.

Christobel did not reply at once. "You'll have to do something about your hair," she exclaimed instead. "You look like an owl in a hedge — quite a pretty owl, and a wild hedge, but all the same — no!"

Harry waited.

"They've been such terrific parents. They've stayed together and they're really fond of each other," Christobel burst out at last. "It seems as if a big lump of virtue like that needs balancing out a little bit, and it's my duty to balance it."

"As if they'd saved up money, and that meant you could spend a bit extra," Harry suggested, beginning to smile.

"Exactly like that!" Christobel agreed and laughed. Unexpectedly she hugged Harry who hugged back, pleased but awkward.

"Old Harry!" Christobel said. "Old owl in a hedge. That's your bed-time story for tonight. Your big sister is signing off and descending to Middle Earth. I'll murder the little ones if they wake me up early tomorrow." She began to climb down the ladder and then stopped with only her head showing.

"Felix found his way back all right, did he?"

"Yes!" Harry said shortly, and Christobel laughed and continued her descent.

"Pleasant dreams!" she called from below, but Harry, putting her head on her pillow, did not want dreams, only a quiet sleep until morning.

PART TWO

Christmas

14
Magical Changes

On the morning of the day that would end with
carols around the piano and empty stockings hung
under the tree, Harry woke out of a bright scat-
ter — bird flight, scraps of poetry, lines from songs,
seagulls' footprints printed on sand like words in a
language older than man. Little pictures whirled
around her, as if waking up had made a tempest in
her head start blowing them around like confetti.
Then they fell away from her. She thought the Hide
murmured around her, giving an uneasy greeting,
for now it never slept. A missing part had been
restored to an old machine, the wheels of memory
had begun to turn, and when people were asleep,
the house tried to twist itself back to another time.
During the night Harry had woken to hear it mutter
and groan. Drawers and cupboard doors chattered
urgently, cups and saucers down in the kitchen
chinked like startled birds. Carnival's Hide was
being stretched and strained by a natural power.
    Earthquake! thought Harry, knowing that oth-

ers in the house, disturbed by the fretful twisting would be lying awake, holding their breaths in case it got worse, ready to leap out and stand under the solid architraves of the nearest door. But it lessened, and after a few seconds of barely detectable quivering, the house had grown quiet once more, Harry had gone back to sleep.

Between midsummer night and the beginning of Christmas, light had sparkled and skipped on a glassy harbour, the air was silky and fresh but still warm, and Harry's early-morning window had framed a lucid sky. But today there was nothing but a grubby, sinister yellow in the frame. Low grey clouds were reflecting the light of an unrisen sun, striking ahead of itself up over the eastern rim of the crater. Scrambling into her tracksuit, Harry watched this threatening colour become a little more glossy, but fail to become true gold. There were footsteps. Someone walked along the verandah, as someone else walked out of the kitchen and through the living room. Harry heard them meet.

"Just take a look at the hall!" she heard Charlie say in a puzzled voice. "Who did that? It wasn't done yesterday, was it? Sometimes I think they're all crazy! Here — grab hold of this. You'll need two hands or the ham will fall out." Another pause. "Did you feel the earthquake last night?" Then, impatiently, "Come on! Do I have to eat it for you?"

She knew they were standing on the edge of the verandah, assessing the wind and weather, eating doorstep sandwiches for breakfast. Robert's words were inaudible through his sandwich.

"Just think of the sailing! Forget the rest!" Charlie said. "Besides, you've always known that Christo can fall in love in ten seconds flat." Robert said something inaudible.

"Well, it's like this," said Charlie. "A few years back when Christo and I grew up a bit and wanted to get out in the world and kick our heels round, I think Ma countered by inviting the world in, and of course we still get all sorts. Anyhow, you can see the way things are — Christo likes these Carnivals, so does Jack, Harry, too (well, one of them anyway), and, after all, it's not as if you and Christo were engaged or anything."

"I know, I know!" said Robert gloomily.

"And I know she's being a bit rough on you," Charlie went on. "But it's partly because she's feeling guilty, and she's no good with guilt."

"I could flatten that Ovid Carnival!" Robert said.

"Ovid, maybe. Hadfield, no," Charlie said. "I think they hunt in a pair, don't you? Let's be off." Harry heard their feet on the verandah. "Anyhow, what about you?" Charlie added unexpectedly. "Christo's not the only one to change."

"What the hell do you mean?" said Robert, his voice suddenly loud with indignation.

"You know what I mean!" Charlie's voice came back with weary significance. "Talk about a mid-summer night's dream . . . Come on!"

Their feet sounded on the step and Harry could hear their voices vanishing down the track, Robert protesting and Charlie still laughing. Then she was the only person awake in Carnival's Hide. For a moment, she was so interested in what Charlie had said, she thought about crawling into the far corner of the roof, reclaiming her hidden book, and writing it all down in the back among her other notes, but the thought of things already written down rather frightened her at present. Instead she opened her trapdoor, climbed down her ladder, looked around and sighed.

Once again the room had shifted as the house tried to move back to what it had been in its very beginning. But beyond the window the yellow sky was fading to heavy grey. Harry went into the kitchen, where, because there was a certain early-morning pleasure in breaking rules, she drank fruit juice straight from the jug, firmly keeping her head full of pine needles and tinsel and other Christmas thoughts. Tonight their stockings would be brought out, each one embroidered over the years by Naomi and also, unexpectedly, by Jack. Harry could even remember him carefully drawing a cat's face on the heel of Serena's stocking (one of his own long walk-ing socks, sacrificed to the season) and then em-broidering around his drawing in bright chainstitch. It was easy to love Jack when you remembered things like that and remembered the careful way he had made whiskers for the cat out of the long hearthbrush bristles. Of course, by the time Serena came, the stockings had grown quite elaborate. Charlie had a mere scarlet "C" on his, but Christobel had golden bells, and Harry herself had a lion with a collar of holly leaves. Mixing Christmas in with other thoughts she did not want to consider too closely just yet, she went through the living room again, opened the door and stepped into a different country.

Where yesterday's white surfaces had flung light backwards and forwards in the hall from one wall to another, a jungle of painted leaves and flowers now stole morning out of the air and turned everything to a greenish twilight. Everywhere she looked, there was the same repetitive pattern of flowers, leaves and lines, clear in a few patches, blurred in others. However, where it vanished altogether, her eyes simply went on by themselves and filled the pattern in, because it was the sort of pattern that got into your head and kept itself going. The Hamilton cartons that had waited, slumped into each other, for the time when they would pack to go home, had vanished, too, though the old coats remained. Harry studied the wallpaper and recognized the flowers as stylized waterlilies. The hall had resumed its earliest dress and now waited to be recognized by old friends.

Someone had polished the dark wood of the hall table and had set a jar of roses on it. They were as perfect as Ovid's silk roses, but their scent was strong in the air. Beside the flowers was an old sewing basket. Rotten silks spilled out of it, hanging down like the hair of Rapunzel, never rescued but grown old and unloved in her tower.

Under the shadow of the roses lay an old book covered with some fabric that was rotting along the edges. The edges were all Harry could see of the cover, for it was held open by a glass paperweight, so that people passing through the hall could stop and read what might be written there. The first page was old and yellow, the writing faint, but Harry knew it was a child's book. It reminded her of her own notebooks, filled, when she was eight or nine, with stories about beautiful wild horses and girls with long hair. She took a step forward. "*Seven Ways to Outwit the Black King*," she read, "*Advice to Mortals by the Goddess of Wisdom and the Boy Enchanter."*

Harry clasped her hands together; something moved at the far end of the hall. Her throat tightened, but it was only her reflection moving unexpectedly in an old mirror, reflecting the hall and the door of coloured glass and the morning beyond it. She stood between the real door and the reflected one, held in the yellowing mirror like a fly in amber. The book on the table filled her with horror.

A memory stabbed her, and then slid away before she could name it. It was colourless — brown and white — and was followed by another slower and completely respectable memory. The mirror had once been part of the complicated collection of junk housed in the storeroom behind the bathhouse. Some of it had been there for many years, waiting to be sold, or given to charity, or thrown away. She could not guess by what power it had materialized here in the hall.

Just for a moment she thought she might go and climb into bed with her father and mother as she used to do when she was small and had bad dreams, when it had seemed like paradise to be safe between them. On those mornings when she woke up Jack used to threaten her with his unshaven cheek, and she would dive, screaming with delight, under the bedclothes. But such times, once they have gone, never come again. She was too old for that particular comfort and, besides, Felix might be waiting up on the hill.

The house had not been changed by any magic of Ovid's. Harry considered that possibility, but a magical illusion would have restored the walls without streaks and stains. The house itself was struggling to reform around a core of memory, recharged by the presence of Ovid, Hadfield and Felix, whatever they might turn out to be. Yet the hall, marked by rich and ruinous transformation from present to past, had become the imagination of the house. Yesterday, all rooms had opened away from it. Now it felt as if all rooms must lead back into it. Harry was glad to leave its strangeness for the open simplicity of the verandah, from which she looked up into a sky grown livid with angry, rolling cloud — thunder made visible. Once seen, the sky actually spoke aloud. The trees lashed around frantically and the whole harbour was transformed into a vast bruise as if a giant had pressed his thumb into the land. Beside her on the verandah the cardboard cartons were stacked inside one another, like a nest of mathematical boxes made to educate a child giant.

Harry gave a great sigh and ran off, turning away from the track down to the beach, running up the hill in a long shallow "S" through bracken and broom. She ran, hoping she might find Felix there, waiting as he had waited during the two mornings since midsummer. At the thought of seeing him, her heart clenched into a fist and thumped in her chest. The worst thing was that, though she did not enjoy that electrical thump, though she was angry at being possessed against her will, and though she deliberately ran Felix's image through her head over and over again trying to exhaust its power by making it commonplace, she did not want to be without the excitement of it. Suddenly she had the unreasonable power to command love, a right which up until now had seemed to belong exclusively to Christobel.

Harry half-feared that Felix might not come out on such a threatening morning, but there he was waiting for her, as he had waited for the two previous mornings, sitting in the grass and bracken and staring out over the blue-black sea. He watched her come up to him, neither smiling nor speaking, and held out a hand to her without letting her know if she was to pull him up or he was to pull her down. But she was used to his hand by now, for it seemed engineered to fit her own, and she took it without hesitation. It was Felix who seemed to hesitate, making up his mind about something. Then he stood up, and they walked together along the ridge with the sea far below them, beating mournfully at the rocks.

"Do you realize we are actually going to see the sunrise, after all?" he said.

Below the cloud and just above the sea was a narrow strip of clear sky and an arc of violent light was being born into it through the long slit of the horizon. For a moment they were bathed in an unearthly glow. On previous mornings the crumpled land had been reflected in water, like green glass, but the sea was dull and rough today, muttering below them in a surly fashion. The brightness of the emerging sun made Harry's eyes water.

"Where do you come from?" she asked. "Who are you?" But by now she did not expect an answer.

"Let's just *be*," said Felix. "I've run off from my brothers to spend time with you. I don't want to answer questions about anything. I just want to walk along with you and look at the morning. Everything looks different to me when I look at it with you. Have I mentioned that?"

"No," said Harry. "Perhaps you open a sort of pineal eye and see with that one as well as the other two."

"What?" said Felix, taken-aback and intrigued. "A what?"

"I think that's what it's called," Harry said doubtfully. "I'm not even sure if it's a real eye. Tuataras have them. Eye number three on the top of the head, all overgrown with scales."

"It's not as silly as it sounds," Felix said. "If I found I had opened a third eye these days, one that saw more deeply into things than the other two, I wouldn't be all that surprised. Shall we hold hands or leave that respectable space between us?"

However, it was no longer the simple, honest space it had been, for it had been crossed once, and they both knew it could be crossed again. Besides, by now they had imagined themselves crossing it so many times that it seemed laced across with actual memories, so that it not only held them apart, but bound them together, too.

"Our hall!" Harry cried across that little, electric distance. "Our hall has changed. Why do you all upset the house so much? Other people will want to know what's going on, not just me."

Felix looked out to sea.

"I know the house is uneasy," he said doubtfully. "Fearsome things happened in it when it was a young house. I think it was stuck through with knives, pinned into the past."

"But it's all over and done with," Harry said.

"So am I," Felix answered at once. "Finished! But I want to be *well* finished — completed, say — that's my problem. Harry, let's stop talking about this. You might make me talk myself out of existence."

Harry could not meet his eyes. She was not only ashamed of her own persistence, but also a little frightened at being on this hilltop alone with him, both besieged by storm and alight with the unnatural radiance of the air. Something was making him look very brilliant, as if, in the absence of a visible sun (for it had now risen behind the upper layer of cloud), he was giving off light. Yet, after all, it was not fear she was feeling, simply something that had some of the same symptoms as fear.

"It isn't fair," she said sadly. "Now something wonderful has happened — something that makes my life less ordinary, and I'm not allowed to ask." Then, for she could not help herself, she cried, "But the hall — what will Ma say about the hall?"

As she spoke Felix took hold of her ears under her hair, as if they were handles, and shook her head in a reproving way, laughing at her a little ruefully, but not in any kind or easy-going way.

"I can stop you asking questions, you know," he said. "I know I can."

Harry looked at him, caught by an alteration in his tone. They stared at each other silently. They were like children playing a game with a line drawn between them, and Felix, stepping over the line to command her silence, would belong to her for ever.

But then, somewhere above them, the sky opened and the rain poured straight down. There was no warning. One moment it was dry, then next the air was ruled with lines of water. They were both soaked within seconds. Streams flowed down over Harry's cheeks and throat. The end of her nose dripped like a faulty tap. They were both astonished to find the outside world capable of touching them in any way, when a moment ago it had felt that they had exclusive rights to act on each other.

"The villain in my book wouldn't be put off by rain," said Harry.

"Well, I can't be a villain then. Proof positive," said Felix. "A ghost perhaps, but not a villain."

"That's what I meant," Harry said. "That I know you're being you yourself and not anything I'd made up. You grow carrot flowers and you're kind to little children."

"You sounded more convinced the other way round on midsummer night," Felix said. "I argued, but I believed you immediately, then. Are you cold?"

"No!" Harry replied. "It's warm rain."

Felix gave a deep sigh, almost a groan. "Harry — " he said at last. "Harry, I know this might sound silly — but you see I'm not what I seem. I'm not . . ."

He looked vulnerable, and for some reason this frightened Harry more than when he had looked threatening.

"You said you'd stop me asking questions," she cried, "and now I've got to stop you giving answers."

"But listen . . ." he began. Harry boldly put her hand over his mouth, and he put his own hand over hers and held it there, not kissing it, but rather as if he were helping her secure him against confession. The rain poured down around them, and they stood there a little longer, poised over the inky sea while the hilltops flicked with lightning and the whole countryside watched them, winking and growling in dismay at their dangerous companionship.

15
Stormy Exchanges

The next person to come into the hall was Anthony, sneaking a small Christmas parcel on to the tree before anyone else was around to catch him at it. Like Harry, he stopped and stared at the hall. Unlike her he touched the walls as if they might tell a secret to fingertips that they denied to eyes. When he saw the book he stood completely still, then moved to read the first page. Unlike Harry he moved the paperweight and read on for a moment or two, paused and frowned around at the jungle of lines and waterlilies. Then he slid the book into the pocket of his dressing-gown, walked through the living-room door and over to the Christmas tree. Even after he had set his present among its branches, he still stood there, gazing into the tree like a crystal-gazer hoping to see prophetic shadows move. A door opened out in the hall, there was a second of silence and a loud cry.

"Benny!" shouted Serena. "Benny, come here!"

Then she changed her summons and began to bleat, "Ma! Ma!" like a spring lamb.

"Ma!" said another voice like an echo, but an echo that refused to take its echoing seriously, and laughed on its own account.

"Shut up, you kids!" cried a third voice, further away, but ominously clear, sleepy and furious all at once. "Get away!"

"Ma!" shouted Serena, too overwhelmed to take any notice of Christobel.

"Shut up and go out or I'll get up and thump you!" screamed Christobel. "For God's sake — I'm trying to sleep."

"Ma! Quickly!" yelled Serena. There was a soft but very powerful plumping sound.

"Now, there's a sound we know and love!" exclaimed Naomi to Jack as she struggled into her dressing-gown.

"Christo's already dealt with Serena," said Jack sleepily, looking at the bedside clock. "Just ring the ambulance and then come back to bed."

"She's only thrown her pillow at the door," Naomi said. "But I'd better get out there all the same to forestall real violence. What on earth is Serena thinking of! Right outside Christo's door and before sunrise, too."

A moment later, staring like Harry, touching like Anthony, Naomi stood in her changed hall. Serena, over her first shock, beamed, and bounced from one foot to the other. Tibby, swollen around the bottom with her nighttime nappy, copied her with the pleased expression of someone mastering a new mature skill.

"Who *did* it?" cried Serena. "Is it for Christmas? Are we going to have a stately home?"

Naomi's mouth hung open incredulously, and she touched the wall as if she might find a secret button that would make the new walls fly up, mere blinds painted to deceive the eye, revealing the familiar white paper and family muddle safely behind them.

"It's as good as new," Serena shouted.

"Hardly!" said Naomi. "It's covered in mildew. Still, I must say it's a heroic effort at restoration on someone's part."

The door burst open and Christobel appeared, electric with fury. But her lips, actually on the point of framing bitter reproaches, grew still, and the reproaches were saved for another time. She stepped into the hall wrapped in her old brocade bedspread. She habitually slept naked and had been so angry at the voices persisting outside her bedroom door that, in the end, she had not been capable of walking across the room to get her dressing-gown and had scrambled to the door wrapping herself in whatever came to hand first. With her hair standing out around her head like white flames she looked as exotic and strange as if she had pushed her way out through the wallpaper pattern instead of using the door. Serena now thought she would get out of Christobel's way and bolted along the verandah to wake Benny up. "Come and see!" she cried. "Come and see what someone's done."

"Is it something grunt?" asked Benny staggering around in his faded summer pyjamas and staring fearfully down the verandah.

"No — it's moo! Very moo!" Serena promised.

By the time she got back Emma, newly emerged, was having her turn at being surprised, while Christobel, recovered, was following Naomi into the living room. She had forgotten about punishing the early-morning lamb who had bleated boldly at her door.

"It wouldn't be them," she was crying. "There'd be no point."

Naomi smiled briefly at Anthony, who was sitting in a chair by the window, trying to lure Crumb on to his knee by rustling paper at him. Crumb, interested in the rustling, put his ears forward, but refused to be lured.

"It's a miracle!" Christobel suggested hopefully. "People will come and stand in our hall to be cured of boils and we'll clean up on the souvenirs."

"Really weird, though," Emma said, coming in after them, Tibby in her arms, "because I keep feeling I've seen it all before. Spooky!"

Naomi was looking up and down the bookcase. "Not at all!" she said over her shoulder. "You've all seen it. There's a photograph in that book — a photo of Edward standing in the hall. And it's more or less the same hall that's out there."

"The same general effect!" agreed Anthony unexpectedly. "But not identical — no roses, no sewing basket."

"You've seen it too, then," Naomi said, hardly paying any attention for she was becoming angry. "Well, you tell Christo that what's out there isn't a miracle. It's an improvisation. The last time I saw that mirror out there it was up the hill in the junk room. Probably the sewing basket was there somewhere, too. It's not magic."

Christobel swished clumsily across the room, the bedspread dragging after her.

"Ma — are you trying to tell me someone came in, stripped off the old paper and hauled that heavy mirror in, all in the very early morning, and all without waking us up?"

"More than one person — say three! And maybe last night's earthquake was only a bit of home decorating. Either way, what's out there has got a real *hey presto*-look about it."

Christobel let the brocade bedspread sag around her. "Ma! It was an earthquake," she said. "Don't be angry with them. Don't make them leave. I'll die. Worse than that, I'll — I'll make terrible scenes. I'll ruin Christmas. You know me, I won't be able to help it. Ma, they've done no real harm."

Naomi turned back from the bookcase. She looked stubborn and calculating, but Christobel, used to reading family faces, read dismay in her mother's — not surrender, but the possibility of surrender.

"It's like this," Naomi said, crossing to the kitchen door, but hesitating before going through it. "Just suppose — just suppose I'd really *liked* the hall the way it was. Not everyone is crazy on mildew! Wouldn't it have been nice to be asked?"

"It's got miles more character than it had before," Christobel argued.

"And it's still a bloody cheek!" Naomi declared with rare violence. "Why don't you go and get dressed, Christo? I'm sure you're embarrassing Anthony."

"Nonsense, I'll bet he loves it," said Christobel, looking furtively down at herself. "I'm perfectly decent. Ma — everyone's innocent until proved guilty."

"There's nothing innocent about those conjurors. They don't even pretend to be innocent," said Naomi. "And what do we know about them, after all?"

"Am I or am I not a member of this family?" Christobel demanded. "I've always been allowed to ask friends."

"Well, this time we were a bit silly — we asked first and made friends afterwards!" Naomi said. "Honestly, Christo, if Attila the Hun turned up pulling six roses out of the air I'm sure you'd let him come in and redecorate the house with his axe."

"Ovid can do real roses, too!" Christobel cried triumphantly, as if this were the real point at issue. "But he says silk ones frighten people less."

At that moment lightning flickered, a sheet of rain stroked across the roof, which purred beneath it at first, then rattled and then roared.

The lightning was followed by a rending sound as if all parts of the sky had been simultaneously torn to black shreds.

"God bless this house and all who sail in her!" cried Christobel looking up. "Aye, it'll be a fearsome, rough day for the poor souls at sea, Jim lad — and serve the idiots right."

"It won't last," Naomi said. "It's just a summer storm. The forecast says it'll clear away and will be a lovely day — fine and warm. Just as well. We'll have visitors in and out all this afternoon and evening."

"Ma!" Christobel pleaded. "Please! Nothing heavy."

"Forget it, Christo, I'm not promising anything," Naomi replied.

"On your own head be it!" Christobel yelled. "Emma, if you're getting breakfast for Tibby, run up a bowl for me, too. My own mother's going to spoil my Christmas, so I'll be adopted by you instead."

She whirled around, a capricious storm of blue and gold. As she did so she met Anthony's eye. Her frown lifted and she laughed.

"Heavens, I've beguiled Anthony!" she exclaimed. "Who'd have thought it. There's more to him than meets the eye."

"Which can hardly be said of you," he replied, looking thoughtfully at her golden legs.

Serena struck a graceful gesture in the background.

"You've got to have plums!" she cried dramatically. "Everyone has to."

"You know what you can do with your plums!" Christobel suddenly recalled her grievances. "Ma!" she yelled. "If you turn against Ovid, I'll never speak to you again."

"Ha! I should be so lucky!" Naomi shouted back as Christobel stormed out of the living room, slamming the door after her. Her trailing brocade caught in it, and she had to open it and slam it more effectively. The house resounded with the impact, mingling inextricably with a new clap of thunder, which bellowed and crackled around the sky, as if both the sound and its echo were struggling to occupy the same space at the same moment of time.

16
Blackmail

The rain rolled monotonously over the roof of Carnival's Hide, and the living room became crowded, for the whole family, with the exception of Robert, Charlie and Harry, were gathered together in the same room. Tibby pursued Crumb from chair to chair and when she had caught him, carried him around, holding him just under his forelegs, with his hindpaws dragging along the ground.

"This Crumb loves me," she boasted, while Crumb dangled down, confused but uncomplaining. Christobel read a few lines of yesterday's newspaper, then stood at the window looking down the slope of the grass, beaten by the storm, while people moved around her cautiously, fearing some extra vibration might set off an explosion. Then she began to play Christmas carols on the piano, making them sound so bad-tempered that Jack bravely got up and took over from her. Christobel promptly took refuge in the kitchen, slamming the door, then sat on the table and stared blankly at the row of unmatched cups on the cuphooks, scarcely looking up when the door opened again and Emma came in.

"Your turn to be a *Sunburst* widow," Christobel said at once, with a needling smile.

"I don't know what you mean," Emma replied, using a stiff voice to hide nervousness.

Christobel's eyes became relentless. Their slight narrowing seemed to intensify their blueness. She looked directly at Emma as if she had all right on her side.

"Yes, you do!" she cried. "Not that I care! But you've always followed after me, picking up what I'd finished with, and now you're taking over Robert. I just know it."

Emma hung her head, but not out of shame. She was trying to keep her temper.

"That's OK," Christobel went on. "You're welcome, but don't think I don't notice. First you took over my old clothes, and then you took over my family, and now you're getting Robert."

Emma scowled at the floor, took a deep breath, and then looked up with a forced smile.

"Christo — don't be bitchy," she begged. "Be fair! You've been spending all your time chasing after Ovid Carnival, so Robert's got a choice of looking silly — or he can talk to someone else. I think he's being very good, really, because his feelings *are* so hurt."

"His feelings *are* so hurt," Christobel mimicked contemptuously. "He's just not a fighter." But then she winced and sighed. Her momentary spite subsided. "Anyhow, really, it's more than that," she went on in a subdued voice. "I know this is true — that Robert looked at you and Tibby — I think I

even know the exact moment — out on the verandah that first night — and suddenly he saw a family,
and that's what he really wants. Not that he'd admit
it straight off. Probably he needs to do some ritual
suffering to feel properly disengaged." She
stretched her arms over her head as if she were
pushing against a ceiling, lowering itself heavily
down on her. "If only this rain would end. I feel
completely shut in. He probably wants to put all
the blame on me. Well — anyhow — what do you
think of my theory?"

"It's only a theory," Emma said, looking away
from her again.

"Only a theory!" Christobel exclaimed. "Very interesting, Albert Einstein, but it's only a theory.
OK — so I can't show you the mathematics of my
idea, I just know it adds up. But what I most want
to know is this! Is there something wrong with
Ovid, or something wrong with me?"

Over the past two days Christobel had stood on
the scalloped edge of the sea, like a heraldic em-
blem — for the sun, which gilded her to a deeper
gold, had also bleached her hair to the colour of
fresh sea foam. Behind her dark glasses her eyes
were as blue as delphiniums, and she stepped along
these shifty margins like a wonderful phoenix of the
tidal zone to meet Ovid, advancing from the whare
with two black shadows trailing behind him — Felix, a resigned prisoner, Hadfield, a bodyguard.

Hadfield's patched eye made a pantomime pirate
of him and, as the two days went by, he developed
his own sinister significance, as if he were the nurse
of a brilliant but dangerous child, prepared to sub-

mit to all whims except one final whim, which would threaten both of them.

Robert frowned at Christobel's elbow while, sitting behind Ovid on the sand, Hadfield rested his own elbows on his knees and covered his mouth with one hand, half-concealing a smile that resembled Crumb's. And no one could tell what Ovid thought, for he courted Christobel with jokes and paradoxes, conjuring flowers and butterflies and rainbows out of the air around her. Sometimes people fell silent, for though his tricks were pretty, they became increasingly inexplicable, causing a little numbness at the heart.

"How do you *do* that?" Serena cried, nervous and entranced as he snapped his fingers, and the sharp sound was transformed into blue and green mayflies which fluttered, grew transparent and vanished.

"I carry them up my sleeve!" Ovid cried joyously, dancing and holding out his bare arms. He juggled not only words but balls painted with wise moons, laughing suns or the masks of animals and kings. He showered Christobel with compliments that would have been fabulous if they had not also been ironic, rather as if Ovid were parodying a genuinely romantic man he carried in his heart and must continually deride. He singled Christobel out in every way but one. If she walked away from him, looking back over her shoulder at him, he would not follow her but would begin laughing with Hadfield, teasing Emma about Tibby, Serena about Anthony. Still, occasionally, Christobel thought she surprised a private face, come and gone in a moment. But it was not a reassuring one, not only sad but childish, too, as if Ovid were not much older than Benny, displaced, perhaps by his own conjuring, into the body of a grown man, which he did not quite know how to use.

"So, what's wrong with me? What is it I haven't got?" Christobel now begged Emma to tell her.

"You seem to me to have everything," Emma said. "Almost everything," she added. Christobel did not hear the qualification.

"But what happens when everything isn't enough!" she cried despairingly. Emma did not answer. Instead she looked wistfully around the kitchen with its red bar stools (leftovers from more social days in Carnival's Hide), at the unmatched cups and last night's supper dishes still in the sink, a burnt saucepan soaking on the stove.

"I love this kitchen," she said. "I know it faces south and gets cold at times, but remember how we used to sit in here and make cocoa and cheese on toast, and play cards and gossip about the visitors who'd just gone. That's exactly what I want to give Tibby. Cocoa, cheese on toast, family gossip and a happy kitchen."

"You make the cocoa and I'll give you something to gossip about," Christobel offered. "But Tibby'll want something different from that. She's fiercer than you."

As she spoke, Christobel was prowling around, opening cupboards, looking vaguely for something to eat, but not because she was hungry. She was dreaming of a wonderful taste, because ecstasy seemed the only reasonable way to pass the time.

"Propose to Robert, why don't you?" she asked,

rather grudgingly. "If ever there was a man who'd sunk so low as to yearn after a mortgage and a home in a nice area it's Robert. Oh, blast! There I go, being nasty again. Two days ago I was thinking, poor Robert — how can I make sure he's happy? And now I'd like him to be slightly more miserable than he is, because I'm not all that happy myself. I've given Ovid plenty of chances, but he won't move around without Hadfield. Why?"

But Emma had no idea. She did not like Ovid and could not explain him.

"Wine!" said Christobel, discovering a bottle. "There's about three thimblefuls left in it. Why is it proper to drink at some times of day and not at others? As far as I'm concerned, first thing in the morning is the time when you most need to escape from reality. Let's drink it out of eggcups and that will make it seem more breakfasty."

The door opened and Anthony came in, sent to find a pair of scissors for Naomi. Christobel danced over to him.

"Here — have half an eggcupful of wine, Anthony. And let me say at once what a particularly nice nose you've got. It's burned red, but the basic design is very sound."

Anthony squinted down at his nose. "I don't think mere flattery will stop it peeling," he said.

"Then I'll back up the flattery with ointment, and you'll look like one of those surf-club life-saver men who go round with brick-red faces and noses white with sunburn cream. I'm glad you've come in because I've been really unpleasant to Emma here, but it didn't work. She's made herself into such a victim already, it only made me feel worse. *And* it's still raining. Anyone would think it was Noah's Flood, not Christmas!"

Anthony looked down into his eggcup. It was shaped like a rabbit, a relic left over from a long-forgotten Easter. Now, a dead moth, previously concealed in the hollow of the rabbit's tail, floated to the surface.

"Jack's reading to the little ones," he said, "including Tibby, though I don't know what she's making of *Coral Island*. Naomi's fixing some shorts for Serena . . ."

"Letting them out, I'll bet," said Christobel meanly. "Grunt!"

". . . and Harry is apparently still reading up in her loft," Anthony said. "Naomi seems quite confident the rain will stop."

Faintly from the next room there came the sound of new voices. Christobel listened and grimaced.

"Robert and Charlie — I'm not going out there," she said and pulled open another cupboard door. "Gosh, look at all this food. This is more what I had in mind." But Emma shut the cupboard door firmly.

"It's for tonight," she said reproachfully.

Christobel did not insist. All the time, she was waiting for the moment when the Carnival brothers might appear, which they did about twenty minutes later, shortly after the rain had stopped. At the sound of Ovid's voice, Christobel made for the door.

"I feel I might have to protect him from Naomi!" she said. "She's chosen to be very old-fashioned about her hall."

"Do you really think they did it?" Emma asked sceptically. "In spite of everything . . ."

"Somebody did," Christobel said reasonably. "I hate to say it — but Ma's probably right."

The living room was crowded. Jack was draped in children — Serena on the arm of his chair, Benny leaning against his knees and Tibby settled on his lap. Naomi had just put her sewing down. She turned to face Ovid and Hadfield as if they were bad children who had been sent to her for reproof.

"Felix!" Ovid explained. "We're looking for Felix. He went out on one of his walks and hasn't come home yet." He sounded more cautious than usual. "Has he called in here?"

"No!" Naomi said. "Though he may have been by, rather earlier. Did you by any chance notice the hall as you came in?"

"Wonderful!" Hadfield said. "Time travel, almost."

"Yes, but suppose I don't want to travel in time?" Naomi replied. "Who ever did it didn't consult me first, you see."

"Oh, you think we did it," said Hadfield at once. He placed his hand on Ovid's shoulder like a ventriloquist drawing attention to a clever doll. "*You* explain it," he said with a smile that Harry would have recognized as belonging to her invented Belen. But where that same smile on Felix's face was being increasingly altered by doubt, on Hadfield's face it was taking on a malicious edge that was not part of Belen, who was merely violent.

"Do you want truth or a confession?" asked Ovid immediately. "The truth is we had nothing to do with it, but of course the confession is more interesting."

It was seldom that Naomi showed the sort of

uncertainty she did now. She appeared to stop and think very carefully about what Ovid had said, and in the pause Jack spoke rather unexpectedly.

"Personally, I don't care, either way," he said, rather coolly, "but it seems to me Naomi's entitled to a less equivocal answer than that."

"Is Ma angry with Ovid?" asked Benny in a stage whisper.

"Not yet," said Jack.

"Good heavens — you're the magicians!" Naomi cried. "Of course I suspect you."

"I confess then," Ovid said, flinging up his hands as if Naomi had pointed a gun at him, "and no one is to interrupt me. Last night I woke up feeling very thirsty — oh, as dry as sand." He held out his right hand and, from between his fingers fine silver sand appeared, falling and glittering, as if, indeed, by magic. He looked at it in apparent astonishment. "I felt you wouldn't mind if I came up and stole a drink of water . . ." And now, as the sand stopped falling, he shook his fingers and water splashed from them, seeming to well out from his skin. "But when I opened the front door, the wind rushed in past me." (A baby nor-wester breathed over them, billowing the curtains at the open windows, rattling the old posters and making the needles of the Christmas tree tremble, but Ovid talked on apparently unaware of it.) "It rushed right in over my shoulder — whoosh — the wallpaper swelled out, as if it was big with a whole litter of wind kittens, then it tore loose and rushed at me like a white, flapping vampire and flopped all over me. The more I tried to push it back into place, the more the past crumbled and the paper fell. And then the whole house shook. Truly, Naomi, its time had come, and there I was wrapped in it like a — a very reluctant — present. I nearly went and lay down with the rest under the Christmas tree."

"But instead you went to get the others to help, I suppose," Naomi said.

Ovid threw up his hands, filling the air with silver grains and droplets. Charlie and Robert, sitting behind him by the window, ducked, but the sand and the water vanished as if they had never existed. Even the wind grew still.

"Exactly," he said. "I remembered a photograph in that scrapbook you lent us, and once I got the idea of all of you waking up in the morning to find the hall shifted back into the past . . ." he broke off, shrugged his shoulders and held out his hands, palm upwards. "Who could resist?" he said, and turned on her the full force of a singular contradiction between the formal prettiness of his curls, thick brown eyelashes and short straight nose, and then, where one expected a pink and white complexion, a ruined surface, slightly pitted as if he were corroded. Now he ran his finger absently over the line of his jaw, smiling all the time, possibly reacquainting himself with irregularities that he himself could not see, trying to discover what they saw when they looked at him. His green eyes were hot and cold together.

"It was very bad of us," Hadfield said repentantly, "though we meant well." However, his easy expression, simply by becoming rigid, had also become very threatening. "We wouldn't want to add to your problems." He sighed, half to himself.

"Such a particularly diverse family to worry

about!" Ovid put in. "And it can't be easy with someone like Christo in the family — someone so temperamental and abusive." He smiled warmly at Christobel, who responded to his smile rather than his words.

"Goodness knows," said Hadfield, his gaze still fixed on Naomi, "we appreciate, probably more than anyone else, how *very* much you must want a quiet Christmas this year of all years."

"Is this a confession, or just another circus act?" Jack cried, fixing his eyes incredulously on Hadfield as if he had only just noticed him and couldn't believe what he was seeing.

"Oh, well — we like to make all occasions glitter with special effects," Ovid admitted. "Are we overdoing the repentance now? Dearest Naomi — don't throw us out. Look — you give us a little Christmas forgiveness and I'll make you a present of Christmas silence all gift wrapped. I won't confess anything, accuse anybody, tell any coming fortunes, or past secrets."

"Ma! You have to forgive them," Christobel declared eagerly.

"And the sun's coming out," Hadfield exclaimed. "That's symbolic."

"Tolerance triumphs!" proclaimed Ovid, while Naomi's mouth hung open uncertainly.

"Either that or self-preservation," said Hadfield quietly, nodding at Naomi, apparently agreeing with something before she said it.

Naomi's expression had certainly become less forbidding. She looked startled and uncertain, as if something had been tossed around over her head and then thrown away before she could even be sure of what it was. Jack began to stand up, but he was hampered by the children, and as he put Tibby on her feet, Naomi had time to lay a firm hand on his arm. He looked at her and then sat quietly back again.

"You're no real trouble," she said to the Carnival brothers, speaking carefully, as if they were armed and dangerous, holding a knife against the throat of Santa Claus. "I don't want arguments just before Christmas — no prizes for guessing that."

"We'd be so missed if we had to go," Ovid pointed out complacently.

Tibby, dislodged from Jack's knee, looked around the room and then made for Robert, watching with Charlie from the window.

"Look at that!" Ovid said admiringly. "It's just as if you're the father of her heart, Robert."

"But it's a wise child who knows," Hadfield appeared to agree, nodding.

"Don't waste your time trying to take the mickey out of me!" Robert replied resentfully. "Anyhow, I wouldn't mind."

"Now *there's* enough truth to fill a well!" exclaimed Hadfield. "Truth *and* a confession, too, though they aren't always the same thing. Lucky Robert to do both at once."

"Here!" said Charlie, looking up unexpectedly from the newspaper. "You two sound very cocky about something."

"Oh, shut up Charlie!" Christobel exclaimed, but Ovid continued to look at Naomi.

"Robert doesn't know *how* to confess properly. He sticks to facts," he said. "We really are forgiven, are we?" he asked.

"Of course you are," Christobel said. "Ma's the greatest forgiver in the world. She forgives me and that takes some doing," and she flung her arms around Naomi's neck and subjected her to a throttling embrace.

Out in the hall they heard the door open, and Hadfield and Ovid both made a half turn to face it.

"This has to be Felix," Christobel said. "We won't have to go through all this grilling again with him, will we?"

"He's as guilty of everything as we are," Hadfield said, "but we'll give you three for the price of two."

Out in the hall, Harry paused. Then, still dripping water from her rained-on hair, she went into the living room, where she found the entire family sitting around, and knew she had arrived rather too late for a performance of some kind. Nor did she have any doubt who the performers had been. Hadfield and Ovid turned to look at her as she came in at the door.

Christobel was as elated as if a weight had been taken away, allowing her to bubble cheerfully once again. Robert frowned over Tibby's soft, thistledown hair. Jack sat, Naomi stood, both looking at her in a troubled way, so that Harry wondered if they saw something new about her, read her face like a map already marked by remarkable advances into the unknown. Or perhaps their concern was for something that had nothing to do with her.

"Harry!" exclaimed Christobel. "I thought you were being your old, antisocial, escapist self upstairs." Then she laughed and said trumphantly to Ovid and Hadfield, "I'll bet you anything Harry's the reason you've lost Felix. Oh well, boys will be boys."

"So they will!" said Hadfield. "I warned Ovid about that, but he refused to believe me."

His face, in spite of his eye, where the fading bruise was marbled yellow and green, presented to Harry the identical features that Felix had turned towards her earlier, but now interpreted differently, for Hadfield looked at her with a great good nature that she knew had nothing to do, at heart, with either goodness or nature, whereas Felix had become a different sort of man.

"I did see him back a bit," she said carelessly, "but he ended up walking in another direction." It was not a lie except in intention. And she met Ovid's eyes quite squarely, though perhaps she was the only person in the room who could see that his smile was less a smile than bared teeth, and his clear green gaze was alive with menace.

"The sun's out," Christobel cried. "Work, everyone. It's party day today."

17
Harry and Ovid

Harry went up, and Christobel went out. Encouraging herself with little presents of praise, Christobel began to plan for the Christmas Eve party, believing that, after all, she still might make Ovid follow her, that she could be a conjurer as well as he.

"Come on, Ma! Snap into it," she called. "Let's get this show on the road."

Naomi went and studied the hall, frowning at the waterlily wallpaper.

"Are we being too sensitive?" Anthony heard her asking Jack and was struck by Jack's expression, affectionate, faintly mocking, but above all else, resigned.

"I think we are being blackmailed," he said.

"I wondered — but it was hard to be sure," Naomi temporized.

"Very hard!" Jack said with mild sarcasm. "And we *do* want a particularly happy Christmas, don't we? I mean, dearest Naomi, we do, really *do*, need it."

"Fancy dress!" Christobel was crying out on the verandah. "Let's cover the beach with wonderful, fantastic people, have late sunshine pouring over them, the sea in front, and the old hills behind them. Let's have a bit of surrealism this Christmas."

"Fancy dress! Fancy dress!" shouted Serena and Benny, and began to moo like nursery-rhyme cows.

Harry heard Christobel on the phone, shouting to friends, determined to bring new colour and strangeness into an old festival. Quite stunned by the events of the morning, she herself, wet clothes peeled away, lay naked on her bed, the smooth surface of the sleeping bag like a cool, friendly, undemanding skin against her own, the familiar weight of her hair on her shoulders and back a welcome caress. Christmas, holidays, family, summer, love and ghosts tumbled through her head until she felt that, under the pressure of this confusion, she might be pushed into becoming a spirit of fire, incandescent in the pointed room. She had parted from Felix at the top of the hill, but did not miss him yet because he still seemed to be coursing around in her blood, wandering through the four chambers of her beating heart.

After a while she sat up, wondered what on earth she could wear to make herself look beautiful, and stared blankly around her attic room as if it might belong to someone else. She finally put on a skirt with a pattern of rearing unicorns and white rose trees and a dark-green shirt with a low neckline, then began to brush her hair slowly like a mermaid — but a mermaid of the upper air, a swimmer in the wind, watching her face in the little looking-glass with her naked eyes, while her glasses squatted back on their own folded legs and quietly studied the ceiling. Harry's brushing hand grew slower and slower, for she thought she looked both tanned and translucent, her eyes large and shining, her hair quite black in the shadows except for the single hairs at the edges, which caught the light and burned like threads of fire.

Suddenly Harry felt certain she was beautiful, not as Christobel was, for her face was too round, her eyebrows too straight, but like an enchantress who could make people think she was beautiful simply by declaring herself so. Her lips parted in bewitched astonishment. She put the brush down and lifted handfuls of hair on either side of her face, sifting it down so that it fell in vague soft fans shot through with coppery red, but as she did this she saw in the glass, through the slowly folding veil of hair on the left side, a twist in the air and then a face taking form and looking at her. Far more than Felix, more, even, than Hadfield, Ovid had the very quality of demonic Belen. If his brothers, infected by Harry's field of imagination, had grown to look like her hero-villain, Ovid had caught ruthlessness from it, and tuned it eagerly to match his own. Harry was shut in with him. However, she turned to face him with a confidence that surprised both of them. She had subdued Hadfield with a blow and Felix with a kiss, and, matching her own magic with Ovid's, she might also assert herself at last over Christobel. Harry picked up her glasses and put them on firmly, so that Ovid's smile came into sharp focus.

"What do you want?" she asked, pleased with her calm voice.

"Oh, everything!" he said fervently. "How about you, Ariadne?"

"Everything, too," she said.

"Well, we can't both have it," he replied, "and I wanted it first. A word to the wise, my dear . . . Learn wisdom quickly."

"How did you get here?" she asked, glancing at the trapdoor, though she knew he had not come into her attic that way. Ovid was already shaking his head.

"I don't have to hide from you that I am *more* than a conjurer," he began. "I'm sure that silly Felix has laid his head on your shoulder and told you all our secrets. And why? You're pretty enough, but not so very pretty."

He could have sounded spiteful, but instead he was, above all else, inquisitive. Harry was pleased to let him think Felix had answered her questions, that she had more power over Felix than he had.

"I can *seem* beautiful," she replied, and saw his expression change as if he suddenly recognized something unexpectedly formidable in her. His cold green eyes grew a little warmer with unwilling speculation, and he grimaced.

"You've upset my poor brother — do you know that?" he asked. "Upset him so that *I* feel it — feel it *here*!" he exclaimed, laying his hand on his heart. "He gives his pillow your name in the dark — reinvents you out of shadows and sleep so he can have you in there with him. But what touches him touches us all. I'll catch this sickness. Be a good girl and leave him alone."

"But you've upset Christobel, so we're even," Harry exclaimed severely. "Besides, Felix doesn't look very upset to me."

"But you don't really know him," Ovid said. "He's mine. We're marked with the same scars. Has he told you about that?"

Harry would not confess to any ignorance. She looked scornfully at Ovid.

"I know about his scar," she said.

"We're not just brothers, we're blood brothers. Cut Felix and I bleed. I can't help being concerned."

Harry thought of a clever thing to say. "Well then, heal Felix and you'll be healed too," she cried.

"There's nothing I want to be healed from," Ovid answered sharply.

Then he seemed to lose interest in what he was saying, peering into the dark reaches under the roof that were made uninhabitable by the slope of the iron, reading the titles of the books by her bed, even picking up her cotton nightdress and holding it against himself, studying his head and shoulders in the mirror, and saying as he did so, "Anyway, why worry about Christobel? Leave her to me and simply watch what happens. You wouldn't mind if she didn't get her own way, would you?"

Harry felt her first hesitation, for Ovid had moved in surely on a weak place in her life. Now he read her face with triumph.

"Confound them! The ones on ahead of us! I know all about *them*, my dear. I was born in the shadow of the Black King and the Goddess of Wisdom, and you were born in Christobel's. Don't you shiver there?"

"I used to," Harry admitted, meaning as little as

four days ago. She would not admit that she did not know anything about the Black King and the Goddess of Wisdom. "But now I don't need to stand in anyone's shadow."

Ovid listened intently. "Really?" he said. "Because of Felix? Well, they say it makes you powerful. I wouldn't know. But find someone else. Leave my Felix alone. I won't have it."

"Tell him, not me!" suggested Harry boldly.

Ovid's smile, which was half alert with curiosity faded. He began to trace the shape of his own lips with his forefinger, staring at her broodingly, saying finally in a very soft voice, "I don't trust him. He's too susceptible."

"Don't be jealous!" Harry said, half-inspired. "You probably couldn't be susceptible yourself if you tried."

Mysteriously she had struck a blow that hurt Ovid, for his face, strange in its marred prettiness, flared with a feeling made up of many other feelings. He was angry, and not only angry but suffering.

"There, you see!" he cried, baring his sharp white teeth, indignant, as if she had given ineradicable proof of Felix's treachery. "You've made him untrue. What will he tell you next?"

She could easily have let him know that Felix had kept almost all his secrets, and that she did not have the ghost of an idea what she had said to make Ovid wince, but she remained silent.

He waited a moment, catching his breath and then said in a more commonplace voice, "I won't take it out on him. Or on you, though I could make you flame like a warning beacon right where you stand — strike you blind and topple you through your own trapdoor, break your neck at the foot of your own ladder . . ." He took a step towards her and shrugged, beginning to smile again. "And who'd suspect me?"

"Felix!" Harry said at once and saw his eyes shift as he considered this.

Outside there came a sudden scream from Benny.

"Crumb's got a mouse — a mouse. Get it off him! Get it off him." Harry could imagine him dancing with anxiety, waving his thin arms, a cross between a boy and a windmill of sticks.

"It's no use," Charlie shouted from somewhere. "Leave it — you'll only make it worse for the mouse."

"Get it off him!" yelled Benny. "Crumb's cruel!"

There was the sound of thudding and probably unsuccessful pursuit.

"I was like that once — like Benny I mean — for a little while," Ovid said unexpectedly. "I really was. But I had to change. Now I'm enjoying feeling more like Crumb. Of course, you're right. Felix would know. We're not private from one another."

He casually placed his hand against the rough wooden diagonal over his head. Smoke immediately poured through his fingers and when, a moment later, he took his hand away, the lines of four fingers and a thumb were charred into the wood. As part of the same movement, he reached across, took her upper arm and drew her towards him, making her gasp and believe she was going to be branded. But though his hand burnt, it burnt with cold as if its natural heat had been seriously overspent.

"Since you've found out so many of our vain secrets," he murmured, "I'll let you into another. I've

taken more of a liking to your sister than I would
have wished. It might be because of what Felix is
feeling. Or possibly not. Because she *is* so beautiful,
of course — and because she wants life to be thrilling every moment of the day. I like people like
that — people who might exhaust me, given half a
chance. I don't always enjoy feeling so — so . . ."
He didn't finish his sentence, but shook his head,
and for a fraction of a second she actually glimpsed,
beyond his Mongolian doll-mask, a perpetual ov-
erloading, an unsuspected torment from which he
had suffered since childhood. "The truly exhausting
things — fury and love, delight, lust — were all
forbidden," he said. "All shut away in the land of
Too Far! And I admit, of course, it isn't rational to
yearn for exhaustion. But I do so long for someone
who would use me all up. Anyhow, because of
Christo I was going to let you all off lightly. But
Harry, sister Harry, Felix is mine. He is *me*, and
if you threaten me by making him want you too
much, I promise you I'll destroy your family, and
I'll use you to do it."

The signature, burnt into the wood over her bed,
spoke eloquently to Harry. At the same time, she
felt certain that there was much more to her family
than Ovid understood. If she had chosen to teeter
along a strand of silk high in the air and over risky
ground, she was sustained by many things — by
the way Jack and Naomi held together, in spite of
midnight arguments and differences of opinion; or
even by the memory of Tibby holding Crumb, the
murderous mouser, in a strangling hold and saying,
"This Crumb loves me," while Crumb swung in her
grasp, legs and tail dangling patiently down, ex-

tending his claws in despair but still not striking.

"We're not yours to destroy," she said breathlessly, and Ovid, uncurled his fingers from her arm, though he left his hand still resting on her, rather as if she actually was a mouse that might run and give him a chance to play. She refused to shrink an inch under his newly-relaxed hold.

"Think it over!" he said.

"Felix just might be able to look after himself," Harry said sternly. Ovid laughed.

"Not he, poor darling. He wants us to be loved for ourselves alone." He straightened the collar of her shirt like a fussy, older sister and touched her breast in the careless, affectionate way he might have touched a troublesome kitten.

"He likes girls," he said, and added, "What do you really think of him? You really think he's attractive?"

"I suppose so," Harry said cautiously, since there seemed to be no reason to deny it. "He is quite."

"He is quite," Ovid mocked her with her own careful voice. "He's tremendous this side . . . but he doesn't really look like that, you know. And Felix isn't his real name either." Ovid suddenly wrapped his arms around himself as if he were very cold. "You don't know what he looks like, do you? Or what he's called, or any real thing about him. And he's a trickster, too, don't forget, so you could have some terrible surprises at any moment of truth. Because we all go together. In the end there's no separation."

Then he was quite gone, hugged out of existence by his own embrace. Harry sat down on the end of her stretcher-bed. She shut her eyes, breathed deeply and gently, and unexpectedly felt an excitement she had never felt before. It was to do with becoming powerful for the first time in her life. If she could not actually combat Christobel, whom she loved, she could at least overcome Ovid and his commandments, for over the last three days it had seemed to her more and more that, from under the invented face Felix wore, another softer, more vulnerable face was trying to make itself seen. Just for a moment, she thought of Ovid's advice and Felix's obscure answers, and lingered a little on their different words. But now she had caught their own longing from them and longed for an extreme place of her own, to go out between the waterlilies to a land where no one (except possibly Felix Carnival) could follow her.

18
Winners and Losers

The beach below Carnival's Hide was crossed by a
wavering frontier (heads of kelp streaming with flat,
brown shiny ribbons instead of hair, feathers, foam,
the frail cases of crabs and sodden wood) repre-
senting the furthest advances of the tide. Sometimes old plastic containers, bright ends of nylon
rope like synthetic blue and yellow worms, and
scraps of homely orange peel reminded the Hamiltons that other people were sharing the harbour
with them. Out beyond this line, other people were
enjoying other Christmases, perhaps as mixed as
their own. And Harry, for example, knew this ran-
dom line must stretch in many different directions
around the world, and sometimes contemplated a
journey for herself that simply consisted of following it, knowing that it would lead her safely through
a strange maze.

However, whenever a beach party was planned
(and in good weather all parties turned into beach
parties), this long, untidy clue had to be raked away.

Serena and Benny, armed with spades and rakes, were set to work, while Jack, Charlie and Robert began to search out the trestles and sheets of hard-board used each year to make tables down on the sand.

Christobel, looking into the kitchen, saw Naomi making mayonnaise, Emma taking tin-foil parcels out of the deep freeze (salmon steaks which would be baked and later served cold), and Harry peeling potatoes for a potato salad. In the centre of the floor, just where people might fall over her, sat Tibby, scraping out a bowl that had recently contained fill-ing for candle-ring bread. The bread itself, swollen with chopped orange, pineapple and almonds, and rich with brown sugar and cinnamon, was waiting to go into the oven. Later it would be frosted with icing, and a fat green candle would be set in the middle of it, but it was still waiting for its moment of glory.

This domestic scene did not appeal to Christobel. "I'll take the tablecloths down," she called, "I'll only get in the way here." She picked up the pile of red and green cloths from the end of the counter, turned and banged into Robert, coming through the kitchen doorway.

"That was nice," she said. "Let's go back and do it again." However rare, uncertainty gave a me-chanical edge to her voice, and, Robert did not smile, simply walking by her into the kitchen. Chris-tobel saw Naomi hesitate and glance anxiously in her direction.

"Talk to me!" she shouted imperiously after Rob-ert. "Don't be childish!"

Robert turned. "I can't say anything clever

enough for you," he replied. "Naomi, do you have another hammer in here? We could use another one."

"*Be* like that, then!" Christobel exclaimed and walked on down to the sea, the tablecloths flapping like flags over her arm. As she approached the orchard, her path intersected with that of Anthony, wrestling with two large deckchairs, both of which were trying to unfold themselves and pinch his fingers.

"I've left the others working in the kitchen," Christobel said immediately. "I'm trying to seem helpful and reliable without actually having to *be* it, not in the kitchen, anyway."

"Tricky!" Anthony said, wrestling with the deckchairs.

"I know you disapprove of me already," Christobel went on, taking one of them from him, "because you give me a very old-fashioned look from time to time, so I've got nothing to lose if I let you in on the worst."

"Sounds interesting," Anthony answered, smiling.

"I don't even *want* to be reliable!" Christobel cried. "Reliable's what people are stuck with when they've got no other choices. I suppose you're in favour of it. You look reliable," she said accusingly and added, rather more uncertainly, "most of the time."

"I'll let *you* in on the worst now," Anthony replied. "It's all an act." The deckchair succeeded in pinching his hand. "Are these things deckchairs or crocodiles?"

"Better than ironing boards, though!" Christobel sympathized, as her own deckchair snapped at her. "In the end you can enjoy deckchairs, but ironing boards are nothing but misery."

They walked on with their deckchairs firmly under control.

"Why bother to act?" Christobel asked.

"To deceive others!" Anthony said. "So forget reliability. But I've got a lot of virtues we could talk about. I'm kind to animals, for instance."

Before them Serena and Benny, neglecting their party duties were fighting a ponderous duel with rakes, giggling and scuffling backwards and forwards in the soft sand.

"You kids!" Christobel roared at them, and they immediately stopped their game and began raking industriously, muttering, "Grunt! Grunt!" to each other. Christobel had roared with such relief and fury that Anthony jumped, too, and looked at her with startled curiosity, just as she looked over at him.

"I'm crying, if you want to know," she said defiantly. "I'll bet you didn't think I could, but I've got a lot of talents."

Anthony promptly opened his deckchair and arranged it facing the sea. Christobel opened her own beside it. They sat down formally, side by side. The hills were bathed in brilliant sunshine, and every grain of sand reflected the light. A faint steam rose from the bush at their backs and from the thin moist films at the edge of the sea, even from the driftwood that Charlie was piling up into a small bonfire at one end of the beach. Christobel and Anthony sat in their own tropic. Robert walked past them, hammer in hand, moving towards Jack and Charlie and the trestles further down the beach.

Christobel waved to them, Jack waved back, Robert turned and then pretended not to have seen her.

"He's really gone off me," Christobel said. "I don't blame him, but it makes me feel bad-tempered with guilt. I suppose you feel sorry for him. Everyone else does," she ended in a rush.

"Not in the long run," Anthony said. "He'll be better off without you."

"Oh, thanks!" Christobel said despondently.

"Actually I'm far more sympathetic towards you than towards Robert," Anthony said unexpectedly. "And just to entertain you, I'll open my heart and tell you why."

Christobel now turned her brilliant gaze towards him, with a lively mixture of apprehension and interest.

"That mythical broken heart!" she said, looking a little shamefaced.

"Not mythical," said Anthony, "but not mine. I was the one that caused it. And, in the end, I couldn't bear its unhappiness, so when I got the chance of the trip out here I moved away."

Christobel now stared at Anthony as if, before her eyes, he was revealed, not as a victim but as an unsuspected conqueror of life.

"So I've seen someone really hurt that way," Anthony continued after a pause, "and although I don't know what promises you might be breaking, I'm certain Robert will recover quickly."

"In a way I think we both knew the end was in

sight," Christobel said, beginning to look easier. "Sometimes he's tried to talk about it, but I wouldn't listen because — because I've known him for ages and ages, and I'm really fond of him, even if he is a bit thick. And then there's Jack and Naomi — they've had such a long love affair themselves that it sits like a great monument in my life, something I've got to do as well as — or better than," she concluded, looking confused.

"I don't think you can afford to worry too much about the examples other people have set," Anthony said. "What I think is that Robert loves sailing almost more than anything else he can think of. He looks misty when he talks about it."

"But I think he might be beginning to love Emma," Christobel added with slight displeasure. "I know I should be pleased about it — it lets me out — but it bugs me at odd times. It's as if I have all the ideas, but Emma picks them up and does them more thoroughly, and they wind up more hers than mine in the end. She's only been original once in her life and that was over Tibby."

"Well, you don't need to envy her that, do you?" Anthony said.

Christobel opened her mouth to reply, then frowned at him suspiciously. At last he turned his head and met her eyes with such an amused expression that Christobel laughed against her will.

"You're getting at me!" she cried. "It's true I do feel cross when she strikes out on her own. I mean *I'd* like the glory of a baby as long as I didn't actually have to *have* one." A tear left behind by the rest squeezed out of her eye. "And I don't really want Robert, I just want him to go on liking me best."

She let Anthony see what she had only hinted at before, that behind her burnished surface she was troubled by these contradictions in herself. "Was yours very unhappy?" she asked.

"Very!" said Anthony. "We were engaged to be married, and I'd told her that I would love her for ever. I believed it myself, so I was very convincing. But her 'for ever' turned out to be a longer-lasting brand than mine. Mine fell to pieces quite quickly."

"It's over-rated anyway, *for ever* is," Christobel said gloomily. "It sounds good in the advertisements, but it comes in such scrappy little pieces these days."

"Will you have the two week *for ever*, or the large economy size with the six-month guarantee, seven days' free trial and no obligations?" Anthony asked rather sadly, holding out his hands as if he had a limp *for ever* draped over them.

"Mind you — think of Jack and Naomi," Christobel said. "That's the trouble. Their *for ever* has been just so classy. In a way it gives me hope that someday I might — I mean I like being the way I am at present, but I want things to get even better. I want them wonderful."

"Choice can be wonderful." Anthony looked out to sea. "But there are traps in choosing . . ." He broke off. "You know I stepped off the plane two weeks ago, and here I was in a country where nobody knew me. It was such a relief, I decided to stay unknown. I didn't see that it mattered, but somehow things have become very difficult. Christobel . . ." He began as if he were going to tell his life story and needed her name to begin it, but then he laughed and shook his head. "This is *your* time for confessing, not mine. Just remember, if ever I seem too reliable it's because I'm over-compensating for past sins."

Christobel's tear had dried on her cheek, making a little steam of its own in the warm, moist air.

"I actually feel better," she said, "knowing I'm not the only changeable one." She drew in the soft sand with a toe. "I don't ever want to be a loser. Deep down, that's the bitter truth. I'm sorry for losers, but I don't want to *be* one or even be with them. And then, every so often, all in a blinding flash, I think that *I'm* already really a loser and haven't faced up to it yet."

"I'm used to victories myself," Anthony said unexpectedly. "This mild exterior hides powerful ambitions. I'm astonished people don't notice more often, but they don't seem to." Christobel looked at him inquisitively. "Are you sure your heart isn't even slightly broken?" she asked.

"It's rugged!" Anthony answered. "I'm recovering well from its success."

Christobel sat a little straighter. "It's not very nice of me to sit here complaining about myself and other men," she said. "Sorry!"

"If I wanted things different, I could make them different," Anthony said lazily. "Heavens above — what's a mere conjurer? I told you, I'm used to victories."

Serena, still raking virtuously, drew alongside their chairs and stared intently as Christobel, her fugitive attention completely caught, regarded Anthony with an open speculation that made him smile.

"Now then! Don't turn that particular look on *me*," he said. "Save it for the conjurer. Anyhow, aren't these deckchairs meant to be further along the beach?"

"Buzz off, Serena!" Christobel said. "Stop spying! Anthony and I are confessing our sins to one another."

"I wasn't spying!" Serena cried, insulted.

"You'll be up at the house in five minutes reporting all to Ma," Christobel said. "All right, Anthony! Shoulder deckchairs. Quick march!"

Serena frowned crossly after them. Then she ran up the path between the native beech and fuchsia, through the orchard, over the verandah, hesitated in the hall, clattered through the living room and into the kitchen. Benny, who had come up a little ahead of her was helping Tibby scrape out another bowl, this time one that had contained white frosting.

"There's love going on everywhere!" she cried in tones of deep disgust and envy. "Christobel is beginning to give looks at Anthony, Robert's got keen on Emma, and Harry keeps watching Felix Carnival."

Harry was glad she had her back to the room, but she still knew when Naomi and Emma turned to look at her.

"Really?" Emma said. "Do you like Felix, Harry? How on earth do you tell him from Hadfield?"

"He looks totally different," Harry mumbled in involuntary surprise. "Well, not totally . . ." and wondered why Emma laughed.

"He's awfully good-looking." Serena sighed, staring longingly at Harry's back, as if she owned a treasure and was refusing to share it. "Hadfield's the wickedest."

"I'm sorry to strike a boring, domestic note," said Naomi apologetically, "but I'm taking this paté out of the deep freeze and putting it in this cupboard. It'll take about three hours to thaw. Don't any of you let me forget I've put it there." She gave Harry her usual smile, which may have been just a little more lopsided than usual.

"When I grow up I'm going to live in a little house on a mountain and I'll have Tibby and Crumb to stay with me," Benny announced. "But she's got to stop wetting her nappies first. I'm not changing a girl's nappies."

Tibby heard her name and the mention of nappies.

"Good, dry girl!" she cried patting her own bottom.

"It sounds a wonderful life," Naomi said sighing. "Dry nappies, Tibby — Crumb, a jug of wine, a book of verse — the wilderness would be happiness indeed."

19
Breaking Free

Before going down to the beach that afternoon, Harry went into her parents' room and stood staring into the big mirror, trying vainly to see again the enchantress who could seem beautiful. But, somehow, making sandwiches and peeling potatoes had made the enchantress hide herself away. Her reflection looked so ordinary she could have cried.

"Oh blast!" she exclaimed despairingly, for an enchantress who could be vanquished by mere potatoes wasn't up to much. In fairy tales people put on cloaks of beauty and dread and wonder, but Harry wanted to draw wonder up out of herself. It was no longer enough to be Ariadne alone up in her room. Revealed to Felix, recognized by Ovid, she now wanted everyone in her family to know her, too. Beyond the attic, other people were disguising themselves with fancy dress, but Harry's fancy dress would have to be her true, astonishing self, inventor of beautiful winged demons, conqueror of the ravishing Hadfield, adversary of Ovid — the very girl who had tempted Felix under the furious blade of the lightning. So she did not want to dress as a witch or gypsy. She wore her black swimming suit and unicorn skirt and left it at that.

As she walked into the hall, Emma, looking lively and mischievous, just as she used to look before Tibby, came out of Christobel's room with a box of makeup.

"Christobel's dissatisfied with herself," she said. "She wants me to paint her face for her — you know — the way I used to," and then she went on, with a pause. "Have you really become keen on Felix Carnival, Harry?"

"Have you really got keen on Robert?" Harry parried quickly.

"I asked first," said Emma, and then added, "I don't know. Maybe! Not like I was over Sam, of course. Robert's all rules, and Sam had no rules at all. Sort of exciting — but I could never imagine living with Sam."

"Can you imagine it with Robert?" Harry asked.

"I'm beginning to, whether I want to or not," Emma said. "You can't help trying out sudden possibilities and seeing what they could lead to — but it might just be holidays, and a rebound from — from everything else. You know! Don't *say* anything, will you?"

"I won't," Harry promised. They were both thinking of Christobel.

"It won't last with Ovid," Emma said, "and then Christo might want him back." Harry thought this was possible. "I don't think she could have him though," Emma went on when they had walked a few more steps down the track. "No real *certain* reason, but Robert and I feel restful together in a way, and I think he likes restfulness. I know *I* do."

Down on the beach, about thirty people were drinking wine and fruit juice, most of them ordinary summer-holiday friends, or other neighbours hurrying on to their own private Christmases. In among them moved two Santa Clauses, a newspaper girl, a pirate, a mad bride, a villainous scarecrow, a giant penguin, an owl, a clown and Frankenstein's melancholy monster, and these few made others look strange as well. Anthony's sunglasses, Jack's wide straw sunhat, Hugh Tavener's scarlet headband and the rings his mother wore, flashing as she waved her hands talking to Naomi about casseroles, lost their everyday look and became fantastic. Like the soldier in *The Twelve Dancing Princesses*, Harry, descending into magic land, had discovered a marvellous company, centaurs and griffins, all half-resembling people she knew. She might almost have been invisible, able to walk up to them, to look *into* them, to turn their skin to glass with her gaze and study the regular crimson clockwork of their hearts, while her own heart remained quite unseen. But then Felix looked over at her, and he either blushed or shifted, so that his face flared with sudden light, turning away almost at once. He stood between Ovid and Hadfield, watching Emma kneel, laughing, in front of Christobel, sitting on a camp-stool.

"Make me completely amazing!" Christobel begged. She was draped in a floating toga, old net curtains patterned with large flowers and humming birds, faded streaks showing where the folds of the original curtains had once fallen. Her tanned skin and white bikini showed through the net, which, though less spectacular than other dresses on the beach, was at least cool. Many fancy-dress people were already discarding pieces of their costumes, and some were already swimming, their heads bobbing among the slow green ripples. But Christobel was watched by Hugh and Debbie Tavener, by the three Carnival brothers and by Serena. Caught unawares, Ovid's face, once he had seen the lipstick, eyeshadow and kohl, the eyebrow pencil, blusher and bronze beach make-up, began to show the same preoccupation he had shown when he had seen the Christmas tree and its decorations. Emma began to sketch — with tiny feathery strokes — dramatic, slender, long science-fiction eyebrows for Christobel.

"You're too used to what you're doing," Ovid cried abruptly. "Let *me* colour her in." Emma blinked eloquently at Christobel and made way for him. Ovid took her over, quickly blending blue, green, grey and brown, turning her before their eyes into a mineral girl, a girl of platinum, gold and bronze touched with verdigris. Her eyes outlined with kohl, shaded with gold, her lips blue, her hair sprayed into a stiff, glittering crest, Christobel grew less and less able to smile of her own accord, took on the iridescent skin of a dragon queen. Hadfield watched with his own kind of sinister amiability. Felix stood impassively at his side.

"Everyone will be able to swim but you," Ovid said caressingly, standing back from Christobel. He was still not quite satisfied and passed his hand over her face, stroking the air half an inch in front of it as if it were a delicate skin. Her face, coming out from under his eclipsing palm, seemed more metallic than mere paint could have made it. She had become the marionette of his dreams, a toy of precious but lifeless treasure. Harry thought this was Ovid's triumph.

"You're nothing less than a work of art," he said to Christobel.

"Nothing more, either," Harry muttered, but Ovid's smile faltered into something wilder and sadder. Something in him grieved at his own success, and he took Christobel's smiling face between his hands and kissed her as if he would breathe his own life back into her. He kissed his own work of art, thought Harry, anxious to experience it by tasting and touching and smelling just what he had made, and she shivered and wondered if there was really a live sister left in the core of that beautiful puppet.

At once Hadfield broke into slow, derisive applause, but Harry noticed something akin to dismay cross his dark face — a sharpening of his attention. Then he turned a singular glance on Felix, a glance challenging, even threatening, but filled with respect, too. Indeed, Harry thought she saw, for the first time, Hadfield becoming apprehensive. Felix laughed and closed his eyes, while Christobel, finished but not yet free, looked at Ovid as if she, too, had questions to ask, even in the middle of the crowd. But he was already turning away from her, his lips stained slightly blue from hers, as if bruised by the kiss. As he did so, he saw Harry watching him and gave her a secret, wincing smile.

Shortly after, food began to come down from the house — at first just mince pies and sandwiches. Naomi had put plastic holly around them as a decoration, but Serena had added sprays of tom-thumb roses from the sprawling bush at the corner of the wash house. Down came the candle-ring bread, the air over its lighted candle quivering with invisible flame, down came the first of two Christmas cakes wrapped in merry red frills.

"Holly and roses!" exclaimed Anthony, rather as if he were making fun of a Christmas that defiantly mixed its summers with story-book winters.

"The holly's just plastic," Serena said anxiously, in case he had been tricked by it.

"No robins?" Anthony asked. "Don't you have a wind-up robin or two?"

But the Christmas birds of Carnival's Beach had red legs not red breasts. Several seagulls settled their wings, like formally dressed gentlemen straightening their ties while waiting for a meal to be served. Serena and Benny raced along the margin of the sea, shrieking with laughter, their bare feet kicking up fans of silver. The seagulls rose in a leisurely fashion, hung casually in the air as the disturbance passed by them, then settled and straightened their ties again.

Harry felt a hand on her shoulder and turned to find Felix behind her.

"I thought you might have decided not to speak to me again," she said.

"It's dangerous," he agreed. "We can't rely on it raining next time."

Harry thought again that he looked both softer and more startled than when she first saw him. His face seemed to be changing, struggling against the outline her villain had imposed on him.

"Ovid decorated Christobel, and now she's his,"

Harry said. "I'm going to decorate you into being mine." And she stole a tom-thumb rose from the edge of the plate of mince pies and put it behind his ear.

"I shall wear it always," he said. "I can feel it suiting me."

"Harry," said Naomi coming up behind her, "I keep feeling I've forgotten something that ought to be here."

"Salad? Chicken?" Harry guessed, shy at having her mother look at the rose in such a resigned way.

"No, that's all for later," Naomi said. "Oh, I know! The paté. Could you be a dear and go and get it for me with the little crackers and the crispbreads?"

"OK," Harry said, wondering if Felix would walk up to the house with her. She understood just how Christobel must feel, walking away from Ovid, wanting him to follow without being asked, but Felix glanced at his brothers and shook his head slightly.

The sunny afternoon seemed to grow hotter rather than cooler as the sand began to pay back the heat it had borrowed earlier in the day. Above the sand on the bank where the rough sea-grass grew, an owl mask sat like a small idol staring blindly out over the table, while its owner herself bobbed in the sea. The mad bride took off her wig and hung it on the back of a deckchair, and one of the Santa Clauses put his heavy suit on a coathanger and hooked it under a tree growing back from the bank a little way, where it kicked restlessly in the light breeze, as if there was an airy, irascible saint still inside it. In due course, Harry, having returned with the paté, climbed with Felix up on to the bank and sat almost at the feet of this vigorous Christmas spirit. Someone gave Felix a cigarette which he accepted gingerly.

"Something's happened," Harry said. "Something between you and your brothers."

"What brothers?" Felix said smiling. "They're disowning me."

"You gave Hadfield's smile all of a sudden," Harry told him, fascinated.

"We're more than brothers," Felix told her, still smiling. "You know that, don't you? Still, in a way, of course we *are* brothers," he added quickly, sounding as if he were covering up an indiscretion. "We're jostling each other for a place in the sun. That's family life, isn't it?"

"Do you really think *we* are jostling each other for a place in the sun?" Harry asked, looking at the children playing, at Jack and Naomi with their guests. Felix nodded, jiggling with the cigarette dubiously.

"Mmmm!" he murmured. "Well, don't you think so?" he added, looking up. "There's Christobel on ahead of you, and Serena coming up behind, trying to get your attention, and you worrying too much about Christobel to notice Serena."

Harry's mouth fell open in astonishment. "I *love* Serena!" she said. "But she wants to be like Christo all over again."

"Listen!" said Felix abruptly. "Don't you even notice? She tries to be on your side. You miss out on her. You look on and up, not back over your shoulder. She's got one beautiful, powerful sister and one mysterious, silent one. She wants the best of both." Harry was too astounded to protest. "Will you pay now or shall I send my account in later?" Felix went on. "I know, you can pay in kind, and I'll be kind back to you." Harry was too startled at the thought that Serena might want to be like her to take any notice of his words or the tone of his voice.

He was still playing with the cigarette, tapping it on the back of his hand, putting it between the index and second finger of his right hand and looking at it curiously.

"You just don't know what to do with it, do you?" Harry said, grinning.

"I didn't ever do it before," he replied vaguely. "But others did."

At this moment the donor of the cigarette, seeing Felix's dilemma, kindly offered a light and Felix lit it clumsily.

"It's no good for you," Harry warned him.

"But I like a dangerous holiday," he said. He puffed it, concentrating, then shook his head, startled at the taste of tobacco. "Good God! What a remarkable habit!"

"How do you know about Serena?" Harry asked.

"Nothing said, but there's a lot of looks I recognize. I know them by heart — by *heart!*" he repeated, putting his hand on his chest. "I've felt some of them on my own face so when I see them here I know just what itchings go to make them. As to what's happening between Ovid, Hadfield and me, we're getting a bit mixed. I'm becoming more eloquent in their lives — that's all."

Harry looked over at Ovid, who was walking around the table with Christobel beside him and

Hadfield half a pace behind. He had stolen all her mobility for himself, so that he was lively and nimble, his face bright with animation, but Christobel, more masked than any of the fancy-dress visitors, was displayed like a jewelled icon in a private procession. Harry felt angry to see her sister so reduced for, though she envied her power, she did not want it stolen away by Ovid Carnival.

"He's turning Christobel into a sort of doll and playing with her," she said.

"Well, that's something you have in common — you and Ovid," Felix said, squinting at her through a delicate veil of blue smoke. "Both being puppet-masters, I mean!"

Harry did not know what he meant.

"Being a novelist . . ." he explained, and his expression was not altogether pleasant. "You said you could rewrite me or cross me out. It's an Ovidish thought, because none of you is anything but fiction to Ovid. He likes to play chess with people, get in there, set traps and alter balances! He can't bear equilibrium."

Harry thought of some of the situations she had invented for her characters to live through. She was not fond of equilibrium herself.

"Ovid and you — " Felix taunted her mildly. "You both like novelty."

"That's only a play on words," Harry said at last. "The paper can't feel — neither can ideas."

"Mmm!" said Felix once more. "Personally, I think one thing runs into the other . . ." He shrugged. "Never mind! Let's go and get something to eat. I think I've totally exhausted the pleasure of this cigarette." So saying, he blotted it out in the sand and put it carefully into his shirt pocket. "Make haste slowly."

As the long late summer afternoon settled gently on the beach and the eastern hills reached up to gather rich gold out of the high air, many of the guests set off for their own Christmases at last, and those that remained were old family friends like the Taveners, or Hamish Price who worked with Jack. He had arrived this year with a new and very young wife (not much older than his daughter, who complained passionately about her father to Debbie Tavener and Charlie). The salads, cold chicken and salmon came down, and the table blossomed again.

"Shall I give Christo a break?" Emma asked Robert, who stood at her elbow holding Tibby for her while she set out paper plates among the salads.

"Do what you like," Robert said, rather shortly. "It's none of my business." Emma scuffled sand from under the legs of one of the trestles.

"Hadfield," she called. "You're looking very strong. Come and help me straighten this table up. It's started to wobble again. Robert's weighed down with Tibby."

Hadfield came promptly, and Christobel was left alone with Ovid for the first time that afternoon. For a moment, caught between various conversations, they were almost as private as if they had indeed been alone.

"Why did you kiss me like that?" Christobel asked at once.

Ovid frowned, almost as if he could not remember what she was talking about, but he answered at last. "Do you always ask?" he said cheerfully. "I thought you'd expect it by now."

"Yes," said Christobel bitterly. "I have been expecting it. But not in the middle of a lot of people! Not with your brother watching."

Ovid grimaced slightly, looking up at her under his long eyelashes. He touched his curls as if he was not quite sure of his own outline.

"I suppose I thought . . ." He broke off, appeared to consider and then ended in a rush of words, "I thought I might carry a guarded citadel by storm," he said.

If he had spoken in the tongues of Babel, Christobel could not have been more mystified.

"What *are* you talking about?" she asked him. "There's nothing guarded about me. *I'm* not a citadel."

At last Ovid lifted his green eyes to look so deeply into hers that she felt his regard wash over her like a sea wave.

"Who's talking about you?" he asked her. "*I'm* the citadel. Or I ought to be," he added. He spoke his riddle as if he were describing an illness. Hadfield, coming back to his side, seemed to know exactly what they were talking about and laid a forefinger like a gun at his brother's temple.

"It all begins here, Christo, and that's where it ends for him," he said. "Or it ought to. It always has until now."

"Damn Felix," Ovid said angrily.

"By all means," Hadfield said. "Shall I stop him?"

"What's going on?" Christobel asked.

"I'm being invaded," Ovid answered. "I'm losing my light-heartedness. Hadfield, don't kill him."

"I'll just remind him who's in power," Hadfield

said. "After all, why shouldn't I be happy, too, in my own way? It *is* Christmas."

"What is it?" Christobel asked anxiously as Hadfield walked off.

"Riddle me ree!" Ovid said. "Let me live, Christobel. Let me stay unanswered."

Down at the edge of the sea, Harry and Felix stood listening to Hamish Price's young wife play the flute. Hamish had talked her into it, for he was anxious to show her off to this crowd of old and slightly reserved friends and to win their unqualified approval for her. Standing barefooted, her cloudy, dark hair lifting in the breeze, her silver flute held to her lips, she looked very beautiful, using her breath to embroider the air with delicate trills, unexpected falls, and bird voices sometimes as sad as the cry of the gulls but always sweeter.

Harry felt a hand close, hard and chilly, on her bare arm and found Hadfield had moved in beside her. Never had she seen him look as terrifying as he did now. Suddenly, she found him far more frightening than Ovid, for he seemed alive with limitless strength, as if he could snap her arm like a twig, or drive steely fingers right through it. Behind him, she saw her family listening intently, caught in the silver, supple tendrils of sound.

"Get out!" he advised her softly. "I want to talk to Felix."

Harry stared at him. Ovid had once said that Hadfield was a predator. Now it showed, for his eyes were round and yellow; he smiled, his smile drawing his lips back from his teeth a little, and breathed quickly and eagerly through his smile. Even his hair seemed to stiffen and bristle like a dog's ruff. Had he been like this, standing behind her in the dark, almost where he was standing now, on this very beach? He pushed the angry hair away from his forehead, and there, at his hairline, was the identical scar.

"Leave her alone," Felix said at once.

"You're affecting Ovid," Hadfield said. "It'll be me going soft next."

"He's ridden me," Felix replied in a similarly quiet voice. Their conversation sounded like a man debating with himself. "Even you have from time to time. My turn now."

"You don't get a turn," Hadfield answered. "I can work with Ovid. But you'd alter me too much. You'd put me out of myself. I can *feel* what's happening, you know. You're shifting me already. That's probably why I let her go, down on the beach that night." He grinned at Harry. "You don't get away from the dog so easily."

Felix laughed, and reaching out, he very gently touched Hadfield's face where the bruise was yellowing and fading.

"Go on!" he said. "She really cracked you with that bit of wood. She's got a dog of her own, and it beat yours, that's all."

"You . . ." Hadfield began, but then, as if he simply couldn't wait long enough to finish his abuse, he flew at his brother and they both fell to the ground rolling over and over, straight into the sea. A small wave broke over them. They fought in silence, without cries or groans, but the family felt the concussion of their struggle through the ground and turned away from the music to see what the thumping and splashing was about.

Ovid came up, Christobel, more herself than she had been, at his heels. He had been watching from a little distance away.

"Stop them!" Christobel cried. "It's wrong to fight at Christmas."

Hadfield reared up in the shallow water, looking as if he would drown Felix. Harry caught his arm, but his strength was huge, and flinging her off with no trouble at all, he struck Felix again, while Ovid turned to Christobel with a strange, sickly smile, making no move. It was someone else who stopped the fight.

"That's *quite* enough!" someone said with tremendous authority. Hadfield froze. Ovid turned, his own lips parting on an unspoken reply. Felix, rolling clear, sat up in the salt water, blinking and overwhelmed, not by his brothers, but by something he heard in the voice. The speaker was Anthony Hesketh.

"If you don't learn to behave, the Black King will never let you out in the world," Anthony told them. It was as if he were speaking to children, using someone else's words in someone else's voice, and then he added in his own familiar tone, "I think that's enough brotherly argument for a Christmas party." He sounded both easy-going and domineering. Ovid's mouth hung open for a moment. He stared at Anthony, as if a spirit had spoken through him, and then over at the concerned people beyond.

"I apologize for both of them," he said briefly. His voice shook slightly. "Great clowns!" He pulled Christobel's arm through his and walked her a few steps away, but she continued to look back over her shoulder at Anthony, facing Hadfield, still apparently transfixed. Felix, sitting up in the sea, laughed aloud. People relaxed, turned away and got on with other conversations.

"How could they! The music was so lovely!" Naomi said reproachfully to Ovid. "Play some more, Jennifer." But Jennifer said she was getting tired anyway. Jack put more music on the tape-recorder. Still, Anthony and Hadfield stared at each other, and Felix and Ovid stared at them both.

Then Hadfield lifted his lip in a doglike snarl. "I was enjoying myself!" he said. "Why should I stop?"

"Because I've spoiled it for you," said Anthony. "I know all about the Black King and the Boy Enchanter, not to mention the Goddess of Wisdom. Bye the bye, did you know she witnessed the final kiss of Suriel?" Hadfield was silent again. "Old riddles are like splinters. They work their own way out because they want to be answered. So answer mine for yourselves."

Anthony walked away, with Ovid looking after him as if he had been overwhelmed all over again. Hadfield forgot Felix, and Felix forgot the red patches on his face which, given a few hours might match him up with Hadfield again, for curiously enough Hadfield's blows had duplicated the bruises on his own face.

"Don't go," Christobel said to Anthony as he went by. "You're the hero. You've stopped the fight."

"Hasn't he just!" Felix muttered dabbing at his lip, which was bleeding.

"Who are you?" Ovid asked suddenly, as Hadfield moved out of the sea to join him. They had both forgotten Felix.

"A descendant of the Goddess herself — direct as a blow!" Anthony answered cheerfully.

Beyond them, Jack took Naomi's hands and then began to dance with her across the sand, Robert turned rather anxiously to Emma, as if he were concerned for her, and after a moment they began to dance, too. Charlie laughed and said to Serena, "How about dancing with me?"

"Oh, moo!" cried Serena beaming.

"This child should be in bed," said Benny severely, but he and Tibby, giggling, spun clumsily together, falling over on purpose every so often. Christobel looked seriously at Ovid.

"I think you've danced enough for one day — in your own way that is," she said. "I think you really dance alone — or with your brothers, but that's the same thing, isn't it? I'm asking Anthony."

Harry helped Felix to his feet and put her hand on his shoulder, not sure if she wanted to comfort or steady him, and they stood for a second watching the dancers. There was an alteration in him as if she were seeing him by a light other than that of common day. At last, Harry thought, at last she had actually squeezed not just a hand but her whole self between the lines of her book and found space for wild and sweeping games, magical acts with no one crowding around her.

"Run!" he suggested. "Shall we run like the wind?" The wind obediently whirled around him as if he were its very vortex. "Run with me."

"It's Christmas! It's a family time!" she cried, but becoming for a second a creature lighter than breath, flying freely through the summer air.

"I'm *all* your family," Felix cried softly back,

"and you're all mine. Come on!" As thrilled as if he had ridden into Carnival's Hide on a white horse and swept her away in front of him, she ran beside him.

"Where are we running?" she called to him.

"Up and away!" he said. "I want to be alone with you!"

Unnoticed they edged around the dancing crowd, up the track and took to the hills as if, on the high horizon, a place that was neither earth nor sky would open for them, close behind them and hold them hidden until they were ready to come back down again. They ran on and on, hand in hand, leaving Carnival's Hide and Christmas behind them.

20
The Great Grandchild
of the Goddess of Wisdom

"It's unnaturally light," Anthony said, as they walked up to the house in the late evening. "A golden, airy Christmas under a sky like glass. And I feel as if I've been eating all day."

"It's got to be light," cried Serena, "because it's only just past midsummer. It'll still be light at ten o'clock — just a little bit light around the edges."

"It's going to cloud over," prophesied Jack, moving ahead of them. "The wind's coming from the east."

Anthony looked around the hilltops, their upper slopes still painted with sunshine. The sky, losing its strong blue, was edging towards grey, and the deep rifts running from the gilded crests down to the sea were filled with shadows, dark but not yet opaque, in which the shapes of trees were still visible. Seagulls called overhead, and a kingfisher, perching on an apple tree, watched their approach, flicked its short tail, then shot off in an arrowish flight towards the sea.

"Strange . . ." Anthony said listening to the gulls, ". . . that bit of sadness in the air."

"Is it still Christmassy for you?" asked Serena, as she had asked him regularly all day, worried over a man who thought of Christmas as a festival for a cold season.

"It's a magical day," he answered. "It's gone through so many changes, and it's still changing. Listen, is that the wind?"

Indeed a wind began to blow strongly enough to sound an occasional booming note on the trees that strung the air, a note similar to that of the sea on the beach below, so in this way the sea invaded the land, followed them up the hill and washed around the corner of the house.

Many people had come and gone during the afternoon and evening at Carnival's Hide, but those now going up to the house were the family members, both the born and adopted ones, mixed inextricably together. Tibby rode triumphantly on Jack's shoulders, her sandy legs on either side of his neck, so that he could hold her feet. She loved being up high in the summer air, and stretched up her arms fearlessly so that she would be even taller.

"Big girl," she cried and drummed her heels against his chest.

"That child's touching the sky," yelled Benny, frisking in circles around Jack, then running up the hill backwards before him. "It's here. Christmas is here and I want it to stop for a minute. I hate it going so quickly." He made a motorbike sound.

"Oh, there's still a lot of Christmas to come —

and to go," Naomi said. "We'll have a few carols when we get inside."

Christobel, walking between Ovid and Hadfield again, her brilliant makeup worn away, appeared much more her own woman than she had even an hour earlier. She bent a little forward as she walked and Naomi followed her gaze, straight and true as the darting kingfisher, to Anthony.

"Anthony," Naomi said to him, walking thoughtfully beside her, "what on earth happened down on the beach there? Why were they fighting?"

"I'm not sure," Anthony replied. "They stopped when I invoked the Goddess of Wisdom."

"Athena," cried Serena triumphantly. "Athens was called after her, wasn't it, Ma?"

"She's got a Roman name, too — Minerva," Anthony said, and then turned to Naomi, speaking with the hurried anxiety of someone who has suddenly made up their mind to say something and can barely wait to say it. "Naomi, there's something I must tell you."

"Urgently?" she asked, rather taken aback by his tone.

"Moderate urgently," he replied. "It's by way of being a confession, my second today."

"Well, I don't expect anyone will think about helping in the kitchen," Naomi said. "They all help early on, but by now enthusiasm is at a low ebb. Is it private?"

They crossed the verandah in an irregular procession and came into the hall. As they did this, it seemed to Naomi, automatically turning to check her family, that there was a visible alteration in both Ovid and Hadfield, something difficult to define — perhaps their skins had become a little more grainy, their eyes shadowed, Hadfield's face paler, Ovid's ringlets less buoyant.

"Are you all right?" she asked them, trying not to be concerned, for she was not feeling at all fond of them. Yet, suddenly, she thought they looked a desolate pair.

"We're anxious as anyone to pay tribute to the Christmas king in the cloak of green needles," said Ovid as they all went into the sitting room, where the king lifted his starry crest and held up welcoming arms hung with seasonal jewels.

Naomi walked past the tree, on into the kitchen, and looked around it with a sigh. The end of every feast is slops, scraps and washing-up. Emma, coming in after her, also looked ruefully at the counter burdened with the detritus of extended hospitality.

"I suppose there must have been at least fifty people in today," she said, "but we *did* have paper plates. You wouldn't think there could possibly be so much washing up if you saw what Charlie was burning on his bonfire. I'll give you a hand, and then we'll start Christmas Day tomorrow clean as a whistle."

"You go and put that Tibby of yours to bed if you can," Naomi said, "and then help them to sing carols around the piano. I'll do a bit of stacking and rinsing. Really, one person's enough for that, but I don't say I wouldn't like some help later on, however."

"It's funny," said Emma, "even having a couple of rooms of your own makes you think about how much work goes into keeping them orderly — nothing wonderful even, just reasonably clean and tidy. Until I started looking after myself and Tibby — absolutely looking after myself, I mean — I'd see tidying going on and even help a bit, but in another way I wouldn't see it, because what I saw didn't count."

"I know exactly what you mean," Naomi said. "If only you knew the number of times I've cleaned up on my own and listened to other people having a good time in the next room, and I've wanted to walk out on it all. Christobel says, 'All right! Walk away! Leave it,' and Harry says, 'I'll help you in a minute.' But I get so sick of the mess I don't want to walk out on it, or leave it for a minute. Sometimes it's easier to do without help. Anyhow, I saw Harry go off with Felix Carnival, so she won't be here to lend a hand until later. Never mind, I'm feeling quite philosophical about it all tonight."

The door opened. Anthony looked in, self-consciously holding a thin little parcel in Christmas paper at his side.

"Off you go," Naomi said, as the lights of the Christmas tree flicked like coloured fingers snapping in the room beyond and Jack struck the first notes on the piano.

"We'll start off with 'Hark the Herald Angels Sing'," they heard him say.

"I feel I might have been a real — I don't know — a real burden this Christmas," Emma said, without turning around to look at the door.

"On the contrary, Emma — you've been more help than almost anyone else," Naomi said. "Don't start worrying at this stage."

"I didn't mean that," Emma began. "You know I don't, Naomi . . ."

Naomi looked beyond her to Anthony in the doorway. "Emma dear, you're not the only one who needs to stand in a state of grace with the past," she said. "I do, too, I truly do, and it helps me having you here — helps Jack as well, much more than he knows. He's a bit inclined to fall in love with his own troubles. Given time, putting the rough edges together, everything will heal over, and there won't even be much of a scar. He's starting to play the piano, so get out and sing. Anthony will help me."

Emma wheeled around, noticing Anthony at last in a startled way.

"Gosh, I didn't hear you come in," she said, rather foolishly. "I was filled up with my own thoughts. Did you want to see Naomi?"

"You can leave us alone together quite safely," Anthony told her gravely.

"The fact is we're having an affair, and you'll be in the way," Naomi said. "Off you go."

Anthony came into the kitchen as Emma went out. He looked after her doubtfully.

"Did I interrupt some private talk?" he asked.

"An old, continuing one," Naomi replied. "A serial! I'd rather hear something new with a snappy plot."

There was a sigh and the window trembled as the wind ran a hand lightly along the side of the house. Naomi bent forward over the sink, not to begin the dishes, but to peer out and up. "It certainly brings the clouds, this wind. We might have a grey Christmas."

"And I've brought you your Christmas present,"

Anthony said, holding out his parcel. Naomi, turning from the window, looked at it in surprise.

"We always open them on Christmas morning," she said. "Or is there some reason that . . ."

"I did put it on the Christmas tree," he said, "but I think it might be better if you opened it now. In a way — not an ominous way — I'm here under false pretenses. It's just too embarrassing to put up with it any longer."

As he spoke, he pulled out a chair for her so that she could sit down at her own kitchen table, and then, turning away, he began scraping dishes into a bucket and throwing screwed-up paper plates and table napkins into a large rubbish bag. "It all looks so sordid, all the ham fat, bones, limp lettuce and stuff," Naomi said, glancing anxiously at the counter. "You don't have to do that. You're a visitor."

He said nothing, but went on tidying, and she unwrapped her small parcel. A plastic envelope held a small limp book — not even a real book — simply a few yellowing pages, folded over one another, given a look of pathos by the faded ribbon threaded along the fold, binding the pages together. The handwritten words were round and childish and so faded as to be nearly illegible. However, there was a feeling of difficult precision about them. It was easy to imagine a child trying very hard to get something right. *"The Goddess of Wisdom and the Boy Enchanter."* Naomi read the title. Her mouth opened in astonishment. "Where did you get this?" she asked.

"It was given to my sisters," Anthony said. "Well, to all of us, originally. I was to donate it to your museum. One of them wrote to you about it. We're Minerva's great-grandchildren."

Naomi's inquiring smile vanished abruptly. She turned a severe look on the folded pages.

"You're free to give it to your museum, if that's what you want to do," he told her. "But I'd rather it stayed here for a while."

"*You're* the one whom we heard was coming," Naomi suddenly declared. "Why didn't you *say* so?" She looked at the door. Beyond it they could hear a carol being sung cheerfully, though not very musically. Jack stopped playing the piano, protesting at the different keys people were choosing to sing in, and struck a firm note to guide them.

"That's not all . . ." Anthony said. He placed a second little book beside the first. "I've practised felony. When I came out this morning into the hall this book was on the stand beside the sewing basket. I stole it because I — well, I recognized the authorship and the characters. I thought it might be a sequel." The book was both pathetic and powerful there on the kitchen table.

"Is it?" Naomi asked gingerly, turning the first stained and faded page. "*Seven Ways to Outwit the Black King. Advice to Mortals by the Goddess of Wisdom and the Boy Enchanter.*"

"It's an earlier one," he said. "They are stories written secretly by two children cut off from other children, frightened of their father inventing mythological lives for themselves."

"The Goddess of Wisdom," Naomi said, "and the Boy Enchanter!"

"The Black King was Edward," explained Anthony.

245

Naomi sighed. "Before I get too confused," she said, putting the stories side by side on the table, "you'd better begin at the beginning."

Anthony was silent.

"I'm listening," she prompted him rather sharply.

"But what is the beginning?" Anthony asked. "I'm not sure myself. I descend from Minerva Carnival through the female line, you might say. I've got many Hesketh relations in England, but because we're rather a matriarchal family I've always known about Carnival's Hide. I knew Minerva. I can tell you all about her. She's a whole story in herself. However, the situation was this — my mother worked, and we children were looked after, when school was over, by our grandmother who also looked after her old mother — Minerva. Minny, we used to call her. She'd have milk and cookies with us, play cards with us. She often told us stories about Carnival's Hide and her childhood long ago with a brother and a stern father who wouldn't let them go to school. She told me all about the garden . . ." Involuntarily he glanced at the wall of the kitchen as if he might see the straggling woody lavender bushes beyond it. "I heard about King Trowley and Lord Rake-Rake. I heard about Suriel. Of course I heard a little about Teddy."

Naomi looked towards the sitting room door again. "Who are *they*?" she asked in a low voice.

"It seems to me," Anthony said, "that Minerva, being older and probably upset by the changes following her mother's death, was rather hard on Teddy. She thought so anyway. It seemed to bother her in old age. However, as children they were also very dependent on one another. They invented this land of garden tools and turned dreams of over-throwing their father and running off together into stories like this. Suriel *is* an angel's name you know. I've looked it up. It's the name of the benevolent angel of death."

"Good heavens!" Naomi looked startled. "I thought it was another, *hey presto!*"

"Minerva was very restless when I knew her," said Anthony. "Towards the end, she found it hard to be comfortable. She would wander from room to room, talking as if her father, even her mother, were still alive. However, she never once talked about Teddy as if *he* were alive. 'He died!' she'd say. 'He went too far and he was struck down.' She never once said he drowned. I somehow formed the impression that, when he was about twelve or thir-teen, Teddy got too much for her. 'He said he was going to work by instinct, not thought,' she told me."

"You remember all this very well," Naomi commented.

"I heard most of it over and over again," Anthony pointed out. "It was like a fairytale from another country, magical but true, too, because there she was telling me about Teddy 'letting his dog loose', as she called it. They were starting to meet people in those days, do a little social calling, entertaining visitors. She said Teddy was clever at manipulating people ('moving the puppets,' she called it)."

There was a sudden distressed jangle of notes from the piano. A chair was pushed back and the door opened.

"Naomi — " Jack said, coming into the room. "Do

come and lead the singing. I've never struck such a tuneless collection in my life. Ovid and Hadfield don't seem to know either the words or the music, Emma does her best but she sounds like a penny whistle, and Christobel hasn't ever been able to sing in tune. As for Serena, she's bellowing in my ear with such feeling it really puts me off. Forget the tidying up — not that you seem to be doing much," he added, looking at them leaning across the table towards one another, linked by secrets. "Emma says you're having an affair with Anthony and it looks as if she's right."

"She is," Naomi agreed. "Off you go and play 'Jingle Bells'. Everyone knows that."

"Oh, come on!" Jack said. "It's Christmas! I'm missing you."

"I won't be a moment," Naomi said optimistically. She turned to Anthony as Jack obediently left the room and said, "They must be Carnivals — they know the family folklore — but not from your family apparently."

"No," Anthony agreed. "I have a number of far-flung cousins, and I certainly don't know them all. I've got uncles in Canada and an aunt in Australia. However, and this is the end of *my* story of Carnival's Hide, when Minerva was very old, shortly before she died, I was sitting by her bed (I'd been reading to her, something we did from time to time), and she suddenly put her old, wrinkly hand on mine and whispered, 'He killed him, you know. My father killed Teddy.' "

"What?" Naomi exclaimed, clapping her hands to her cheeks and staring at him rather wildly.

"I can only repeat what she said." Anthony

looked defensive. "I said 'What?' probably just as you did, and she said, 'I don't want to go without telling someone. Someone ought to be told, now that it doesn't matter.' She used to wander a bit, but her voice was quite clear — matter of fact."

"What did *you* say?" asked Naomi.

"Nothing much," Anthony replied. "I was probably quite confused. Then she said, 'It was a self-defence. Teddy would have torn him to bits. He had got so strong and so furious.' According to Minny, Edward struck Teddy with the spade — the executioner of their childish games. She ran through the kitchen door — *that* door — shut it behind her, and never saw Teddy again."

A silence descended on the kitchen that seemed as if it might not be broken, for it lasted a whole minute. It was not an empty silence. Naomi looked at Anthony, then back to her Christmas present, and then stared around the kitchen as if reassuring herself that it had not gone back to an earlier state. Outside, they heard the wind rise again and give a huge melancholy sigh that so encompassed the house it was like a vibration from wood and iron, even from the electrical flowers of the Christmas tree.

"You seriously maintain that Edward murdered Teddy?" Naomi said at last.

"No — how can I? What I heard was just a story told by a very old woman who often got things wrong," Anthony said. "All the same, many of the things the Carnival brothers have said have had overtones of Minny's story. She grew apart from Teddy as you know, because, though they were close as children, he turned into a very — well, a tormented and tormenting young man, from all accounts. That matches up with what you told me, doesn't it? And besides, she was furious as they grew up when he was ultimately granted liberties that were denied to her."

"So there's no proof," Naomi persisted. "You could be making it all up."

"Why should I?" Anthony asked, looking astounded. "It's an old story, as far as I'm concerned. There's no one left to praise or blame. Although being here in the house has made it come alive again for me — more than I imagined it would. But I don't even suggest that you believe it, if you don't want to. It's just family gossip."

"She didn't say anything you could check up on," Naomi said.

"If she did, I don't remember," Anthony replied. "I wasn't thinking of it as history. After a moment she began to talk about her dinner and then suddenly she said, 'Teddy forced our father to kill him, although my father loved him best and meant well. That was Teddy's triumph.' "

Naomi rose and began pacing up and down the kitchen. She opened the kitchen door and looked out into the night. The kitchen was filled with the sound of the sea. "You believe it, don't you?" she said restlessly.

"I suppose we always believe a story the way we hear it the first time," Anthony said. "I've always imagined that for most of her life she wanted to protect her father because — well — he *was* her father — but there, right at the end, she had to let someone know. She died about a week later, and as far as I can tell she never said a word to anyone else. Perhaps she picked me because I look a little bit like Edward — or so they tell me — or perhaps I just happened to be there when the moment came."

"So you don't know anything about Ovid and Hadfield and Felix?" she asked again.

"I could almost believe they're ghosts," he said lightly. "I don't know anything about them except that, when I spoke to them down there on the beach, I heard myself using the same intonations old Minny used to use. She had a very imperious style. 'That's *quite* enough!' she used to say, and we'd all take notice. I didn't plan it exactly, but I thought it had a remarkable effect."

Coming back to the table, turning over the frail pages, Naomi studied the little books, looking sadder and sadder. "Poor children!" she said at last. "I wonder if Harry is still out there with Felix."

"Felix seems pleasant enough," Anthony replied, watching her put the books together and wrap them very carefully in the Christmas paper. "They may all be. I don't want you to think that they were the Carnivals who wrote to your museum, however. Besides, I've really blown my cover, speaking to them as I did. Better for you to hear my story from me than in hints from others."

"Much better," Naomi agreed. "But I haven't heard your story — not all of it. Why didn't you mention who you were before? It's not natural to be so secretive."

"It's all very humiliating for me," Anthony said, without looking particularly humiliated, however. "In a few words, until earlier this year I was engaged to the daughter of my mother's best friend, and then we decided — no — *I* decided that it wouldn't work out. The broken engagement caused so much bad feeling, particularly between my mother and myself that I decided now was the time to leave home in real earnest."

"You ran away," Naomi said.

"I certainly wanted to make it harder for my mother to get in touch with me," Anthony replied. "God alone knows I felt all the guilt she could have wished. Anyhow, I applied for the fellowship, though I was completely taken aback when I got it — I was a late applicant, for one thing. So I came out here, quite enchanted with the prospect of anonymity. But, though I enjoyed being unknown, I did want to see Carnival's Hide, so I used the forestry angle to get in touch with people who knew about Edward Carnival."

"I see," Naomi said doubtfully. "I suppose that's understandable."

"Then, all of a sudden, it was too late to start saying, 'Oh, by the way, I forgot to mention it but Edward Carnival was my great-great grandfather,' " Anthony continued. "And then Jack invited me to stay. Talk about holidaying among my own myths. Because to you, it's Teddy's home, but to me it's Minerva's, and it is a fairytale — a real fairytale — peopled with monsters, as well as fairy godmothers. In the end, I thought I'd get over it all by making you a Christmas present of the little book. I didn't anticipate that the other one would appear."

Naomi sighed deeply. "I feel very mixed up over them — the ones out there. I've had reason to feel doubtful about them more than once today." She paced up to the kitchen counter, wheeled around and paced back again.

"We've had funny people staying here over the years," she said at last, "because Charlie and Christobel have had a very mixed bag of friends, but Ovid and Hadfield — Anthony, I don't want to go into any more stories, but I've got an idea they — they've caught on to something personal — something I'd rather keep a secret for just a little longer. It seems to me they threatened us this morning. Well, what I'm getting at is this. I don't want any fuss until *after* Christmas — not even then, if I can avoid it. Besides, I believe — I've always believed — there is something healing in sharing the season. I want us all to share it as warmly as we can. Would you think it very cowardly of me if I just let things be for a couple of days? After all, I accepted the Carnivals very easily, didn't I?"

"It's none of my business, really," Anthony said, "provided things are understood between you and me and I don't feel as if I'm abusing you in any way. However . . ."

"Yes?" Naomi turned back from the window.

"Well, I think your other guests out there have got problems within their own ranks. I hope they keep it to themselves — that's all."

"Oh dear," Naomi said. "Ovid is the sort of person who likes a — a *large* effect, I think, don't you?"

"Very much so," Anthony agreed. "He's what he says he is. He's a showman, and when he's got nothing to show, he forces something to show itself."

"I think we might leave the dishes, after all," Naomi said, studying the counter. "You've done a good job of rinsing and stacking everything, I must say. It wouldn't even be too piggy to go off and leave them like that overnight — because there's almost too much to think about in what you said — and we've been in here for ages — but thanks for telling me, anyway. And I hope we won't have to organize a search-party for Harry. It's the first time she's ever really taken a fancy to a boy — and I think it feels very serious to her."

"On the other hand, I think she's on her guard against the Carnival brothers." Anthony stood up. "More than anyone else, though I can't for the life of me think why."

"Well — shall we leave real life in the kitchen and go out into the haunted house and sing with the ghosts?" Naomi stopped and listened. "I'm not sure," she said at last. "The singing seems to have stopped, doesn't it? It's gone very quiet. No — I can hear Christobel talking. Trust her."

She went to the door and opened it on to a room where all lights but those on the Christmas tree had been turned out. Candles had been lit and set in pottery candlesticks. Curled up in a large chair, Christobel read aloud by this soft uneven glow.

"They fell together on to the quilt of fallen blossoms as if on to a bed of silver and ivory. 'Now you will be mine,' said Belen. 'You can't escape. In the end you will beg me to possess you.'"

"Gosh," said Serena's voice, somewhere in the shadows.

"No one ever talks like that," Christobel said. "Don't you dare be impressed by it. It's dreadful!"

Naomi stood and Anthony moved carefully into the dim room looking for an unoccupied chair.

"Ma!" cried Christobel looking up as Naomi came

in. Her face glowed in the candlelight, so that once again she resembled a nativity angel on an old Christmas card. "Look at this ancient old book Hadfield found down in the whare — up in the whare roof you said?" She looked towards Hadfield, dim and bulky, at the edge of the room, who inclined his head. "It's covered in cobwebs and soot. But it can't be all that old. We can't work out who could have left it there. It's very, very romantic."

"Perhaps it was left behind by Teddy Carnival himself," Naomi said lightly, and felt a shift in the room, a refocusing of attention, rather like the physical drag of an intensified gravity.

"Well, Christmas is a time when dumb beasts talk," said Ovid, "and maybe that goes for all sorts of ghosts, too. They have to speak."

". . . and hidden stories float up, determined to be revealed at last," Hadfield agreed. They both sat back from the light of the candles like an audience watching a play.

"It's a year or two since we actually had anyone staying in the whare," Jack remarked, "but I suppose we might have had a tenant or two we don't know anything about. I mean, it's there, right on the shoreline. Anyone might sail in and spend the night without us knowing about it."

Christobel gave a hoot.

"Listen to this bit," she said. *"Her hair flowed over her naked shoulders like black wine. Her mouth was bruised and swollen with the violence of his kisses.* There's whole pages of it. Go and sit down, Ma, and we'll have a Christmas reading from a turbulent book."

"I shall enjoy that," Ovid said out of the shadows,

"and so will Hadfield. I feel quite at home with the characters already."

"They're all jerks," Charlie said, yawning.

"Oh no, I think they're charming," Ovid said. "I think Prince Valery is particularly attractive. Go on reading, Christo."

21
The True Carnival Magician

"We'll have to go down again and face whatever music they happen to be playing there," Felix told Harry.

They both looked down through the dusk of Christmas Eve in the direction of Carnival's Hide.

"I wouldn't have thought your brothers would have let you go in the first place," Harry said. They sat together in a hollow at the very crest of the hill behind Carnival's Hide, surrounded by the ruin of a flowery season grown luminous in the dusk under a brief, eerie, reflected shine. Harry picked up her clothes and looked at them in surprise, for she felt they belonged to some other, earlier girl and that the nor-west wind and later sunshine were all she would ever wear again.

But the sun had given up its long rule, and left its high places. The wind had turned to the east. Clouds were creeping in, and behind Harry and Felix the hills were capped in mist, the upward flow of the land cut short by greyness that was less a veil than a pillow held down over the breathing face of the land.

"We've been as rich in time as anyone ever is," Felix said. He had gathered a little knot of wild flowers that had lain on her breast. Now he occupied their last moments as lovers with picking the grass stems out from among them and plaiting them together.

"Felix," Harry said, partly because she wanted to speak his name aloud, but the pause turned into the beginning of a question.

"Hello — yes?"

"Are you — are you really Teddy Carnival?"

"Part of him," Felix answered. "The best part," he added with a smile.

"Have I made love with a ghost?"

Felix smiled.

"It's what writers do, isn't it?" he said. "Make love with ghosts." Now he took her hand and put a plaited green ring on her finger.

"It won't stand up in a court of law," Harry said, peering at it in the deep twilight, smiling and touching the ring gingerly in case it suddenly unwound or disappeared.

"Married by grass, witnessed by clouds and stones, I don't see why it shouldn't stand up," Felix said, turning away.

But Harry touched his shoulder saying imperiously, "Let me look at you," and he turned back again, smiling, but reluctant, too, so that she could push his hair away and see a face altered in so many ways from the one he had worn when he came into the living room at Carnival's Hide that first morning. Felix had taken over Belen, and the features that Harry had invented, putting words on to blank paper, were now animated by a kinder spirit and by a passion where confidence and doubt were at odds with one another. Nor was this the only contradiction. Felix looked solid and strong, but Harry also thought he looked as if in some peculiar way he were dying.

"It's just a game," Harry argued, a little stiffly. "But which of us is playing the game? Teddy Carnival's dead. How can you stay?"

"It's never enough — time, I mean," Felix said, not answering, "and yet it feels enough to fix me for ever. One transfixing hour — perhaps you've made me immortal after all."

"A game!" Harry persisted, standing up boldly and facing the sea.

Felix stood up beside her.

"No," he said reflectively. "No, I love you. It doesn't change *much*, but it changes *me* at least. Suppose you've got money (which I don't have), you must have a time when you think of all the things you can spend it on — a paint box, a dress, a — I don't know . . ."

"A book!" said Harry.

"Of course. A book, or a goldfish, or a flower in a pot. And then you make up your mind, and you spend it, and all the money's gone, and all the possibilities are gone too except for that one thing. Well, I feel as if I've spent my savings, and now I'm poor except for the thing I chose."

"Not very sensible to spend it on something you can't take out of the country," said Harry. To be in love was supposed to make lovers happy, but Harry could not recognize ordinary happiness in her feelings, unless an achieved mystery at the heart of her life should turn out to be happiness after all. A profound secret had begun to yield to her.

"Wait a moment," said Felix, as she began to put on her shirt. "Your turn to be looked at!" He stared at her so intently and strangely she grew shy and still, for all he could take away with him was memory. Besides, she thought he could barely see her in this light, but he touched her shoulder where the grass had imprinted a pattern of disordered, crimson lace, and she thought that what he would remember of her was this rubric that the grass had scribbled on her skin, and that would have to stand for everything. And then she wondered if spirits such as he could have memories, or if everything would dissolve with the temporary bodies they had wrung out of a world that no longer had a place for them.

Down below she could see Carnival's Hide bloom with light. Beneath the roof, if she had had the power to look through the gathering darkness and then through iron, she would have seen her own bed, the empty boxes waiting to be filled again with the Christmas decorations, and her hidden book in whose unfinished pages Belen and Lady Jessica had come to a standstill. Unlike Harry and Felix, the winged man and the girl in rose-pink silk would never move on. The house looked so far below, it was easy for Harry to imagine that she would arrive back and find herself grey and wrinkled, old age fallen over her out of the air, as if she had spent a perilous hour in fairyland making love to a ghost who needed love, returning pregnant with phantoms.

At last they began to climb down, scrambling from one stone to another, from one tussock to the next. As they went, the sorrel, the dock, the last foxgloves lost their faint luminosity and became, if anything, blacker than the grass and stones.

"Well, there we were, Minerva and I," Felix said reflectively, "and Edward. Our father! The widower. Edward was too sensible not to know he'd been widowed by nothing but a reasonably common happening. Yet really he *did* believe in his heart that he'd been punished for passion. He thought it was his fault — the fault of human appetite that our mother had died in childbirth. He felt such guilt it made him believe that he was at fault for loving, and in a way he punished himself through us, though he didn't understand what he was doing. He was easier on Minerva. But we came to exist all split up in Teddy. I was the sickly one in those days. No one ever dreamed of me, though they knew Ovid — and Hadfield sometimes. My father could encourage Ovid and countenance Hadfield, but he couldn't stand it when I showed. I hid all the time. I think in the end we all wanted to have revenge on him, Ovid and Hadfield most passionately, for it's my job to make allowances and show compassion and inform them, but, with me so weak, they could scarcely support their own existences. I mean we lived without joy."

Harry felt the grasses blowing against her ankles, licking her skin with silky green tongues.

"Does it matter?" she asked. "Isn't it over?"

"Of course it matters," he said, "that's why we came back — to finish it — finish ourselves. Ovid and Hadfield mocked Edward and taunted him over his wife's death, out there in the garden where the old gooseberry bushes have gone wild. Hadfield would have fallen on him, but Edward lifted the spade — the one Minerva had christened Suriel after the benevolent angel of death — and he hit Teddy and killed him — killed us all. And then his sufferings really began, which was what Ovid wanted, I suppose . . . to bring him face to face with his despair by closing the circle. He'd hoped to make a perfect man, but ended by killing his creation."

Felix helped her to climb the five-bar gate and she let him help her, although she could easily climb it herself and had often done so. "We didn't know it, but apparently Minerva saw what happened and must have left some sort of a record. That's what Anthony meant, down on the beach."

"Anthony?" Harry asked.

"I'd say he was some sort of great-nephew of Teddy's," Felix said, "though all those old connections are dissolved." His voice grew dreamy. "Because I dissolved. We all dissolved. Edward undressed Teddy and forced him into his swimming suit and slipped him into the sea, sweating with horror at himself, and Teddy drifted — I drifted — and turned gently in the tide, and slowly sank — because Edward had weighed him down. And in due course he came to pieces, but I could never — I couldn't dissolve . . ." Felix said. "I'm sorry to be so confused — so confusing. We were tied to that strip of beach, struggling between each other, head, heart and that instinct." He was talking to himself, not to her. "Then this year, all the things came right — first, the invocation, and perhaps there was a feeling of Minerva in the air too, and the time of year was right, and there was a vehicle — you." He looked sideways at her. "He tried to come back all of a piece, but you pushed him out, you filled your head with images connected with Teddy, but *not* Teddy, as it were. We were caught up in your storybook people, but it didn't matter. It suited us all to argue as separate men, rather than struggle as one. And in a way it set me free, to make my bid for power, to grow strong."

And now, as they crossed the winding road for a second time and the boards in the walls of Carnival's Hide became distinguishable through branches and leaves, a strange realization came to Harry.

Time was too much a part of love, for even in fairytales the proof of love was not its first moment, but its latest ones — that people lived happily ever after. Love at first sight was nothing but infatuation until proved by time, and time was what Felix and Harry didn't have.

Felix turned his head and spoke.

"Even if we had a hundred years, if we were happy it would end too soon," he said. "A hundred years, a hundred minutes — it still goes too fast." He had been thinking the same thoughts that she had.

"I love you," Harry said.

"No — " he said. "Perhaps you love what's lovable in a divided man. But I love you and that might be enough to . . ." He broke off. "It might be enough," he said, and left it at that.

They could hear family voices laughing in the living room. They were back at Carnival's Hide and there was no time left. Their stolen time had shrunk from hours, to minutes, to seconds and now to fractions of a second. Each half second between staying and going seemed as if it must have eternity hidden in it, but it went by, mercilessly.

"It's not possible," Harry said and heard in the room behind her Ovid's leisurely voice. She could not hear the words, only the familiar smoky accent of his voice. She looked relieved, but Felix became suddenly guarded.

"Oh glory!" he murmured. "Harry, we're nothing but tricksters. I'll never become a true angel. Oh, well, whatever's going on, the worst has probably happened."

They walked together into the hall, the jungle of Carnival's Hide, and then paused.

The living-room door was a little open, and the easterly wind pushed past them to open it further still, coming from behind them, chilly, even slightly damp. The whole family, except for Tibby, who was probably in bed asleep, was sitting around the Christmas tree. Harry had the curious feeling that its arms were upheld, not in benediction or peace, but in a sudden start of horror. Its lights had become lights of warning.

Christobel was reading a story in a room lit by Christmas lights and candles. Like Jack she was a good reader and chose to read, on this occasion, in the arch voice of a proper person trying to tell a dirty story and not getting it quite right, so that people were laughing at her voice as much as at the events of the tale. Charlie, idly exercising for sailing in a corner of the room, barely seemed to notice the story, but Serena listened seriously, her mouth hanging open, while beside her, Emma and Naomi both folded Tibby's nappies in from the line, a little stiff with wind and sun. Jack listened carefully, smiling in the candlelight and sweeping up a little pile of pine needles, threads, and crumbs. He made his dustpile with the slow craftsmanship of someone who sweeps floors only rarely and is rather fascinated by what a mere floor has to tell about the lives of the people who walk over it. He had thoughtfully arranged a red-handled pan and broom so that he could pick up his completed dustpile and carry it away.

"*Belen snarled like a wolf,*" Christobel read, with dreadful primness. "*Her heart grew faint at the expression in his eyes but she could not look away. In vain she tried to cover herself with her flowing hair.*"

"Not much good against a bloke who could see through — what was it? — pink silk," commented Robert, watching Emma fold harmoniously, like someone arranging flowers.

"Listen to the next bit!" commanded Christobel. "*The silver streaks in his hair flashed a signal she could not resist. She lost the power to think clearly.*"

"Moo!" breathed Serena heavily, her eyes round with enthusiasm.

"A flasher, too!" Charlie groaned from the stool where, a little apart from everyone else he was strengthening his stomach muscles. His feet were hooked under the sofa so that he could lean slowly back holding himself at an angle corresponding to the one he must hold if, for some reason, he had to balance a bending sail by hanging out over the side of *Sunburst*. "It isn't 'moo', Serena, it's 'grunt', very 'grunt'. Hadfield should apologize for inflicting it on us."

"I didn't write it — I merely found it," Hadfield replied. He and Ovid, sitting close to the door, had watched Harry and Felix come in, Ovid with a dreamy smile, Hadfield with malice that slowly changed to wariness as Felix moved into the light.

"It isn't 'grunt'," argued Serena, "because it's got true bits in it. Hadfield's got hair just like that, hasn't he?"

Naomi shot a puzzled and faintly troubled look at Hadfield's hair. "If it comes to that, all the descriptions of the wicked, black angel match up with you, Hadfield," she said. "Confess! You did write it yourself, didn't you? You're having us on."

"Not guilty," said Hadfield. "No, I'm not a writer, though Felix used to write in the past."

"I wrote!" Ovid exclaimed, turning angrily on Hadfield. "I was the one."

"You used Felix's ideas," Hadfield replied, without interest or condemnation.

"It's too mature for Benny and Tibby to listen to," said Serena with satisfaction.

"It isn't," Benny exclaimed. "I know about sexy things."

Christobel, seeing Ovid and Hadfield staring at the doorway, turned.

"Hello there, Harry — and Felix, too," she cried with great good humour. "You've arrived just in time to hear the end of a remarkably dreadful book, written by someone who's devoted their life to good works and square dancing at the Y.M.C.A. and is secretly longing to be raped by a winged stallion."

"A winged stallion, fancy!" marvelled Hadfield,

266

grinning derisively at Felix, standing in the doorway.

Harry wished she could die. She did not want to think or feel another thing. All she wanted was to break into dust, be swept up into the red-handled pan and emptied mercifully away. Every single thing the day had held for her — the Christmas of family and friends that had tied her back into her childhood, Felix calling out to her, "I'm your family," his kisses, his love-making on the hillside which seemed to her beautiful and thrilling, but at times unbearably sad — all these happenings, loaded with mingled joy and dread, shrivelled and blistered back into the stilted image of her own story through which she had tried to reach ahead of herself, using words like oracles to wring amazement out of the reluctant world. But Christobel had turned on spotlights, and Harry had woken out of a dream to find she was performing before an audience which was laughing at her.

"Winged stallion? Who wouldn't love to be that? But not everyone can, can they?" said Felix beside her, nodding at Hadfield and Ovid.

From behind the table Anthony slowly stood up, like a man anticipating trouble, staring at Harry's rigid face.

"Perhaps . . ." he began, speaking into a suddenly silent room.

"Perhaps Harry's read it already!" Ovid observed quickly. "It was in her attic."

Jack turned. "You said it was in the whare!" he cried.

"Did I?" Ovid snapped his fingers, miming irritability. "Silly me. I meant the attic."

"It was covered in dust," Hadfield said. "It had been hidden away for a hundred years. I found it when you sent me up to get a box of rubbish."

Harry faced him boldly. She had been ashamed of her book, but it was still hers, and she had hidden it to protect it from the very humiliation it was now suffering.

"Here!" exclaimed Naomi sharply, suddenly standing up, too. "Let me see that book!"

"*I* wrote it!" Harry said quickly, coming farther into the room. "Didn't you recognize my handwriting, Christo?" She didn't dare look into any faces, but burned before them like a witch at the stake.

"Well, Harry . . ." Jack began, looking horribly shocked, but Christobel spoke over him. She had been enjoying reading and making people laugh, and, though she was often prepared to acknowledge guilt, she could not bear to have it forced on her.

"God, how could you write such stuff!" she cried angrily. "Of course I'd never ever insult you by thinking you wrote it."

"Just give it to me!" Harry cried back, in a high, harsh voice. She wanted to fling herself on Christobel and hit her with her fists, but instead she simply snatched the book away. Christobel, who surrendered it without a struggle, looked intensely irritated.

"Well, how was I to know?"

"That's right — how *could* you know?" Harry said, hearing her own unnatural voice mock Christobel and then begin to tear apart. "You don't know anything about me. No one in the whole bloody family knows anything about me, but I know all about you." She struggled to hold her voice steady, but it began to rasp, and her head and her heart split; a thousand bitter memories crowded out through the rents, longing to be set free. She became both Pandora and the box of troubles, remembering her birthday parties when Christobel just couldn't help seeming like the true birthday girl, remembering days when Christobel had forced her into spending her saved-up money on things Christobel wanted and she didn't. She saw the table at home in front of the fireplace, spread across with Christobel's homework so that there was not one little corner for her own, and no time for Naomi to help her work out a heading or check her punctuation. She thought of the time when it had suddenly seemed to her that Naomi's attention had jumped straight from Christobel to Benny with his bronchitis and occasional attacks of asthma. It was not that Naomi or Jack loved her less, but love was sometimes limited in what it could do, and it could not quite make things fair in a family where some people not only wanted but needed so much more than others. Now Harry wanted to scream at them and pour out all this old, sad, forgotten rubbish, making her pain less by spreading it out through everyone else. Ovid watched her, alert and smiling — remorseless.

"It's terrible, drippy, purple stuff!" Christobel declared in a measured voice. "Nothing can change that, even knowing who wrote it."

"Art is art," said Ovid, "and bad art is bad art."

"Christobel — stop it," cried Naomi ignoring him. "This isn't fair."

But Christobel wanted to make Harry agree publicly that her story deserved ridicule. "Come on —

admit it! You've always had your nose stuck in a book, so you must have learned something about writing."

Harry, at the foot of her ladder, turned, as if an invisible master had taken her shoulders and spun her round. Even without a mirror before her, she knew she was wearing her enchantress face. She could see it, as if she had caught fire and was reflecting a hot light on all the other family faces turned towards her. She let her book fall heedlessly.

"You don't know anything about me!" she cried, speaking through Christobel to all of them. "All you ever think of is yourself. You're so used to seeing your own face in the sun, the moon — on every single star — that you never once wonder why it's on Tibby, for example. You just think everyone ought to look the way you look and be the way you are, and if they don't it's their fault. You don't recognize me. No wonder! You don't recognize yourself."

"Tibby!" cried Christobel. "What's Tibby got to do with it?"

"You're *so* stupid!" screamed Harry.

As she spoke, she saw Ovid, beaming and nodding at her, and knew she had done what he had intended all along, and also, from the enormous relief that accompanied her dismay, that she had always wanted to be the one to tell Christobel this secret, and now it was told.

Naomi, Jack and Charlie all spoke at once and then all stopped to make way for one another, just as if they were doing a crowd scene they had rehearsed many times. Emma sitting quietly in her corner, gaped in horror, and was dyed with a blush that did not creep over her but struck her like an instantaneous rash, so that even the hands she put up to her face were red with shame. Jack presented arms with the broom, like a soldier who knows he will be forced to defend himself.

"Charlie?" asked Christobel, half turning, but then, without a pause, in the very same breath, she cried out, "Oh no! Oh, that's too horrible! Not Jack, Ma, not Jack!"

"Christobel," said Jack and repeated her name in a curious rough voice. He sounded ashamed; he sounded defiant; he sounded miserably triumphant. His words came in little rushes. "Christo — I wish Harry hadn't — but she did — and — Christo, Tibby *is* mine — no, not mine, but I *am* her father. It's old news by now."

Christobel threw her arms over her head as if fire were descending from heaven.

"Ma!" whispered Serena's voice. "Ma — is Jack Tibby's father?" but no one heard her. Naomi put her arms around Christobel, just as if she would turn herself into a place Christobel could hide in, while Robert, in a curious counterpoint, rose and sat firmly down by Emma. Christobel was aware of this movement and turned towards it.

"You bitch!" she screamed at Emma, while Charlie, trying to disentangle his feet from under the settee, began shouting, "It was three years ago — three years ago. It's over!" causing Jack, still clasping his broom and looking terrified, to turn to him in surprise, and then everyone except Harry, trembling at the eye of the storm, spoke at once.

"It isn't the end of the world!" Naomi was insisting, and hers became the first distinguishable voice. "The worst is over for us all. It isn't so bad."

But Christobel turned her face to the ceiling and began to scream short, thin cries, one after the other, slashing the air with bright razors of sound.

"Is Tibby my little sister?" cried Serena again, panic-stricken, but so much else was going on that only Felix heard her, put out his hand and took hers. She clung to him, as if she had been drowning and he had offered her recognizable help.

"I knew she was," Benny said, but no one, not even Felix, heard Benny.

"Christobel," said Anthony. His voice was not loud but commanding enough to be heard above all others. "Come on! Be wonderful!" and for some reason this made her stop and gasp, as if she too had found a hand held out to her in deep water.

"Listen a moment," cried Naomi. She spoke with great urgency and concentration and a bewildering eagerness, as if a long-awaited chance had been offered her. Her words almost sounded rehearsed. "I know you won't believe this straight away, but, Christo — it isn't so bad. None of us thought we would get through as well as we have. It isn't so bad. It really isn't so bad," she repeated as if repetition alone would force Christobel to believe what she was being told. "We may even — if we learn to understand, that is — we may even be made richer — our lives may become better, in ways we could never ever guess at — " But her voice was stumbling under its burden of desperate sincerity. "I meant to tell you after this Christmas, when you'd had a chance to see . . . We have to take the chances that life gives us and — and — "

" — and ice them over — " Jack said, desperately, and actually laughed with despair.

Harry could not look at them, but, beyond Naomi struggling to reach Christobel, stood Felix, holding Serena's hand and letting her half-hide her shocked, round face against him. Harry wondered savagely if he had lured her out of the house so that Hadfield could steal her book and Ovid could use it to strike at her family. As she thought this, she actually spoke her thought aloud, and though her voice was lost among other voices, Felix heard it and now, as if he had been suddenly drenched, his face shone and trickled with a thousand springs of slick dew that sprang out of him. He began to flow like a man brought out of the sea.

"Oh, this is real family life," marvelled Ovid, looking over at Felix, almost as if he hoped for agreement. "I recognize this quality." But then he seized Hadfield by the arm. Hadfield exclaimed softly, and they rose as one man, edging around the room, almost unnoticed, for Christobel was crying aloud.

"But I can't bear it, Ma, I just can't bear it," and Naomi was saying, "I know things are unbearable, but in spite of that we have to bear them," at which point Ovid and Hadfield, on either side of their white and sweating brother, turned as one man and applauded her enthusiastically, holding their hands high, almost in front of their faces.

"Tremendous!" cried Ovid. "You're all tremendous. Encore."

Both Charlie, untangled at last, and Robert tried to advance around the people in the centre of the floor. Charlie's eyes, as simple and blue as Tibby's, had grown hard and furious. His face, reddened by sun and wind, wore an unfamiliar complexity of expression. Felix pushed Serena gently to one side.

"I'm not going to bear it," Christobel cried violently. "Why the hell should I? I'll hate everyone if I want to." The lights from the tree falling on Felix allowed anyone interested to see the terrible quivering that had seized him, familiar only to Harry, not a mere nervous twitching of the skin or fluttering of the eye but a fluctuation of his entire substance. For fractions of a second he ceased to exist, and though Harry's eye carried him on over these gaps, she could feel that he was no longer continuous, but only an intermittent presence trying to move on in a world where there was nowhere for him to move on.

"It's the kingdom of Too Far," he said to Ovid, "but now we're here, I'm its king, not you. You're nothing but its special-effects man."

And, as he spoke, Hadfield, like an iron man, met the double charge of Robert and Charlie, flicking Charlie back into Robert's arms and sending them both stumbling backwards over one of the chairs. Its back snapped with the sharp sound of a gun firing. Benny wailed as if he had been shot.

Felix, white as death, but *triumphant* death, flung his arms protectively around his brothers, embracing them tightly — one arm over Ovid and one over Hadfield. "Behold how mind and instinct become the servants of the heart," he announced like a showman. "*I* am the true Carnival magician. Hey presto!" and he crumpled like a jigsaw-puzzle man falling apart. His disintegration instantly infected his brothers. They dissolved, they vanished, while Christobel, looking beyond Naomi, saw confusion, fury and inexplicable disappearance, which must have seemed entirely extraneous to her own shock, and, saturated with distress and bewilderment, screamed again.

"Get her out!" Anthony said to Naomi. "Let's get her out through the kitchen door."

"Everything's gone grunt!" Serena wept, Benny crept behind the Christmas tree, and Crumb streaked out from under the couch, leaped up on to the piano in a scrambling jangle, then hissed and puffed out his fur as if suddenly in the presence of deadly enemies. Christobel followed Anthony's guiding hand obediently, but as she moved, she met her father's stunned and guilty stare, stared back at him blankly, then kicked his careful dustpile apart. Anthony and Naomi hustled her out of the room and into the kitchen, where Harry heard her crying.

"She's taken over everything I ever had. I've got nothing left. It's all Emma's now. You're all Emma's. I've got nothing of my own," and then in a last, despairing cry, "Oh Ma! Did everyone know but me?"

"Where have they gone? By God, that was quick!" Charlie yelled, rushing into the hall looking for the vanished brothers. No one except Harry, clutching her book against her once more, believed what they had seen. Yet now quietness fell on them, and they stared at one another as if each of them had woken up in a room full of strangers. However, the old, faded room contained only its usual Christmas people, the same people it was used to, though now shaken up and fallen into different arrangements. The Carnivals had come and gone, leaving no clear evidence of their passage except the alterations in the family they left behind them.

22
Words and Dust

Left to themselves Robert and Emma, Charlie and
Jack, Serena and Harry gave each other unbelieving
glances like survivors rising up from the field after
a murderous battle has swept across it.

"Well, that's the funniest Christmas Eve I've
ever spent," Charlie said, "and that's saying something. Peace on earth and goodwill towards all men,
that's my motto. I suppose Ma and Christobel will
stumble around the hills in the dark, telling each
other this and that, and arguing and crying, and it
might be nice for them to have the place to themselves when they get back."

"But we can't just walk out on Naomi!" Emma
said. "Oh Charlie — I'm so sorry! Charlie, I
don't know what to say — I didn't even realize you
knew . . ."

"I'll stay behind," said Jack. He had automatically begun sweeping his dustpile up again. "You
get out of it, Emmie, because you know what

Christo is. I don't want her coming back and calling you names or taking it out on you."

Harry thought she had never seen him look so sad in his life before.

"But Ma won't need any of us," Charlie argued. "Come on, Jack! It's going to take Christo a while to work her way round to a different idea of everything. How on earth could you think I didn't know? I knew, even before Emma was expecting Tibby. I didn't say anything because — well, I didn't know what to say." He looked rather reprovingly at Harry. "I didn't ever *think* of telling Christo," he added. There was trepidation in his glance, too, as if from now on, dramatic revelations were going to drop continually from Harry's lips like toads and frogs from the lips of a wicked sister. "But don't worry! Ma will fix it up now. It'll be OK given a bit of time."

"Charlie," said Jack heavily. "You astonish me, really you do. I just don't see how it can be put right."

"The trouble is you're so conceited," Charlie said, warmly. "Do you think everything you do is so terrific that the bad things can't be made better?"

"Daddy," said Serena, staring painfully at Jack. "I mean, Jack. Are you Tibby's father?"

Jack looked at her sadly.

"Serena dear, you heard me say so. And call me Daddy," he went on, laughing unhappily and flopping down on the sofa. "I've played Jack with you all for long enough."

"Serena-Serena!" said Charlie, doubling her name into an endearment and patting her on the head. "We've got our health, we've got each other, and I'm going to win the trophy on New Year's Day. God's in his heaven, and all is fairly right with the world. We're OK. We're all right, Jack! Come out from behind the tree, Benny. It's over, and we're OK."

"I think we are, too," Emma said, "but all the same I think I'd better go home." Her voice trembled, but with trouble, not weakness. "Charlie — you're a darling."

"I'll have those words engraved on the trophy when I win it," Charlie said, looking at her thoughtfully. "It might be a good idea if you *did* go home," he added, "because over the next day or two things could be a bit . . ." he waggled his fingers in the air to suggest a delicate balance, ". . . a bit iffy!" he conceded.

"It wasn't Emma's fault," began Jack, but Charlie interrupted him.

"Look — who cares who's fault it was? I don't! Not now. We could argue the rights and wrongs of it until the cows come home. I'll leave it to Christo to thrash all that out with you, because sooner or later she will. It's what to do over the next few hours or the next few days — that's what bothers me. We don't want too much lashing around and screaming and calling names. So why don't we all pack into the station wagon and go and finish Christmas Eve at — at Emma's place, and go home afterwards. It'll still be a family Christmas. The place doesn't matter as much as the people."

"It's so bleak there," Emma objected.

"Who says?" Charlie asked, vaguely patting Benny's shoulder. "I don't expect anyone's hungry, but I'll steal some goodies if there are any left. We'll take Jack's tape-recorder, hug each other at midnight and say Happy Christmas. Go and pack up your baby — go and pack up my *sister*," Charlie said, as Emma hesitated. "Good God, do I have to be the only spirit of good will around? People don't have to sit around picking their sores. You're the ones who are supposed to have imagination — well, not Robert, of course, everyone knows he's dense — but Jack and you, Emma, and old Harry there — so go on. Prove it! Make the jump. Come on, Emma — worry about Christo tomorrow."

"I do need a bit of space at home for a while," said Emma.

"Then I'll come with you," Robert decided, looking around challengingly. "If you don't mind, that is," he added apologetically. "I'll stay over in town so I'll pack, too."

"Oh great!" said Charlie, suddenly frantic. "And who's going to crew for me?"

"I will," Benny cried fervently. "I will, Charlie."

"You're a bit on the light side," Charlie told him. "In a year or two — "

"Get Debbie Tavener," Robert said, grinning unexpectedly. "You make the jump, too." And Charlie sighed and looked thoughtful.

Jack now turned and, unexpectedly, hugged first Emma, then Charlie and Serena. "I've got a better family than I deserve," he said. "Harry, I do wish you hadn't done it — but on the other hand Naomi and I have been dithering over it for so long we might never have got around to it. There might never have been a right time to tell Christo."

Harry couldn't help crying, as she turned to climb her ladder.

"Harry," called Charlie, "come with us. Don't just shut yourself away up there."

Harry turned at the top of her ladder.

"I'd rather stay," she said. "I want to put the pillowcase over my head and not think about anything. I want to burn my book."

"Ah, Mephistopheles!" sighed Jack, as if printed words had the devil in them.

"Oh, no!" cried Serena, distracted. "I thought it was terrific."

Harry thought of Belen ravishing Jessica on flower petals and of the wild feelings locked into lines of handwriting. All to produce a book that Serena thought was terrific. She saw Serena's eyes turned on her with the intense, worshipping stare that was usually reserved for Christobel. She did not know what to say, being unable to explain that it wasn't just the betrayed book that had upset her. Through it, she and Felix had been held up for mockery.

She lay on her stretcher-bed, heard the house move nervously, as Emma packed in her room, and Robert packed out on the porch, and as Jack looked for a pen to write a note for Christobel and Naomi. Harry heard him laugh. "Poor Anthony!" he said. "Promised a typical New Zealand Christmas."

"That's one Englishman that's really had his money's worth," Charlie replied. "As for Ovid Carnival, if I see him again . . ." He broke off. "Isn't Hadfield something, though?" he exclaimed in unwilling admiration. "More like earth-moving machinery than anything human."

A little while later, Harry heard them leaving, shouting out to each other, glad to be on the move.

Having something to do held snapping thoughts at bay.

Harry lay on her stretcher-bed for a while, and snuffled into her pillow, until she began to hear herself sounding like a summer hedgehog looking for the cat's saucer. She sat up. Soon after she went down her ladder into the deserted room where Jack had turned off the Christmas-tree lights. Harry did not turn them on again. They would have to wait until next year. Instead she switched on the main light and looked around the room.

After any party, at the end of every long day of celebration, there is a strange desolation that visits houses, and Harry felt it now. Very slowly she walked around the room, saw a film of dust on Jack's piano, and the Christmas cards on top of the piano with the Christmas music, many of them fallen over, their good wishes spilled. Harry picked one up. "To the Hamiltons," she read, "the best Christmas wishes, from Alan, Judy and family," but the good cheer had run out of the card, which already belonged to a Christmas past. She saw how the points of the tree had drooped, and how the floor and the diminished pile of presents beneath it (for some of them had departed with the departing family) were covered with needles of yellow and brown, and how the virtue had gone out of the green needles still on the branches so that the whole tree looked faded. Its decorations, with no life, no freshness to stand against, had become not true gold and silver, scarlet and blue, but mere tinsel, glitter without depth. Yet something had happened in the house. Harry could feel it, just as she felt the coolness the easterly wind had brought with it. The ghosts had quite gone. Carnival's Hide was no longer a haunted house. It lamented its ghosts, but it had been set free from them and would begin to belong more truly to the Hamiltons than it had ever belonged. Harry's prowling around the room brought her face to face with the bookcase and she looked into it as though into a looking-glass. *Metamorphoses* by Ovid, she read there, *The Book of Love*, edited by John Hadfield, *Felix Holt* by George Eliot. Ovid, Hadfield and Felix already seemed like the names of fabulous beasts. She thought how strange it was that Hadfield, so violent, so amiable, had taken his name from *The Book of Love* and Ovid his from *Metamorphoses*. But though Ovid had helped the metamorphoses along, he hadn't caused them. The changes had been there, planted in their family life, ready to occur in the right season. Harry looked around the room in wonder. Here, on midsummer night, she was sure Emma had confessed to Robert, and maybe Robert had kissed her. Earlier, on the same night, Felix had said, "Let's kiss once and then just be good friends," and three years earlier it was possible that Jack, resplendent in his chef's apron, trying to remember who out of all his guests had their steak rare, had nevertheless been distracted by Emma following Christobel's instructions and keeping an eye on him in case of possible wife-swapping. Perhaps this very room had seen them change from being an almost-father and daughter to being actual lovers.

But now something was concluded. Tormented Edward with his tormented son had been surrendered, their secret told, their knot untied. Harry walked on to the verandah and stared into the darkness of an easterly night — no stars, no moon, low clouds, only the wind occasionally lifting its voice around the house, but almost indistinguishable from the sound of the sea, that persistent and even movement out somewhere in front of her. And now Harry saw something that looked like a swarm of little golden flies leap up swirling into the air. The pattern of their flight told her that they were not real flies, but sparks blown by the wind. Down on the beach, Charlie's fire, lit earlier to burn party rubbish, had come alive again, or perhaps someone had lit another. Either way she knew she should go down and check on it, since it was the season of fire restriction. Notices would probably have gone up that very day, at various points on the road, forbidding barbecues or camp fires, in case a moment's carelessness made the dry land flash up like tinder. Harry stared out into the dark for a moment longer. Then she went into the living room, picked up her book, and walked down to the sea.

The day had offered and taken so much, she felt quite light-headed, and even her anguish over her own actions felt as if it really belonged to somebody else and she was just taking a turn with it. Walking in the dark, Harry wondered if she herself was replacing Teddy as the ghost of the house and half hoped she was. Drifting on down the path, her abused book clasped to her once more, she came face to face as always with the sea and also with the rekindled fire.

Down here, the night was alive with the wash of the waves, each one rearing up, then falling face forward on to the sand, but beyond that the thousand separate voices of the sea made one voice, and it was the sound of time itself, lapping at the edge of the land.

Harry walked past the place where the brothers had fought and kneeled by the rekindled Christmas Eve fire. Without hesitating, she fed it with the first page of her book, then the second, then a complete chapter. The fire ate the paper, burning up brightly and greedily. The ghosts of words appeared momentarily and then vanished for ever; names like grey spells came and went over the charring surfaces. Ovid had wished to blaze, rather than live indistinguishably. Felix and Hadfield blazed with him as Harry burned her book. Yet suddenly her hand grew still. Something in the fire crumpled and fell with a soft ashy sound. Harry looked up over the little spears of flame and found she was not alone.

A man was kneeling on the other side of the fire watching her. Lit from below, his face shifted with shadows, but she could make out his wonderful curls and guess at his honey-brown eyes. He streamed with water as though he were the source of many springs, but he did not seem to be cold. Along his hairline a terrible wound gaped but he did not seem to feel pain. His lips moved slightly, yet Harry could not hear a word. She bent over her book, tore more pages and let them burn until there was only one page left. Then she could not resist looking up once more. He was still there. A slug of blood was crawling down over his cheek. Ovid, Hadfield and Felix looked back at her out of this strange, reflective face. His lips moved again.

"Carne vale!" he was saying soundlessly, smiling at her.

Harry tore out the last page and touched the flame with it, keeping her eyes on him. Suddenly she felt the fire bite her, as the flame ran up to her fingers. She gasped and glanced down letting a piece of the last page fall into the ashes. When she looked up again, he was quite gone.

"Do you love me?" she asked, but of course there was no answer. So she lay back on the sand and looked up at the sky while her last pages crumpled to fine ash. Directly above her, she saw Sirius and Canopus. Orion climbed up to lie above her. The easterly wind lifted the ash beside her and tumbled it off into the night. Some flakes whirled away and were lost in the dark. Some fell to powder. Idly, Harry turned on her side and banged the words that were left with a piece of charred driftwood until they became part of the sand and the sea and air. They could be breathed in like pollen, could fertilize or give hay-fever, make people dream or sneeze.

Harry was left with nothing but the dust of a dishonoured book, a ring of grass and a memory of love that even within a second or two became faltering and inexact, indistinguishable from legend.

I mustn't forget, she thought desperately, but she was already forgetting.

Further down the beach someone came out of the trees, stopped at the sight of her, then moved towards her.

"Harry?" said the questioning voice. "Is that you? We thought you'd gone with the others."

It was Anthony.

"How's Christo?" Harry asked.

"Quieter now!" Anthony replied. "Your mother's

worrying about you. Go up to the house and let her know you're all right."

"But I told," Harry said foolishly.

"She's been wanting to tell Christo herself for a long time," Anthony said. "Always waiting for the moment that never came."

Harry was pleased to take his outstretched hand and walk away from the surge and sigh of the sea. Crumb, mousing out of the shadows, walked ahead, his tail held up in the air as if he were leading a procession.

They walked through the hall, and into the living room where Christobel and Naomi sat on either side of the table, holding hands across it. They looked up as she came in. They had both been crying, but that was over now. Naomi looked peaceful but exhausted, and for the first time Harry saw with a pang that she looked old. As for Christobel, her face was so swollen and bruised with crying that Harry thought it looked as if she had been beaten with a hammer. Christobel and Naomi stared back at her as if she had changed, too, but what changes they saw there she could not guess.

"I could have been nicer about your silly book," Christobel said, "but I hate apologizing."

"I already knew it was rotten, anyway," Harry said. "It was just the surprise."

She and Christobel hugged each other in front of the Christmas tree.

"What the hell — it's Christmas Day," Christobel cried.

"Happy Christmas!" Harry said to Christobel, and to Carnival's Hide.

PART THREE

New Year

23
Once upon a Time

Christmas did not linger and fade into New Year
with swimming, sailing and eating, as it usually did,
but fell to pieces almost at once. The family came
home again, slept, and later in the morning (much
later than was usual for Christmas Day, as Benny
and Serena were tired) they sat in a curious state
of peace, all debates suspended, and opened their
Christmas presents. They had a midday meal so
simple it could hardly be called a Christmas dinner,
walked and talked a little and then the family divided. Jack, Naomi and Christobel longed for
change, for different walls, another garden and, unexpectedly, for relief from vistas of sea and of hill-
sides mottled with gold and brown. But Charlie,
Harry, Serena and Benny wanted to stay at Carnival's Hide, Charlie for the sailing, the little ones
for the swimming and Harry because, whatever
mistakes she might make, hawks still soared in the
updrafts from warm slopes, the waves still reared
and flung themselves forward on to the sand, mak-

ing a sound that was pretty, melancholy and old beyond memory. While Jack and Naomi collected the things they might need, and Harry bobbed out in the waves with Serena and Benny, Christobel took Anthony firmly by the hand and led him along the beach.

"Jack!" she exclaimed. "I can scarcely bear to be in the same room with him. Naomi says you can come home with us — if you will, that is. Then we can help each other get over the sufferings we've inflicted on others."

She sounded like a clever imitation of herself, an almost familiar voice coming from an almost familiar face.

Anthony turned into the wind which had shifted a little toward the north overnight. Low clouds came scudding in before it, but up above the clouds blue sky showed cool and clear, and seagulls hovered, or, striking some fiercer draft, whirled upwards to calmer air where they resumed a steady glide over the sea. Christobel was alarmed at Anthony's slow response.

"You said you were used to victories," she reminded him. "Try being victorious over me, just to stay in practice. Mind you," she added, "I'm feeling weak. It wouldn't be fair to take advantage."

"Not take advantage? You must be mad," Anthony said. "Do you think victories are won by being fair?"

"You seemed such a well-mannered young man," Christobel replied doubtfully.

"So I am," agreed Anthony. "If you're a reasonably ruthless person you need to conceal it as much as possible."

"You're not ruthless," Christobel said. The sea put out a fingerless hand and patted her bare foot. "Are you?" she asked.

"If I wasn't, I'd be unhappily married by now," Anthony answered. Christobel studied him without appearing to do so, and then, when he continued to seem unaware of it, told him what she was doing.

"I'm looking at you from under my eyelashes," she said.

"I know," said Anthony.

"Did you guess about . . ." she began and broke off. "No, no, I won't even think about that. Why did you break off your engagement? Any good reason?"

"No universal agreement on that," Anthony said, "but I thought so. Good, but not nice!"

Christobel waited expectantly but he said nothing more.

"Talk to me," she said. "Be a man of mystery to the others but not to me. Tell me why you broke your engagement."

"Well," said Anthony, "we often used to walk together through a little park to her flat and make love there, but more and more, as we walked through the park I'd find myself looking at other women and wanting them more."

"You did the right thing," said Christobel warmly. "Wasn't she very pretty?"

Anthony laughed. "Yes," he said. "She was very, very pretty. Everyone thought I was amazingly lucky that she had chosen me. That's probably why they were all so angry when I showed that I didn't think so."

They had reached the edge of the beach and now

walked back again, a winding course as they re-treated up the beach from time to time in order to evade the encroaching sea. Christobel had fallen silent.

"You're a bit too clever, you know," she suddenly declared.

"I have to be," Anthony answered. "I mix with clever people."

"Will you come back to the city and stay with us for a few days?" Christobel asked him. "We'll prob-ably be back here for New Year, though right at this moment I don't care if I never come here again."

"Of course I'll come," Anthony said. "I think I've had enough of Carnival's Hide for a while myself."

Harry watched them walk up the hill. Between the miniature headlands, the sea was as smooth as glass. Serena and Benny were trying to float with-out creating any ripples at all; their eyes were round with the effort of stillness. Then they laughed and began trying to duck each other.

"I already knew Tibby was my little sister," Benny said unexpectedly. "Don't cry!" he said to Serena as the corners of her mouth turned down. He was as pleased as if he had guessed a riddle correctly. But then it turned out that in some strange way of his own he had concluded she must be his sister because he liked her so much, and had decided they had been forced to give her away be-cause they had run out of bedrooms. Harry was astounded by this. Serena and Benny stood arguing about it, only their heads protruding from a glassy sea. She thought the world was too inscrutable to be easily lived in. The sun came out and turned the children's heads to gold. Then her name was called, not by mystery but by Naomi on the sand. Harry walked out of the water and Naomi hugged her, wet as she was.

"We're off," Naomi said, and added, "Christo's really dreadfully upset. She adored Jack. I want to keep her moving — keep her ideas moving, too, so that bitterness can't settle down in her like some kind of dreadful silt. If I can just get her through the next few days . . ."

"I'm sorry," said Harry wretchedly. "I thought I'd never, never tell, and then when I did it was like revenge."

They were both silent, remembering for a moment Harry's fierce cries of the night before.

"How *did* you know?" Naomi asked at last. "I had no idea you knew."

"I listened," Harry said. "I stood outside the door, listening." She thought this sounded shameful. "That's what writers do — listen in," she said. "It's a sort of research. Not that I'm a writer now, but I was then."

"They really fell in love," said Naomi. "I didn't know what to do. There was nothing I could do. It was all done." She broke off, then said, "It was just after Sam left and she was lonely, but she'd always been half in love with Jack. We used to make jokes about it, Jack and I did. We both thought she'd grow out of it, but neither of us imagined Jack would grow into it." She broke off to wave to Serena. "But quite suddenly he did," she said.

"It must have been dreadful," was all Harry could think of saying. She wanted to use bigger, more rending words, but the time for those was past. Naomi stood very still, as if she were trying to prevent the air rippling around her. Harry knew that sort of stillness. Naomi was trying not to cry, so perhaps time past was not really time past.

"It was," Naomi said at last. "Now, I think that I'd always been a little bit jealous of Emma, not being young and pretty myself. I've never had a go at being pretty. Sexy perhaps, but not pretty."

Harry found she was embarrassed by her mother thinking of herself as sexy.

"I got quite frantic," Naomi said. "I tried to take everything over . . . first I wanted to adopt Tibby, and then I tried to have another baby myself. We all got so terribly unhappy that all feelings changed under pressure, like metamorphic rock — remember your geology: *rock altered after formation by heat and pressure*," she quoted in a school-teacherish voice, looking around her at the old volcano.

"*Metamorphoses* by Ovid," Harry couldn't help saying, remembering his fingers burning into the naked wooden bracing under the iron of the roof.

"Thank goodness *they've* gone. One problem the less," Naomi said. "They certainly outlived their welcome." She was not interested in the vanished Carnivals. "Jack's suffered over it longer than I did," she said. "Never forget that." She was making excuses for him. "I know, I just *know* there's some trick in all this, and if only I can get the hang of it our lives will end up better for it all, richer and stronger. If only I could be certain what the trick is. But I'm reduced to crossing my fingers. I think it's right that we take Christo back to the city because she can do things there, and visit people, take Anthony around a bit. I should spend more time with you, too, but you've had a chance to get used to it all, and it's new to Christo and particularly terrible. Understand, won't you?"

"No problem," Harry said briefly. She couldn't help thinking she'd had a lot of practice at this particular sort of understanding. "Oh, Ma! It'll be all right."

"Yes, but only if we try hard," Naomi said.

Six long, slow, sunny days faded into evenings as clear as glass when the hills became suffused in the strange pink that Harry had never seen anywhere else. Every morning Debbie Tavener's little Fiat bounced down the track, and she and Charlie set out together, returning later in the morning, elated with their progress, drawing diagrams of wind-flow, arguing about sails and wind and water.

"I didn't think I knew anyone who could write a book," Serena said to Harry quite seriously. "Did she marry that winged man? Did she get carried off by him?"

"It won't ever be finished," Harry said. "There are lots of books like that."

"I'll finish it," Serena said at once. "I want the winged man to get her."

"I can't," Harry said, trying to sound gentle. "It's just — it's just died on the page. I'm never going to write another book. I write rubbishy stuff and then people laugh at it."

"People laugh at me all the time," Serena said. "If I try to be beautiful or to dance or anything, people laugh at me."

Harry found Serena's longing to be beautiful and adored no longer seemed comical to her, but part of a great commandment laid on every person born.

"I don't care," Serena added cheerfully. "I still give it a go."

Benny helped them pack away the Christmas decorations. They took down the cards and polished the piano again, while Charlie carried the tree out of doors in a shower of brittle needles. It was taken up the hill and put behind the wash-house next to the grey skeleton of last year's tree. They lay there side by side — effigies to dead Christmases.

"I'll borrow the Taveners' chain saw and cut them up, but not until after New Year. Nothing but sailing until then," Charlie said.

Harry actually enjoyed doing a little housework and tidied a cupboard a day, an extra offering for the house. She could read down on the beach or lie with her sunhat over her face. The six days seemed endlessly long, but she welcomed the gentle tedium. Certain shapes of cloud, the flat flowers of wild horse parsley gone to seed reminded her of Felix. Sometimes it seemed the real Ariadne Hamilton was still on the hilltop, transfixed by an hour as by an arrow. Sometimes it seemed to her that she had had a dream, or been the victim of an intricate illusion, which had filled her with memories indistinguishable from the memories of real events.

Sometimes it seemed to her she had misunderstood everything that went on. Other people remembered the Carnival brothers as troublesome and mischievous, entertaining, but above all, as ordinary men who had come and gone, leaving chaos behind them.

Standing in the hall, staring at the dense pattern on its walls, she could not be certain she was not embroidering facts with the colours of the imagination. Everyone else seemed prepared to believe Felix, Hadfield and Ovid had been nothing more than troublesome guests, to believe a wind had blown the wallpaper loose, and the brothers had finished the work it had begun. Sometimes she tried to remember the times she had spent with Felix alone, but what she remembered most clearly were straight lines of heavy rain, or the wild flowers, hauntingly luminous in the dusk. Felix himself was barely distinguishable.

On the 31st of December Naomi rang.

"We'll be over later in the day," she said. "We must see the New Year in together, particularly after such an incoherent Christmas. Things aren't too bad. Thanks for holding the fort . . . Someday I'll sit down and have a real talk with you, Harry, I promise I will."

Harry was warmed by her voice, but knew that, though there were some things it was never too late for, there were parts of life where she and Naomi had missed each other for ever.

At six o'clock that evening two motors sang a chugging duet outside the front door and then fell silent together. Serena shouted with pleasure. Naomi, Jack and Christobel, Harry thought, closing the oven door on a trayful of baked potatoes, but then she realized that there were too many voices and came out to find Naomi, Jack, Christobel, Anthony, Emma and Tibby climbing on to the verandah to meet her. Except for Robert, the Christmas household was restored. They all looked at the house and then at her, all of them with stories that would be told in due course.

Once again there was an arriving and an unpacking, voices shouting from room to room. Once again Serena danced and pointed her toes, hoping people would look at her and suddenly think, why didn't I see it before? That child's a born dancer.

"This Crumb loves me!" cried Tibby triumphantly, hoisting the cat off the floor. Crumb squeezed his eyes tight with discontent. His soft velvety stomach was stretched out for all to see. Benny rescued him.

"This child doesn't deserve to have a cat," he said sternly, and used Crumb's tail to tickle Tibby's face, making the house sound again with her ready laughter.

"No show without Punch!" Christobel said, picking her up and staring into a face that looked back at her with her own eager animation.

"Big hug!" said Tibby confidently.

"I should say so," said Christobel, complying. "You'd better keep in my good books because you're going to need me in years to come. Emma's only your mother, but I'll be there to take your side against her . . . and against Robert too, probably."

"What do you mean, 'and Robert too'?" Emma asked rather feebly.

"Go on — make my day!" Christobel said looking amused. "Tell me you haven't been seeing each other." But Emma gave a silly grin and did not insist on it.

Later, as Harry put on a sweater just before dinner she heard someone coming up her ladder and Christobel rose, like a pantomine Venus, up through the open trapdoor and into the attic. The trapdoor slammed shut behind her.

"Hello you!" she said. "Are you surprised? What do you think?"

"I didn't think you'd ever speak to Emma again," Harry said, her whisper undulating along under the iron roof. She could not get over her astonishment at having Emma in the house again.

"I've *conned* myself into it," Christobel said, half whispering back. "Life is *just too short*," she emphasized each word with a nod of her head, "to waste it moaning about things that can't be helped." She looked at her face in Harry's mirror with discontent. "I don't even look any different. For God's sake, you'd think I could be matured by suffering or something, wouldn't you?"

"You might change a bit and not know it — not straight off," Harry suggested, remembering the hammered face Christobel had worn six days earlier.

"Maybe!" said Christobel. "I feel as if I've given up on some great ideal, but for the life of me I can't think what it was in the first place." She sat down on the end of the stretcher.

"I'll tell you what," she said. "I don't care how reasonable Ma makes it sound, I utterly hate the idea that Emma knows something about Jack that we don't. She knows him as a man, and I only know him as a father. It's not one of those psychological things," she added quickly. "I mean I'm not secretly in love with Jack myself. It's more ordinary than that."

"I don't like it either," Harry said, and Christobel's face lightened.

"If I stop speaking to Emma I lose my best

friend," she said. "I mean we're not as close now as we were a few years back, but there's no one who's replaced her. And we've been through a lot together. It's more useful to think about that idea than the other one."

"It's a trick — getting the right thought to concentrate on," Harry said, and Christobel nodded and frowned.

"It's trick, not truth." She sighed. "But the real trick is to *use* the tricks, but never forget the truth. You do what works. But what am I telling you all the deep stuff for?"

"I'm a good listener," Harry said.

"You can say plenty, too, when you put your mind to it," Christobel added ruefully. She looked up at the roofing iron as if she could see through it to the summer sky. "I know most people think I don't care, and I wouldn't let on to everyone, but I — I *covet* a good life, and I've always felt I might inherit one in due course from Jack and Naomi. But no go! I'm going to have to be good on my own behalf. I mean it's obviously not fair to expect them to be good for me, after all. And why not have a bit of style as well? *I* was the one who rang Emma and asked her to come over to the Hide for New Year. No one told me to. 'Oh, I couldn't!' she said, you know — sort of shuddering at me over the phone, so *I* said, 'Well, if I've got the guts to invite you, you can bloody well have the guts to accept.'"

Harry laughed. For no certain reason, quite apart from sisterly love, she liked Christobel. Christobel grinned back, not knowing she was being liked as a friend. "No, but the really funny thing is this," she persisted. "I had to force myself to ring her.

My hand had to be *made* to dial her number, but by the end of our talk I was so — I don't know — so enchanted with myself that I'd got all sincere. I really *meant* it. I'm nothing but another Toad."

Harry found she was impressed by Christobel's wrestling with the problems of leading a good life.

"You're not a toad, really," she said comfortingly.

"Not *a* toad, *the* Toad! Capital 'T' Toad of Toad Hall! Remember, at the end of the book, he's found a marvellous way to be conceited by *seeming modest*? He was indeed an altered Toad."

Harry thought this over slowly, and Christobel, encouraged by her smile, said proudly, "Subtle, isn't it? Still self-centered, but getting extra credit."

"It's diabolical," Harry said. "Good acting!"

"No," said Christobel, puzzled. "It's not just acting. I don't quite know what it is. It's going to be all right with Emma," she added. "I expect there'll be a few rough patches but that's not too bad. But what I can't quite . . . I mean what about Jack? It's all very well for Ma to go on about how he was scared of getting old, and how *she* was so thrilled by her job that she wasn't much comfort to him, and how pretty and docile and admiring Emma was, and not quite his daughter after all — I can understand all that. It's in a thousand books already. But who wants to have to *understand* their father? I just want him to be marvellous and leave it at that — blow being human!"

Harry listened to Christobel spinning those thoughts out of herself and felt relief, for Christobel was speaking a truth that she herself recognized and had never quite managed to come to terms with. If talking thoughts like these aloud gave Christobel some sort of release, Harry was released too, simply by listening to them.

"*And* then," Christobel said with new vehemence, "it's hard not to feel Emma somehow fixed me with her eye, while I was at school, and set herself to invade me, and now she's got *my face* for her baby. And I feel I'm the one who's been possessed through Jack, and all without the chance of saying yes or no."

"It might have influenced Robert too," Harry said at last. "I mean, without realizing it. Looking at Tibby he saw you again, made all innocent and manageable."

Christobel laughed. She appeared to be engaged in a private argument.

"Well," she said at last, "I'm telling you now: it's just as well I'm on the tough side, because I'm going to force happy endings out of all this." And she leaped up and began studying her face in the looking-glass, now pleased at what she saw.

"It mightn't come to anything, Robert and Emma, I mean," Harry said, pursuing her own thoughts.

"Ha, ha, to that!" Christobel said. "They want the same thing too much. Never mind them! What do you think of Anthony?"

"For you?" Harry asked, astonished.

"Well, let's pretend," said Christobel.

"A bit quiet!" Harry said doubtfully. "Very low key."

"He is not!" exclaimed Christobel indignantly.

"Well, you said you wanted fury, and he isn't furious," Harry retorted.

"Forget what I said, you parrot! I'd say anything," Christobel declared crossly. "Anyhow he *is* furious in a way, but not in great big lumps. If you're sparing, fury might last a lifetime. Actually I think he's stalking me, but very delicately. He'd better watch out, that's all."

There was no cooking for New Year's Eve that year, because Naomi had brought all sorts of things from home.

"No plums!" Serena said with deep thankfulness. "We've eaten them all."

"Great!" Naomi said. "Just in time for the new crop!"

"Don't you dare!" exclaimed Christobel.

"Joking, only joking!" Naomi said, flinging up her hands. "Nothing but plum sauce this year."

It was a very quiet New Year, almost as if they were — not strangers — but people accidentally thrown together, knowing each other well enough to be friendly, but still with a great deal to find out about each other. At midnight they sang and danced together, going from partner to partner.

"Oh, Harry!" said Jack. "I gave you the right name after all. Ariadne is a beautiful name, and you grow into it more every year."

"I might match up with it by next New Year," Harry said, and they hugged each other before they changed partners again.

The radio counted the old year out. It melted away and became another intangible part of the old volcano. On the other side of the harbour ships in the port boomed and hooted like water beasts, and people shot flares into the air, which fell very slowly, like burning petals of scarlet and green, floating on the water for a few moments before they finally went out.

"This time tomorrow, I'll have the trophy," Charlie promised himself. The day after that they would all go back to the city together. Christobel was due to start work again on the third. They toasted the New Year and talked about what they hoped for. Down on the beach everything was dark and quiet. The tide once again adjusted its long ribbon of salty litter. Out in the dark a seagull cried, circling in the air, and another called from across the harbour. They searched for each other in the early morning of the New Year calling and answering in melancholy, harsh, but beautiful voices.

Harry woke very early.

A new year, she thought and was surprised to feel her heart leap a little, as if it were looking forward to what the new year might have to offer. Once again she heard Debbie's Fiat arrive, and Charlie talking as he went down to the water.

"Don't you worry!" Debbie said. "I won't drop the spinnaker. You just concentrate on your job and leave me to work at mine."

Harry came down after them and saw the little boat setting off over the sea, around the coast to Gorse Bay. At that time of day it looked unearthly, a vessel from another world, edged with silver, sailing over silver, softened by early mist. Harry sat on the beach, drew up her legs and rested her chin on her knees. She sat dreaming, aware of little pictures but not concentrating on any of them. The silence sang around her. All colours were muted. On such a morning as this, one might expect to find a message scribbled on the sand, or pictures of flying cats and dancing fish, all smiling tricky smiles. But indeed the tricksters had gone. She looked at the sand, smoothed over by the reliable tide, unmarked except that, within her reach, there was a little streak of white where something was partly buried. Harry scrabbled in the sand and found she was holding a ring of white shell, the collar of a vanished mollusc, the rest of the shell broken off and carried away. It looked the same as the one she had worn just before she dived deep and, putting her hand into the tunnel under the sea, had felt words whispered against its palm. Felix had made her a ring of grasses, which she had in a little box of precious things in her room. He wouldn't mind if she wore once again the ring the sea had offered her. She slipped it on her finger.

"There," she said aloud to herself, "I've married the sea. I'm Mrs Oceanus. Everything comes out of me." As she spoke something indescribable happened. She *saw* everything . . . every blade of grass, every grain of sand, every wave on the beach . . . things that she had seen many times before, but which now made themselves known to her in a wonderful way. She blinked. The world shifted mysteriously. Harry believed she might be having a vision, if only she were quick enough to see it properly. She was not wearing her glasses.

The tide marked its furthest reaches with a line of seaweed and shells that went on and on around the world, and she had been on one side, the sea on the other. Now she felt there was no longer the same separation between them.

Harry took off her morning clothes and walked

into the sea. Once in it, it flowed over her, warm and cool at once, if that were possible, more sensuous than Christobel's silk dressing-gown. The ripples wrote lines of light around her, until Harry felt that she might begin to shine. When she spoke, glowing words would come out of her mouth. On the sand again, she turned almost instinctively, it seemed, and saw the sunrise. A little notch in the broken skyline filled up with fire, and Harry was filled with fire too. In the end she was indeed possessed by the brute blood of the air so powerfully but so delicately it was like no possession she had ever imagined. And even when things turned ordinary again, which they did in due course, they could not take back the gift they had made of themselves. Harry, walking back to the house, turned and looked behind her in case she was leaving footprints filled with light. She felt remarkable.

As the house came into sight, drenched in the first New Year sun, already wearing its skirt of shade, garlanded in green and purple, Harry felt the ground undulate beneath her feet. She saw a wave of movement run past her like a wind through grass. It was a small earthquake.

"Rescue Crumb!" Benny began shouting from somewhere, but he was excited rather than frightened by this familiar, even homely twitching of the solid earth, reminding him who was powerful. It hardly seemed possible, but everyone was up, and part of the reason was because of Robert's car, parked in front of the house. He was going to drive Emma round to Gorse Bay for a picnic and help Charlie and Debbie with the boat if they needed him.

"You're up early," Harry said.

"You too!" he told her and then said that he hadn't been to bed all night. He had come straight from a New Year's party.

"Of course I'll look after your damned baby," Christobel was shouting in the living room as Harry went through it to her attic. "Just get out and take that accountant with you, or I might be tempted by him. He's the best-looking man I know." Later, Harry came down her ladder and found Christobel watching Tibby with a mixture of amusement and repulsion. Tibby was sitting on her pink pot singing to herself and shifting herself industriously across the floor.

"Gosh, motherhood must be terrible," Christobel was grumbling. "The things you've got to praise people for!"

"You used to insist on a lot of congratulation yourself," Naomi called through from the kitchen.

"At least I'm beyond that now," Christobel said. "Oh, happy New Year, Harry! There's a present for you on the end of the table — that square thing in the pink paper. You can probably guess what it is from the shape."

Serena bounced up and down beside the table.

"I think it's a book, the one you turn into yourself, the one you wanted for Christmas." She was longing to see the parcel opened. Harry gave Christobel a tentative glance and then unwrapped a great big fat day-to-a-page diary full of white space.

"There's nothing in it," said Serena disappointed.

"No!" Christobel agreed. "It'll be Harry's job to corrupt it."

"It might be the one the world copies," Harry

said to Serena. "It's got the possibility of everything in it."

"Get out!" Christobel said. "I don't want to start the New Year listening to stuff like this."

Tibby leaped to her feet. "Good girl!" she announced.

"You haven't!" exclaimed Christobel also leaping up. "Stone the crows! Ma!" But Naomi did not answer. "Good girl! Good girl!" Christobel shouted. Tibby almost bowed. She laughed, obviously enjoying feeling successful.

Holding the bright pink pot at arm's length Christobel made for the door.

"Just think!" she said. "The first view the New Year will have of me is doing good for others. Everyone take notice," she yelled. Then she winked at Harry and Serena and walked on out on to the verandah.

Harry looked after the sister above her and down at the sister below.

"When I've written something, I'll read it to you if you like," she told Serena, "but all you're allowed to say is, 'good girl'."

Crumb arched his back, and rubbed his head against her leg and gave a small miaow.

"No cat calls!" Harry said, scratching him around the ears. Serena was thrilled.

"Start now," she suggested, "then you can read it to me tonight."

Harry climbed up her ladder and sat under the witch's cap of the roof. Free from its old ghost, the house shrugged last year away and began the new one, light, airy and sunny. Jack and Anthony wandered out on to the verandah and shouted over to

Christobel, trekking up the hill with the pink pot in her hand. Harry opened the big book and looked at its first wonderful blank page. She remembered her rule that she must not put the book away without having written something in it first. The page was pure and certain, words were uncertain, but their uncertainty was what made them magical. At last she carefully wrote the words, "Once upon a time . . ." and thought that the looping line the pen made was a world line, like the one left behind by the tide, and that lines left on beaches and pages everywhere must wind up by going all around the world if one could only follow them. Once the first words were written she had plenty to think about, for they might lead in any direction. She shut the book and put it under her pillow, then put her head on the pillow, lying back, whistling softly to herself, staring over the top of her glasses at the roof of Carnival's Hide, waiting for whatever was going to happen next.

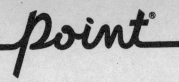

Other books you will enjoy,
about real kids like you!